BRUSH STROKES

Sophie was squealing like anything as I forced her into position for the cane, making a fine show of herself with her bum wiggling in her panties as I lifted her skirt and fastened it up with the safety pin that was still attached to the hem. I took my time about stripping her bottom, standing beside her so that everybody could see as I peeled the big green knickers down off her bum cheeks to the level of her thighs.

'I see you've already been punished this evening,' I remarked, running a finger along one of her welts, where Angel's cane had made twin tramlines of puffy reddened flesh.

'Yes, Miss,' she answered, snivelling slightly over her words, 'By Angel, Miss.'

'No doubt you deserved it,' I told her. 'And you know what happens to girls who have to be punished twice in one day, don't you?'

Sophie looked round, genuinely puzzled, as I reached into my bag.

Why not visit Penny's website at
www.pennybirch.com

BRUSH STROKES

Penny Birch

This book is a work of fiction.
In real life, make sure you practise safe, sane and
consensual sex.

First published in 2006 by
Nexus
Thames Wharf Studios
Rainville Rd
London W6 9HA

www.nexus-books.co.uk

Typeset by TW Typesetting, Plymouth, Devon
Printed in the UK By CPI Bookmarque, Croydon, CR0 4TD

ISBN 0 352 34072 X
ISBN 978 0 352 34072 6

One

'Knickers down, Kay.'

She turned to me, her lower lip pushed out in a moue of resentment. But her thumbs had already gone into the waistband of the lacy white knickers that she was wearing. Her jeans were already down in a denim puddle around her ankles and I watched as the knickers joined them, pulled off over her cheeky apple bottom and on down her legs. Now bare behind, her expression turned to apprehension as she spoke.

'Not too hard, please, Amber. At least I confessed!'

'Which is why you're going over my knee instead of getting the cane,' I told her. 'Now come on – let's get you spanked.'

Kay began to speak again but thought better of it, contenting herself with another pout as she came to me and laid herself across my lap. I got comfortable, holding her around the waist as I reached for the hairbrush on my bedside table. She'd been looking back and realised at once what was about to happen.

'Not the hairbrush, Amber. You said fifty over your knee!'

'You *are* over my knee,' I pointed out, lifting one leg to bring her bottom up a little and make her cheeks spread to show the tiny dark brown dimple of her anus between. 'And I am going to give you fifty.'

'I thought you meant just a hand spanking!' she

1

wailed, her voice full of frustration. 'The hairbrush hurts far more! This isn't *fair*, Amber!'

Kay had begun to wriggle but I held on tight, trying to remind myself that I was supposed to be punishing her and not enjoying the state she was getting herself into, nor the feel of her wriggling body, nor the sight of her pretty bottom laid bare for spanking. But I've never really got the hang of pure domestic discipline and it was impossible. As I tapped the hairbrush against her upraised bottom cheeks I knew full well that I'd end up aroused. How could I not, with such a juicy little peach of a bottom to spank, so well formed, so cheeky for such a slim girl, well tucked under even as she bent for spanking and so bulbous that she seemed to defy gravity. I leant a little to one side so that I could admire the neat pout of her fanny where it showed between her thighs. No matter how often I played with her I never grew tired of her body.

'Amber!' she protested. 'If you're going to spank me, get it over with. Please?'

'You're right,' I told her. 'After all, it *is* a punishment spanking.'

As I spoke I tightened my grip on Kay's waist and began to apply the hairbrush to her bottom, not with the gentle taps I'd have used to start off an erotic spanking but hard and fast, full across her bum cheeks. She broke immediately, her legs kicking frantically as she gasped and begged for mercy. But I clung on tight, ignoring her pleas as I smacked the brush down on her squirming bottom. Her flesh was getting pink and she was bucking like anything, showing off the tiny brown star of her bumhole and the rear view of her fanny, making it even harder for me to concentrate on what I was doing.

'Fifty,' I said at last and released her. 'Now put your nose against the wall and stay there.'

Kay climbed quickly off my lap and scampered across the room, clutching her smacked backside.

'Hands on your head,' I reminded her as she pressed her nose to the wall.

She obeyed, snivelling slightly as her hands went up, her fingers interlocked in her tawny blonde hair. Her bottom was very red, the fleshy tuck of her cheeks now just peeping out beneath the hem of her blouse. The temptation to have her lick me was close to overwhelming, but I reminded myself again that it was supposed to be a punishment. She deserved it too, after all the fuss she had made about not doing anything in front of men and then going into the peep box with Sophie Cherwell at Morris Rathwell's club.

'Why did you do it?' I asked, more curious than accusing. After all, she'd been spanked and that was supposed to be the end of it, the whole purpose of our domestic discipline arrangement being to avoid quarrels.

'I just wanted to be a bit more adventurous, that's all,' Kay said, not quite managing to keep the sulky tone out of her voice.

'Fair enough. But you should have asked, at least,' I pointed out.

'Sorry,' she answered.

There was genuine contrition in her voice, despite her sulky attitude. It made me want to cuddle her but she was supposed to spend a full half-hour with her nose pressed to the wall, her hands on her head and her bare red bottom showing to the room. I made myself comfortable on the bed, once more ignoring the urge to push down my jodhpurs and the knickers beneath so that she could lick me to ecstasy.

'That's the last time you go to a club on your own,' I told her. 'Although I do appreciate that Sophie can be hard to resist.'

'She was! You ought to spank her too, really.'

'She's not my girlfriend.'

'Yes, but she knows your rules.'

3

'That's true. Maybe I *will* spank her.'

'Do it – it's the least she deserves. With the hairbrush, too.'

'Maybe I'll spank you again as well – for being such a little sneak!'

Kay made a face, the corner of her mouth just visible to me as it twitched up. As we both knew, Sophie Cherwell would be more than willing to have my hairbrush applied to her bare bottom and, punishment or not, she would enjoy every smack. It was still tempting, if only for my private satisfaction, and more tempting still to deal with the two of them together. The thought made my stomach flutter.

'Any news?' I asked, trying to distract myself.

'Nothing much,' Kay answered. 'There's some new club, apparently. It's run by somebody called Hannah Riley.'

'Hannah Riley? Never heard of her.'

'Nor has anyone else, but apparently she thinks she knows it all. She's really got Morris's back up.'

'I bet she has! He hates rivals at any time, let alone complete newcomers. Maybe we should go?'

'Morris would not be happy with us. Riley came to the club a couple of months ago, it seems, and tried to get Sophie to work for her. Sophie turned her down but Morris was still livid.'

'I bet he was but that's no reason we shouldn't go. Just the opposite, in fact. I'm not having Morris and Melody Rathwell tell me where I can and cannot go.'

Kay didn't answer, leaving me to my thoughts. It was tempting, because I do like to go out occasionally and Morris's club was getting impossible. There was always pressure on me to perform and Mel in particular never gave up her attempts to get me over her lap – or worse. Not that I mind her so very much, but she knows what gets to me and has a nasty habit of doing it in front of people like the ultra-dominant American, Hudson

Staebler, or Morris's paying clients, especially the unspeakably horrible Mr Protheroe. The consequences were pretty well inevitable – and deeply shameful, culminating in the utter disgrace I'd made of myself at a club in Belfast.

Kay knew all about it and accepted it. But she often used to tease me in the hope that I'd punish her, and for deeper reasons. It turned her on and her approval made me more vulnerable still. Over a year had passed since I'd last been and an alternative venue would really be quite welcome, especially if it was run by a woman – a woman who didn't really know what she was doing, by the sound of things. No doubt my experience would be very welcome.

On the other hand, Morris was far and away the best customer for the kinky secret side of my saddlery business and I didn't want to lose his custom. Not that he was likely to go that far. Anyway, the new club would undoubtedly need tack and a lot of it if they were making a serious effort to rival Morris. At the very least it made sense to pay Hannah Riley a visit.

'What's Riley's place called?' I asked.

'Carnival Bizarre. Apparently Hannah runs a circus of sorts, but they can't get some new licences or can't afford them or something, so they've gone into clubbing instead. That's another thing Morris is cross about. He says they're only in it for the money.'

'And he's not? Well, not entirely, I suppose, but he certainly likes his profit. Nose against the wall, Kay.'

She had moved, just a little bit, and although she quickly resumed her position I caught the same sulky look that I'd seen before. Evidently she didn't think she should have been disciplined. I picked up the hairbrush.

'Kay, do you want another spanking?'

'No!'

'Then show a bit of remorse. I spanked you because you deliberately broke our boundaries.'

Again she made a face, this time looking right at me, her mouth working in indecision for a moment before she spoke.

'Amber . . . I only wanted to play with Sophie.'

'Yes, Kay, but . . .' I began. Then I stopped, thinking of what it had cost me to keep her from the prying eyes of men. Being done up as a French poodle on stage in Belfast, for one thing. Worse, what had been done to me afterwards by the ghastly Mr Protheroe and others. 'Come here – now!'

Kay's expression grew furiously sulky. But she came anyway, shuffling in her lowered jeans and panties. As soon as she was close enough I reached out and grabbed her, pulling her hard across my thighs. She squeaked once in alarm, and then again as I pushed up one leg to lift her bottom. At the same time I twisted my hand hard into the back of her blouse.

'Amber, no . . .' she started. Then she broke off in a chorus of squeals and half-formed pleas for mercy as I set to work on her with the hairbrush, hard now, so that she was kicking and thrashing immediately.

I'd barely begun before I was reminding myself never to spank in anger. I stopped, leaving her gasping across my legs with her fingers clawed into the bedspread.

'Sorry, Kay, but –'

'Ow! My bum!' she interrupted. 'That was *hard*, Amber.'

'I'm sorry,' I repeated. 'But you make me really cross. Think of all I've done to spare your blushes when there are men around – and then you go and put on a show with Sophie, in front of dozens of them!'

'Not dozens,' Kay protested. 'And it was in the peep box – so we didn't even know who was looking!'

'That's not the point,' I insisted.

'Anyway, I want to experiment a bit more,' she went on, her voice more sulky than ever as she bent back to inspect her smacked bottom.

'In front of me?'

'Maybe. Look what you've done to my bum!'

Kay was bruised. The crests of both cheeks showed a touch of angry purple, and her eyes were wide with shock as she looked back at me.

'I said I'm sorry. Now give me a cuddle.'

I put my arms out for her and she crawled on top of me, hugging me but not trembling in the way she usually did after a spanking. Guilt washed over me and I cuddled her tighter, suddenly deeply afraid of her rejection. Maybe I was being too stern with her. Certainly I shouldn't have spanked her so hard, not with the hairbrush. And not when I was angry.

'I'm sorry,' I said for the third time as I began to stroke her hair. I also took hold of her bottom.

Her skin felt hot and oddly thick, the way bottom flesh always does after a hard spanking. I began to caress Kay, very gently, stroking her smacked cheeks and her hair as I thought of how much I loved her and how awful it would be without her. Three years we'd been together, and she was getting bolder and more self-confident. Maybe I should adapt, change the rules, because the thought of losing what we had together put a lump in my throat.

'I . . . I shouldn't have done that,' I told her. 'Not so hard, anyway. Do you want to punish me?'

It was a loaded question. Since I'd been giving her discipline I had felt more and more that it was something I should have myself, just occasionally, so that I didn't have to take the full weight of responsibility. The problem was, who could give it to me? My pride was too strong to admit to anyone but Kay, that I needed it, and she didn't want to inflict it, although she'd hinted that she'd like me to get it from another woman, not just occasionally but on a regular basis. Sure enough, she shook her head, snuggling closer into my neck. Then she spoke, barely above a whisper.

'No . . . but if the right woman was here – or maybe the way you got it in Belfast?'

'Kay! You can be really disgusting sometimes!'

She broke into giggles as I slapped her bottom, just playfully, and with that things were all right between us once more. I continued to stroke her, my arousal warring with my misgivings as I felt the lush swell of her cheeks. Kay gave a little purr, encouraging me, and I let my finger slip into the deep warm crease, tickling her to make her giggle, and then probing deeper still to find the tiny moist dimple of her anus. As I touched her she sighed and pulled herself closer still to my body. I took a moment to open her, stroking her bottom-hole until her ring had begun to loosen before easing the top joint of my finger inside. She moaned, wriggling against me as I fingered her bottom. Finally kicking free of her panties and jeans, she brought one leg up, spreading her sex across my hip. I put my free arm down to cup her fanny and slip a finger deep inside.

Maybe I had spanked her too hard. But whatever the reason she was wet and my finger slid deep inside her without difficulty. Kay moaned as she was penetrated and lifted her head to kiss my mouth as I manipulated her, now with both fingers deep in the hot wet cavities of her body. Our tongues met and we were kissing urgently as I masturbated her, rubbing my palm on the mushy open flesh of her fanny. She began to clutch at me, growing urgent, one hand grabbing at my jumper to pull it up and then pulling aside my bra to expose my breasts.

Now she was mine, completely, as it should be, wriggling in ecstasy in my arms, dishevelled and wanton, her bottom hot from spanking and her body penetrated, kissing me with urgent passion and groping at my breasts. I held on, letting her ride her pleasure, my fingers moving in and out of her sticky open bottom-hole and gaping fanny as I masturbated her towards orgasm. As it started I felt her go tight, her butt cheeks squeezing on my hand, her bumhole and sex going into contractions. Then she was there, her body jerking as she whimpered out her emotions into my open mouth.

I kept hold, tight, until her tension was all gone and she lay limp on top of me, her only motion the fingers of one hand as she gently caressed my breast, her head now cradled into my neck. Very gently I eased my fingers free, looking her in the eye as she lifted her head, her face now set in a sleepy, happy smile.

'Open wide,' I told her. She obeyed without hesitation, letting me feed in the fingers that I'd just drawn from her body.

Kay sucked, her stare locked to mine, her expression sulky as always as she lapped up her own juices. But there was none of the resentment that she'd shown for her spanking. Rather, she wanted me to appreciate the depth of humiliation I was giving her. I waited until she'd thoroughly cleaned both fingers before pushing down my jodhpurs and knickers, all the way to my ankles.

Kay climbed off, immediately crawling round between my thighs. I'd already taken my breasts in my hands as she began to lick and my eyes closed in blissful relaxation as her tongue worked on my body. First it was my thighs and the tuck of my bottom, kissing and licking the sensitive flesh until I'd begun to grow desperate, clutching the covers and shaking my head from side to side in my need. Only then did she grow more intimate still, her tongue flicking at the lips of my fanny and in the crease of my bottom, just an inch of so from my bumhole.

'Lick it, Kay,' I told her. 'Lick my bottom-hole.'

She giggled, and an instant later I felt the pressure of her thumbs as she pushed them down between my cheeks, holding me open. Then came the more gentle pressure of her lips as she planted a single delicate kiss on my anus. I pulled my legs up to spread my bottom to her face – hardly a dignified position but it didn't matter, not when she was about to put her tongue up my bottom-hole.

'Right in,' I ordered. 'Be a good girl.'

Again she giggled and again her lips pressed to my bumhole, only more firmly this time, with her tongue poking out between them, first to lick my anus, then to probe, pushing in as I opened for her. I couldn't help but sigh, not just for the exquisite sensation of having my bumhole licked but for what it represented: her utter submission to me. Her pretty face pressed between my naked bottom cheeks as her lips parted around my anal ring, her tongue pushing in up my bumhole.

I linked my hands, holding myself rolled up for her as Kay licked my bottom, with her nose pressed firmly to my fanny and her arms around my thighs. A little pressure and she'd parted my legs. One hand found my sex and then she was rubbing between my fanny lips, right on my clitty. She was going to make me come while she licked my bottom-hole out, something so dirty, so intimate and so submissive. It was perfect, just right: a good spanking, then her tongue up my bottom – willingly, obediently, so sweet yet so dirty – and as I came in her face I knew that I could never, ever bear to lose her.

Domestic discipline is all very well but it is not always easy to administer. It was something that Kay had come first to want and then to *need* as part of our relationship, giving herself over completely to my authority, so that when and how she was spanked was now entirely my choice. Unfortunately with the right to punish her as I pleased came the responsibility to do it when she deserved it – and she and I didn't always see eye to eye on when spankings were merited.

We'd talked it over again and again, trying to lay down rules and decide what kind of behaviour warranted a spanking for her and what didn't. My argument was that if I was truly to be in charge then the decision should be solely mine. Yet every time I punished Kay for something she felt was unjust – as when I'd given her the hairbrush for playing with Sophie in the peep box at Morris's club – she began to get sulky.

Her solution was for me to find somebody who would discipline *me*, perhaps once a month, when I would be punished in front of her if it was necessary. She felt that would make it fair and deep down I agreed with her – not that I could admit it easily, even to myself. Choosing a woman to do it was harder still. I needed it to be private, discreet and, above all, fair.

In addition to wanting regular discipline, Kay also wanted to explore the boundaries of the world I'd introduced her to. That was fine, only I preferred people to come to us rather than for us to go out, especially to Morris's club. But as her confidence grew she wanted to go there as often as possible. I didn't feel I should stop her but I was scared of losing her, especially to Melody Rathwell. That would be unbearable.

With a rival club, which presumably Morris and Melody would not be attending, I could give Kay the opportunity to explore as much as she liked, within our agreed limit. Carnival Bizarre was thus very welcome indeed. I knew that Kay was even wondering if Hannah Riley might prove to be the woman to give me discipline, but as she seemed to be some sort of glorified gypsy it was highly unlikely.

That also made her a bit difficult to pin down because of the way they operated, moving from venue to venue and putting out flyers just a couple of weeks before the event. But after I'd discovered their website we soon found them: they were running the club at a venue in

Harrow on the coming Saturday. My request for a meeting with Hannah Riley prompted a suggestion that I should go to an address on the A41. I wasn't sure what to expect – certainly not the field full of caravans and sideshows clustered around a huge yellow-and-red-striped tent that I encountered – but it was obviously the right place, with posters advertising *Hannah Riley's Circus* plastered over every available surface. I've never liked travelling carnivals as they always seem to be run by the most uncouth people and I hesitated as we climbed from the car. Not so Kay.

'I love these places!' she said happily. 'And they've got a Big Top and everything. This is so cool!'

She was already walking quickly away between the ranks of parked cars and I had little choice but to follow, wincing at the blare of music and the screech of the rides as we approached. The circus wasn't all that big in fact, and to judge by the run-down state of the caravans and equipment I could see that it might be in need of some extra income. Rusted patches, dented aluminium, even rotten wood showed through the bright paint of the shows and rides, while on closer inspection it was obvious that the red and yellow of the Big Top was badly faded from long exposure to the sun.

Kay was oblivious, smiling happily as we walked in among the stalls and immediately buying herself a bag of rainbow-coloured sweets from one of them. I sucked on one as we moved round to where the majority of the caravans were parked. We passed a coconut shy, an air-rifle range and then an enormous plastic pillory, beside which a clown in a baggy peppermint-striped costume and with a face painted into a ludicrous grin posed. He was encouraging children to throw wet sponges at an imprisoned colleague in the same costume but whose face was painted into an equally exaggerated expression of theatrical misery. Both clowns wore enormous Afro wigs, the happy one's scarlet, the unhappy one's a virulent green.

'Three goes for a pound!' the grinning clown yelled, thrusting a handful of dripping sponges towards us.

'I'm on for that,' Kay answered before I could turn him down, already fishing in her pocket for change. 'A go each, please.'

I took my sponges. The clowns were just the sort of people I'd always loathed: brash, noisy and coarse. But if I had to associate with them it was better to be throwing wet sponges in their faces than to be getting ripped off, which always seems to me to be the main aim of carnivals.

'Me first,' Kay said happily, and hurled a sponge.

She missed completely, the sponge sailing right over the pillory and more water going down her sleeve than landed on the clown. His response was to go into an absurd dance, waggling his bottom from side to side, a move which his colleague imitated and which for some reason I found deeply embarrassing. Kay's second shot was worse, landing on the ground and not even splashing her target. Again he gave his victorious waggle, raising a gust of laughter from the audience. I took her third sponge away from her.

'Honestly, Kay, that's no way to do it. Watch.'

I adjusted my bag so that it was out of the way, took careful aim and threw the sponge, not hard but well aimed, full into the clown's idiotic face. This left him blinking and spluttering water, with yet more of his badly applied make-up dripping down his face.

'Fine shot! Fine shot!' the grinning clown called. 'I see you are an expert, madame! Pray proceed, with the compliments of Baffo the clown!'

He performed a low, sweeping bow to me, promptly spun around, waggled his bottom at us and began to walk among the crowd with his face cheeks blown up and his elbows tucked into his sides. Even Kay thought it was funny, but I felt sure he was somehow imitating me because his bottom was stuck out and he had pushed up the front of his costume with his hands in an insulting parody of the female form. I ignored him, taking a petty revenge by launching another sponge at the clown in the pillory and for a second time catching him in the face but slightly to one side, so that his absurd puff of bright green hair was knocked out of place.

'Bad one for Buffo!' the grinning clown roared. He began what I imagined was meant to be a chicken imitation, crouched low to the ground with his elbows waggling at his sides and his bottom stuck out even further than before. 'Good shot, Madame Boobfontaine!'

Immediately I felt myself go red. I could not resist a glance down at my chest, which is admittedly ample. But that did not give him the right to give me an insulting nickname because of the way I'm built. As he stood up with a crow of laughter and began to go into the next stage of his absurd act, I gave him both my remaining sponges as one, catching him in the face and chest to leave him dripping water as I took Kay by the hand and marched her away to the sound of children's laughter.

The pillory was the last stall. The crowds vanished as we walked in among the caravans and lorries until only one person was visible, a lanky individual who was presumably the guard to judge from the sleek Alsatian trotting by his side and the aggressive expression on his face. He was coming towards us and was obviously about to order us out of the caravan area. But I got in first.

'We have an appointment with Hannah Riley. Perhaps you could direct me to her caravan?'

He answered, his voice no friendlier than his expression.

'You want to see Fat Hannah, you come with me.'

'By all means,' I told him, determined to remain polite in the face of his coarse behaviour. It was exactly what I would have expected from carnival people.

He led us between an enormous red lorry cab and the rear of another shabby vehicle, ignoring Kay's attempts at friendly conversation. Beyond was a big caravan. The car parked beside it was a BMW, a five-series model only a year older than my dad's. Obviously there was some money around – unless the car was stolen, which didn't seem at all unlikely.

'Fat Hannah's caravan,' the guard told us, jerking his thumb at it.

'How about it?' Kay whispered as soon as we were out of earshot. 'Belfast style?'

I slapped her bottom, more than happy to have the security guard see her embarrassment for what she'd suggested. He had stayed where he was, watching us until I'd climbed the retractable steps that led up to the caravan door and knocked. There was no response. I was about to knock again when there was a faint creak and the steps shifted slightly beneath me, making me steady myself against the side. A moment later the door opened to reveal a big, solid woman, as tall as me but maybe twice my weight, with unkempt hair and a slatternly look to both her face and her clothes. A cigarette dangled from her lower lip.

'Mrs Riley?' I enquired. 'I'm Amber –'

'Uh-uh,' she broke in, gesturing behind her with her thumb much as the guard had done and moving out of the doorway.

'Thank you,' I said, climbing in and glancing around the gaudy interior, then at the woman who was seated in a chair at the far end.

She was huge, certainly taller than me, with immense shoulders and a stupendous bosom half hidden beneath a pink coat trimmed with fake fur. That was all she

15

seemed to have on, except for a pair of slippers, also pink and furry. Her tree-trunk legs protruded bare from beneath the coat's hem and a long, deep gash of mottled cleavage showed higher up. She was also smoking but she stubbed her cigarette out as Kay came in behind me.

'Shut the door, Maggie,' she said to the slatternly woman. Then she addressed me. 'So you're Amber Oakley?

Hannah's voice was oddly mocking, as if for some reason she didn't believe that it was my real name.

'Yes,' I confirmed, somewhat puzzled. 'I emailed you –'

'Sure you did, ducks,' she interrupted. 'And you're a lesbian couple into corporal punishment and that, and you make the gear?'

Again there was the mocking tone in her voice, stronger than before. My answer was defensive as I took hold of Kay's arm.

'Yes, as I said. Kay and I have been together three years. Do you object to that?'

'I don't object to lezzers, no,' Hannah answered, 'seeing as how I don't mind a bit of that myself. What I object to is council snoops sticking their noses into my business.'

'Council snoops?' Kay answered. 'We're not council snoops.'

'We're nothing of the kind!' I added.

'Prove it,' Hannah demanded.

'By all means,' I assured her. 'I believe you know the Rathwells, or at least you've heard of them. I have their number on my mobile if you want to ring up and ask about me.'

She laughed.

'Yeah, right, like that bastard Morris hasn't set it all up. I'm not fucking stupid, I'm not. I know what goes on. He makes out to the council that I'm doing something illegal and agrees to stick up for the snoops when they come round.'

'No, really,' I assured her, 'it's not like that at all. I'm sure Morris wouldn't do anything of the sort . . .'

Again she laughed.

'You can leave the bullshit. I've had it all, the council, the pigs, the *News of the Screws*, every nosy bastard out there. But I've never seen such a crap effort at getting in under the wire. You're not into kinky stuff – what a joke! You two are straight out of the fucking office, aren't you?'

'No!' I insisted.

'Yeah, right,' Hannah went on, 'in your neat little two-piece suit and your M&S tights? Don't make me laugh! Got any tats, eh? Got any piercings?'

'No,' I admitted, 'but that doesn't necessarily mean . . .'

I broke off. She was already laughing. It had never occurred to me for a moment that she might doubt my identity and I wasn't at all sure what to do.

'I thought you'd only just started the club?' Kay spoke up. 'Why would the council be interested in a carnival anyway, let alone the police or the papers?'

Fat Hannah just stared at her for a moment, then laughed.

'You've a nerve on you,' she said. 'I suss you out and you're still asking your nosy questions. Now go on, fuck off, the pair of you, before I put you both over my knee. Then we'll see how you like a bit of CP!'

'Would that satisfy you?' I asked. 'Perhaps if I was to spank Kay?'

'Amber!' Kay squeaked. 'You must be joking!'

'No, I'm serious,' I assured her. 'Mrs Riley thinks we're from the council, but I'm sure she'll agree that nobody attempting to infiltrate her club would agree to take a spanking to prove herself?'

Still the huge woman looked doubtful. But I'd given her pause for thought.

'Come on,' I urged, challenging her. 'What vanilla woman would accept a spanking, for any reason?'

'Might do,' Hannah replied.

Her voice was full of doubt. She obviously knew as well as I did that the sort of woman the council were likely to send would never accept a spanking under any circumstances – even if the council *did* send in people undercover, which didn't seem very likely to me. I took a chair, upholstered in red plush but with a straight back, therefore ideal for my purposes. Sitting down, I patted my lap.

'Pop your knickers down, Kay. Let's prove to Mrs Riley that we're the real thing.'

'On the bare?' Kay queried. 'I haven't –'

'Pop your knickers down, I said, and get over my knee,' I ordered, more firmly. 'No nonsense.'

'But Amber . . .'

'Knickers *down*, Kay!'

She made a face but reached up under her skirt to ease her knickers down to her knees. I patted my lap again and, her sulky expression intensifying, she tucked her skirt up into her waist band to lay her bottom bare. She draped herself across my knee. Taking a firm hold around her waist I began to spank, not hard, but it didn't have to be. No vanilla woman would ever let herself be put across another's knee, let alone bare-bottom and in front of other people.

'Are you convinced?' I asked, looking up to Fat Hannah, who now had a smile on her face and was watching Kay spanked with every evidence of amusement.

'Don't know,' she answered. 'What do you reckon, Maggie?'

'I reckon the little tart's well up for it,' the slatternly woman answered. 'The cream's already coming out her cunt.'

Kay gave a sob of humiliation at the woman's words. But I continued to spank, a little harder now, to bring a flush to her bum cheeks and make sure she juiced

18

properly if that was going to be what it took to convince Fat Hannah.

Sure enough ... 'Flip her around,' the big woman demanded.

I lifted Kay and helped turn her, until her bottom was to Fat Hannah and her face to Maggie. Kay was pink at both ends, her face flushed with embarrassment just as her bottom was flushed with spanking. But she let it happen, uncomplaining as I eased her thighs a little apart to show how wet she was. Fat Hannah nodded, then spoke again.

'Show me her arsehole.'

I nodded back, wondering just how much humiliation Kay would have to suffer before the bulky female was satisfied. Taking hold of Kay's bulbous cheeks, I hauled them apart, exposing her tiny dark brown anus for inspection. She gave another sob, louder than before, and I immediately realised why she hadn't wanted to be spanked bare. One or two tiny flecks of pale blue loo paper were caught in the crevices of her anal star, with a rather larger piece blocking the hole itself. I let go of her cheeks, feeling embarrassed for her, but Fat Hannah didn't seem to have noticed.

'Give her a few hard ones,' Maggie suggested.

'Fair enough,' I agreed and began to spank properly, applying a dozen hard swats to the plumpest part of Kay's bottom to set her gasping and kicking before I stopped.

'All right, she's the real deal,' Fat Hannah said. 'How about you?'

She was addressing me. I shrugged as Kay clambered off my lap, adjusting her skirt and panties as quickly as she could.

'I spank my girlfriend. What more proof do you need?'

'What's to say the little one isn't some tart of Morris's?' Maggie suggested.

'Could be,' Fat Hannah agreed.

'I hardly think that's likely,' I pointed out hurriedly, because I could see exactly where the conversation was going. But before I could go any further Kay spoke up, her voice deliberately mocking.

'Pop your knickers down, Amber – show Mrs Riley that we're the real thing.'

'Yeah,' Fat Hannah added, nodding towards Kay. 'Get over your tart's knee for what you gave her, then we'll believe you.'

Maggie laughed and I felt myself going red as I answered.

'I'm the dominant partner . . .'

'Up herself – might have known it,' Maggie put in from behind me. She continued, her voice high-pitched and drawling in grotesque imitation of my accent. 'I'm the dominant partner. I only give, never receive.'

'No,' I began, immediately angry, 'that's not how we work at all. It's just –'

'All right then,' Fat Hannah interrupted. 'If your tart doesn't like to do you, I don't mind. The more up themselves they are, the better I like to spank them – eh, Maggie? Oh, and don't worry about your knicks, ducks, I like to pull 'em down myself, I do.'

'Look . . .' I began to bluster, but Kay broke in.

'Over you go, Amber. Spankies time.'

'You are in *real* trouble, Kay.'

'Promises, promises!' she teased.

I looked from her to Fat Hannah. Both were waiting. I hadn't been spanked in over a year, having done my best to avoid anything that might risk me having to expose the carefully hidden submissive side of my nature. Also I was wary of the Rathwells and their sneaky tricks. Moreover, Fat Hannah Riley was very definitely not my ideal dominant woman. I could walk out, but I was going to feel a complete idiot, and weak, while Kay obviously wanted me to get the same as her after I'd made her show her dirty bottom.

'Oh, very well!' I snapped, glaring at Kay and stepping forward to lay myself across the expanse of Fat Hannah's thighs.

She took hold of my waist, pulling me closer so that I could feel the bulk of her enormous breasts pressing down on my back. I knew that with her huge brawny arm around me there would be no getting up in the middle of whatever I had coming to me. The smell of strong cheap scent was now so powerful that it made my nose wrinkle and added to my sense of how unsuitable it was that I should be put across her knee. I was there, though, ready to be stripped and spanked, and I was struggling not to pout as her fingers took hold of the hem of my skirt. It was impossible. She was going to spank me, bare-bottom across her knee, and not only in front of my own girlfriend but the slovenly Maggie as well. All I could do was take it, try as hard as possible not to make too big a fuss and pray I didn't get obviously turned on.

'Not in tights, then?' she said as my skirt came up high enough to show my stocking tops. 'Very nice. Posh, ain't she, Maggie?'

'Let's see her knickers before we decide on that,' Maggie replied. Fat Hannah laughed.

I screwed my face up, biting my lip in humiliation as they casually inspected my underwear, my skirt rucked up into the small of my back and the tail of my blouse with it, to leave the seat of my knickers on show. They were culottes – black silk with a broad fringe of lace – but quite small, leaving a lot of cheek showing. I felt a truly laughable touch of pride for being in expensive underwear, along with shame for how much bottom I was showing.

'Very fancy,' Fat Hannah remarked. She began to stroke my bottom, fondling me with an awful casual intimacy that put a lump in my throat in moments.

'Got a fat bum, ain't she?' Maggie said. Before I could stop myself my mouth opened in protest at the

21

sheer injustice of the remark, especially coming from her.

'Hardly – not by *your* standards!'

'Cheek!' Maggie answered. 'It don't pay to get lippy around here, girl, especially not when you're over Ma Riley's knee. Use the hairbrush on the cheeky cow, Hannah.'

'I might just do that,' Fat Hannah answered. I felt her shift beneath me as fresh fear welled up inside me.

'No, please!' I begged, babbling immediately. 'Not the hairbrush – you said a spanking!'

'It *will* be a spanking,' she answered me. 'With my hairbrush.'

'How ironic,' Kay said quietly.

'What d'you say?' Fat Hannah demanded.

'I said it was ironic,' Kay answered, stumbling slightly over her words. 'Amber likes to use a hairbrush, too.'

'She does, does she?' Fat Hannah laughed. 'Well, let's see how she likes one used on her, shall we?'

Kay gave a shy chuckle and my consternation grew to new and furious proportions as I remembered how I'd made her suffer in exactly the same way just a few days before. Now *I* was the one being held down to have my bottom smacked with a wooden brush and I could fully understand the fuss she'd made about it. Pouting furiously, I forced myself to stay still, braced for the pain, only to have the horrid thing laid on the small of my back and Fat Hannah's thumbs pushed in down the back of my French knickers. I'd forgotten I was to be done bare and I fought back a sob as that last precious barrier for my modesty started to come down.

'This is the part I like best,' Fat Hannah said happily. 'Taking down their knicks. I love it, I do, getting a nice fat girlie bum all bare for a good spanking.'

She'd taken them down as she spoke, easing them off my bottom with deliberate taunting slowness until I was quite bare, the full expanse of my cheeks showing to all three of them – plump, pale and naked and ready for spanking.

'Right down, Hannah,' Maggie urged, laughing. 'I want to see the little tart's cunt.'

There was no restraining the sob that broke from my throat at the woman's words. Then it had been done, my French knickers down around my thighs so that I was showing naked behind, a picture I could imagine all too easily, my broad pale bottom completely bare, my thighs closed but with the lips of my fanny peeping out between them. Maggie gave a satisfied cluck as she saw them.

Once more Fat Hannah began to stroke my bottom. I screwed my eyes shut in a desperate effort not to react. Yet I couldn't help myself as my body responded to the caress of her fingers and to the awful feeling of exposure and shame. My fanny was showing behind – my cunt, as Maggie had called it, that awful harsh word that still brings a flush to my cheeks for its sheer crudeness. Yet it could have been worse, because thankfully my cheeks have always been plump enough to conceal that last and most intimate detail, my bottom-hole.

'You clean?' Fat Hannah said suddenly, and then my cheeks had been hauled apart.

I gasped in shock and shame as I was put on show. Maggie gave a brief cruel laugh, Kay an embarrassed titter. Fat Hannah didn't react, save to lean forward a little, inspecting my anus. I could picture myself as intimately as she could, every secret detail: the broad star of lines between my cheeks, the dun-coloured ring of my sphincter, the bright pink pit at the very centre, all on show, to be inspected in minute detail. I could only pray that unlike Kay I had wiped myself properly.

'Tidy little number, ain't you?' Hannah said when she'd had me open for what seemed like an eternity. A wave of relief swept over me as she let go and my bottom cheeks closed. 'Now, let's get you spanked.'

I swallowed the huge lump that had risen in my throat as I was given my anal inspection. My sense of shame was burning in my head, my excitement rising despite myself, because everything about Hannah Riley, everything she did, brought out that rare need in me, the need to be thoroughly disciplined across an older woman's knee. Maybe I was wrong. Maybe she was not the one to spank me. I was going to get it anyway, but still I was determined not to show my true feelings, nor to make an exhibition of myself in front of the others. Not that it would be easy. If she spanked me hard I might be OK, in pain but no worse. If she spanked me gently I was in trouble, because I was already fighting the urge to stick my bottom up to her teasing hand. Yet maybe, just maybe, there was a way out.

'Doesn't this satisfy you?' I asked. 'What woman from the council would put up with this?'

'Oh yeah, I'm satisfied you're for real,' she answered me. 'But I'm still going to spank your fat girlie arse.'

As Hannah spoke she had picked the hairbrush up again, and on the last word she tapped it against my bottom. I felt my cheeks go tight, another sob escaped my throat and it had begun. Immediately I knew that I was in trouble. I'd thought she'd be brutal, using the full force of her massive arm so that it hurt too much for me to let my feelings build until afterwards, when I could have taken out my shameful excitement on myself in private, under my own fingers. Instead she had begun merely to tap the brush onto my bottom, peppering both cheeks with gentle smacks, never too hard, all of them on target.

I tried to fight it but it was all too much. Put across Hannah's knee, having my bottom stripped, being fondled, being smacked, and worse, knowing that Kay was looking on, fully aware of what was happening to me, I was gradually, inexorably being brought on heat.

'Oh, she's for real, OK,' Fat Hannah remarked after a while. 'Just watch the way her cunt creams.'

I knew it was true, because I could already feel the warmth in my fanny and the moisture as I started to juice. That didn't stop the painful stab of humiliation at her words and I tried to rise a last, pathetic effort at escape. She merely tightened her grip and gave me a single, harder swat, bringing a harsher sob to my throat as she spoke.

'Oh no you don't, my girl. When you're over Hannah Riley's knee that's the way you stay until she says you can get up.'

'Please, you're only supposed to be testing me,' I managed. But she didn't even bother to reply, just carried on spanking.

All I could do was close my eyes to shut out the view of Kay and Maggie as they watched me, but it made little difference. My bottom was warming to a firm matronly spanking, one thing I have never, ever been able to resist. It was too late, anyway. My fanny was already juicy and swollen, my bum cheeks were rosy and hot, my nipples stiff in my bra. Hannah had me completely, so gentle yet so firm, each smack of the hairbrush taking me that little bit closer to breaking point.

The smacks were getting harder, and she was applying more and more to the swell of my cheeks, right over my bottom-hole, so that every one sent a jolt straight to my fanny. It had started to hurt too, and the meaty sound of the hairbrush on my bottom was growing louder, so loud that I wondered if it could be heard from outside. That was almost too much, to think of the sleazy security guard, even the two horrible clowns, passing by and hearing my spanking, knowing that I was being punished, laughing to think of me lying bare-bottom across their boss's knee . . .

'Oh God, no, please!' I gasped. But it was too late.

I'd broken, giving in to the pain and humiliation, my mouth wide, my legs kicking up and down as the smacks suddenly grew harder and my will to resist snapped. Fat Hannah laughed: her grip tightened and now I was getting a full-blown hairbrush spanking, hard across my fat bare bottom, all dignity gone as I kicked and wriggled across my tormentor's lap. My legs were scissoring to show off my fanny, my hips bucking to make my cheeks spread, giving the onlookers glimpses of the pinky-brown star between.

Maggie was laughing openly now, well pleased by the ludicrous display I was making of myself, even slapping her fat thighs when my desperate efforts to escape the pain put me in some particularly absurd posture. Sometimes my legs kicked out sideways at the knees to stretch my fancy knickers tight, or were cocked apart to give the fullest possible view of my puffy excited fanny.

Hannah just kept on spanking, firm and even, never missing despite my frantic wriggling but catching me again and again across the fat of my bum cheeks, taking me closer and closer to that second breaking point. Already my dignity was gone, and now it would be worse as I started to show my excitement. Yet I couldn't help it – my bottom was too hot, the humiliation of being knickers-down across a big woman's lap was too strong, the heat in my fanny was irresistible.

'Not so posh now, eh?' Maggie laughed. 'Go on, Hannah, bring the little tart off – that'll be a laugh.'

'Yeah?' Hannah laughed. 'Why not? Need your cunt frigged, do you, darling? I bet you do!'

'No!' I gasped. But I didn't mean it. I *couldn't* mean it.

I gave a last despairing wail as Fat Hannah tucked one huge arm around my thigh. Her fingers found my fanny and then I was being masturbated as I was beaten. My pose was more humiliating than ever, held spread across her lap with my legs splayed, my fancy

French knickers stretched taut between my knees, my bottom bouncing fat and rosy to the smacks of the hairbrush and her fingers busy in the wet mushy folds of my open fanny ... my cunt, my open, sopping cunt.

Just two touches and I'd broken to my pleasure, utterly unable to resist as Hannah's fat fingers worked on my flesh, right on my clitty, even as she began to spank harder still. I'd given in, gasping and squirming myself on her hand, pushing my bottom up to receive the smacks, with Kay's giggles and Maggie's ribald laughter at my condition driving me higher still. I was going to come.

'Spank me,' I gasped. 'Spank me hard, Hannah, spank my naughty bottom.'

'My pleasure,' she answered.

She set up a rhythm on my cheeks, the hairbrush smacking down on the same spot, right across my spread bottom-hole, again and again, harder and harder. I felt my thighs start to tighten, my sphincter and my fanny start to contract, begging for it in pathetic wanton ecstasy as I was beaten and masturbated to orgasm.

'Do it,' I begged. 'Do it hard. Beat me, Hannah ... spank me ... spank my naughty bottom, harder ... harder ... yes, that's it, beat me, beat me, beat me!'

I screamed as it hit me, unable to stop myself as she brought me off so skilfully, simultaneously spanked and frigged as she held me, reducing me to no more than a dirty abject little slut. I was allowing myself to be spanked, and in front of other people, and I was begging for my own degradation as it was done.

Hannah let go of me while I was still coming so that I slipped off her lap and sat down hard on my smacked bottom, drawing a last gust of thigh-slapping laughter from Maggie. Kay put her arms out and I crawled to her for a cuddle, too far gone to care about the exhibition I was making of myself. After all, when I'd

27

just been spanked and frigged off what did it matter if I was crawling around the floor with my knickers down?

'Sorry, Amber,' Kay began, 'only –'

'Don't be,' I cut her off. I shook my head, trying to clear the fog of my pleasure. 'It was . . . it was OK, just a bit strong, that's all.'

'Count yourself lucky, darling,' Fat Hannah laughed. 'Normally I make 'em go down on me. So what's this about the kinky gear you make?'

Two

I left Hannah Riley's Circus with one of the biggest orders I'd ever taken, which went a long way to make up for my sore bottom and lingering sense of shame. There's no point in denying that a good spanking arouses me. Yet I will never, ever come to accept that it's appropriate for me from somebody like Fat Hannah Riley, however I might have felt while I was lying face down over her lap. If I do have to be spanked it should be by a bigger, older woman and Hannah Riley was certainly all of that. But it should be a bigger, older woman to whom I can look up and her status as the owner of a travelling circus was far from ideal. Yet it was too late to quibble – and it *had* been a good spanking.

In fact, it had been a *very* good spanking, one of the best, so good that deep down I wanted to go back for more, while what she had said afterwards filled me with both disgust and a sort of horrid compulsion. I knew I'd have done it, too, especially if she'd left me just short of orgasm before putting me on my knees. The thought of having my head pulled in between those gargantuan thighs and my face pressed to Hannah's sex for a licking was enough to send shivers through me every time I thought about it.

If my spanking had left me with mixed feelings, then the incident immediately afterwards held nothing but shame and embarrassment for me. As I'd stood up to adjust my clothing I'd glimpsed a fleeting movement at one of the caravan windows, a flash of hair that was an unmistakable shade of green. The thought that Buffo the clown and possibly the even more ghastly Baffo might have watched me getting my spanking, never mind being masturbated afterwards, was more deeply humiliating even than actually having it done to me. All I could do was tell Hannah Riley, who merely laughed at first. But when I insisted she promised to admonish them, with which I had to be content.

Maggie had been sent off to seek out the clowns while Hannah Riley and I discussed equipment. Carnival Bizarre had run three times so far, which was enough for Hannah to realise that she needed customised gear rather than relying on props from the circus. Apparently they had even used the brightly coloured plastic pillory from the clowns' stall, which had to be about as inappropriate for a club devoted to SM as a stuffed fox at an anti-blood sports meeting.

Hannah had ordered a new pillory, in dark wood and black leather, also a set of stocks, two whipping stools and a Berkley Horse to match. That alone would have been enough to keep me busy for a couple of weeks. But she also wanted a range of whips, paddles and straps, a set of school canes, and enough restraints to cope with a dozen people at a time. By the time I'd written everything down and we'd agreed a price I had enough work to keep me occupied for a whole month. I was looking forward to a profit sufficient to pay off my extortionate council tax bill in one go.

Kay was as happy as I was, maybe more so, and was clearly very pleased indeed to have seen me get a spanking, giggling as we drove back up the A41 over the show that I'd made of myself. I pointed out to her that every sting of Hannah Riley's hairbrush and every pang of shame I'd felt was going to be taken out tenfold on her when we got home, but that only made her laugh more.

I put her on a punishment routine: twenty of the hairbrush every morning before breakfast, bare and across my knee. It was after the first session that she pointed out something that I'd been trying not to think about, still rubbing her rosy bottom as she came out of the corner.

'You're going to have to go and make your peace with Morris, Amber.'

'Do you want another twenty, Kay?'

'No – but it's true, isn't it?'

'I suppose so,' I admitted. 'He's bound to find out sooner or later, after all.'

'Probably sooner,' she agreed. 'In fact, knowing Morris he's probably got video footage of you getting it in Fat Hannah's caravan.'

She was joking, although with Morris it wouldn't have surprised me. Certainly he would have had somebody go along to Carnival Bizarre, and if they'd been snooping when Kay and I were there our presence would have been reported back. It was best to tell him first.

'I'll call him,' I sighed, leaning over to reach for the phone.

'Wouldn't it be best to do it face to face?' Kay suggested.

I hesitated, not entirely sure about her motives, although she looked entirely sincere. Most likely she just wanted to play, reminding me of the need to keep her satisfied. At the least I'd have to give her to Melody for a while, which as always brought me a stab of jealousy. Yet if Mel was happy then Morris would be happy, which meant no recriminations for associating with Hannah Riley. I bit my lip as I tried to choose between emotion and reason.

'It's the only sensible thing to do,' Kay insisted.

'Oh, all right,' I answered, caving in. 'But you're to behave yourself.'

'Yes, Mistress,' she answered as she bent to pull up her knickers, briefly hiding her face and leaving me unsure whether or not her tone had held just a hint of mockery.

We didn't go to the Saturday club in the end because I was worried that Hannah would want me to take a spanking in public, something very different from what had happened to me in her caravan. It would have been hard to turn her down with my order still unpaid for but I really didn't feel I could cope with the sort of audience I'd be likely to have, especially not the appalling clowns. So Kay and I made our excuses, pleading a prior engagement and promising to come to the next one, by which time Hannah would have paid me my first instalment and I would be in a stronger position to negotiate.

On the Sunday we drove into London and to Morris's extravagant Hampstead mansion. We'd been invited to eat and, Morris being Morris, even a simple thing like Sunday lunch was done with vulgar ostentation. His dining room was also the one in which he held his private spanking parties, making it impossible not to think of all that had happened there as Harmony showed us in and poured out glasses of pink Dom Perignon, always their favourite. She was in a thigh-length dress of banana yellow velvet, low cut to show off several inches of chocolate-brown cleavage but otherwise decent.

'Where is everyone?' I asked, surprised that her sister and Morris hadn't come to the door.

'In the kitchen,' she told me. 'Mel was having a bit of trouble with Annabelle.'

'Oh?' I asked, surprised, as Annabelle was usually only too willing to take on whatever Melody chose for her.

'Nothing like that,' Harmony said casually, catching the tone of my voice. 'The bottle wouldn't fit, that's all, so Mel had to fist her.'

I wasn't quite sure what she meant. But I soon found out as Annabelle scampered into the room, holding something between her legs. Mel was behind, and helped her slave onto the table as Kay and I stood gaping. Annabelle was stark naked except for a delicate silver collar, and as she knelt down on the table I saw what was in her: a bottle, just as Harmony had said. A wine bottle, pushed deep in up her fanny, with a collar of lubricant squashed out around the straining pink ring of her flesh.

'Château Monbousquet, 'eighty-five,' Morris said as he came into the room.

'Isn't body temperature a little warm for claret?' I said, struggling to find some suitable quip to cover my shock and astonishment.

'It's not a claret,' he told me. 'It's a Madiran. Old Percy Ottershaw swears by it.'

I managed a weak nod, wondering if Percy Ottershaw also served it from his girlfriend's vagina. Mel came close and kissed me, as usual allowing a hand to steal down to my bottom as we hugged. I responded in kind, determined not to allow her any gesture that might conceivably be interpreted as dominant and also enjoying the full meaty feel of her cheeks. Like her sister, she was in a short velvet dress, only red rather than yellow. Judging by the feel of her bottom underneath the material and the way her breasts pushed to mine, she was otherwise quite bare.

'That's what I like to see,' Morris said happily, beaming as he watched his wife and me cuddling. 'But don't get carried away. Dinner first. I'm so hungry I could eat a horse.'

He made for the head of the table and Kay sat down just in time to avoid having her bottom pinched. She

33

and I were on either side of him, which meant that Annabelle's bare bottom was pushed up pretty well in our faces. Her slim bum cheeks were well parted to show off her anus, which was somewhat squashed out of shape by the bottle in her vagina, as was the tattoo on her bare pubic mound, which marked her as Melody's personal property. Harmony made for the kitchen as Morris picked up a corkscrew from beside his mat.

'What have you been up to?' he asked, taking a grip on the bottle's neck and touching the blade of the corkscrew to the lead sheating. 'We haven't seen you in months.'

'This and that,' I answered, unable to keep my stare from the way the flesh of Annabelle's straining vagina moved as he peeled the lead foil from the bottle. 'We had a week in Paris in May, and . . . doesn't that hurt, Annabelle?'

Her answer was a muffled sob, in response to which Mel took a small red apple from a bowl on the sideboard and jammed it between her hapless slave's jaws.

'It's forbidden to talk,' she told me, 'for making such a fuss over having a little bottle put up its hole.'

'Yes,' Morris agreed, twisting the screw deep into the cork. 'Get your back in, girl, or you'll spill the wine.'

Annabelle obeyed, making a tight curve of her back so that her bottom was thrust higher than before and her cheeks spread wider still. Morris peered in from one side, making sure that the level of the wine was right. Then pushed down on the levers of the corkscrew. I watched as the cork slowly emerged, with the pressure pushing the bottle deeper still up into Annabelle's body. A final 'pop' and the bottle was open.

'Excellent,' Morris declared. 'It works. You must excuse me for using you two as guinea pigs, Amber, but this is something we were planning for a party and I wanted to be sure it worked. Keep that bum up, Annabelle, until I say otherwise.'

He sat down and began to sharpen his carving knife, leaving the bottle trembling ever so slightly in its envelope of taut pink flesh. I caught the smell of roast beef a moment before Harmony reappeared carrying a heavily laden platter. Conversation paused as we went through the little ritual of serving Sunday lunch, no doubt almost exactly as it was being enacted in thousands of homes up and down the country. Except that ours was probably the only one with a naked girl kneeling on the table with a bottle of fine wine inserted in her vagina.

Only when all five of us had our plates and I was taking a little mustard did Morris turn his attention back to Annabelle. He took a glass and poised it carefully beneath the neck of the bottle as he spoke.

'OK, Annabelle, now lift your back – slowly. That's it, nice and elegant.'

The bottle had begun to tilt as she moved and dark red wine was now pouring into Morris's glass. He waited until it was nearly full, peering close before giving the command to stop. Annabelle immediately dipped her back once more, cutting off the flow.

'Excellent!' Morris announced. 'If you would pass your glass, Kay?'

Five times poor Annabelle was made to go through the same shameful routine, first under spoken command, and then with just a slap on her bottom to make her go through the pouring motion. Not that her exposure mattered, as for the time being she was no more than a pretty – and useful – table ornament. Even when she had dispensed all five glasses she had to stay in position, leaving the bottle less than half full and the glistening flesh of the inside of her vagina visible through the deep green glass.

'L'Chaim,' Morris intoned, lifting his glass.

35

I responded in kind and took a sip, trying with difficulty not to stare at Annabelle's spread bottom cheeks. We began to eat, for the most part in silence, until Morris had just about polished off the contents of his plate. He sat back to dab at his lips with his napkin and take a good swallow of wine before turning to me.

'So, Amber, what's this I hear about you visiting Fat Hannah Riley?'

'It didn't take you long to find out,' I answered, wondering just how much he knew.

'I have my ways,' Morris told me.

'Let me guess. One of the clowns?'

'No, nothing like that. They're a tight-knit crew, that lot.'

'How then?'

Morris just tapped the side of his nose. I wondered again how much he knew, and in particular if he'd found out about my spanking. The thought threatened to bring a flush to my cheeks and I went on quickly, eager to show that I wasn't trying to hide anything from him.

'I was thinking that she might want some things from me, since they're setting up a new club. As it happens I got a very good order.'

'Oh, right?' he replied. 'Good for you.'

I felt myself relax a little, not only because if Morris didn't know about my order then he presumably didn't know about my spanking either. I was also relieved that he didn't seem annoyed by what I'd been afraid he would see as a betrayal.

'I hope you don't mind?' I queried, despite feeling rather pathetic for asking the question when it was really nothing to do with him. 'I know it's a rival club, but –'

'A rival club?' he broke in, with a laugh. 'Hardly that. They're a bunch of amateurs, that's all. They don't know the first thing about it.'

At least *one* of them knew quite a bit, judging by the way Hannah Riley had spanked me. But I kept quiet as Morris took another sip of wine and slapped Annabelle's bottom to make her refill his glass before he went on.

'No, I'm not that worried, so long as they don't try running events too near mine or on the same evenings.'

That wasn't the impression Kay had given me, but still I held my peace.

'I *would* like a bit of inside information now and then, though,' he went on. 'Which venues they're going to be using and when, that sort of stuff – so it's great that you've got in with them.'

'Morris, I can't spy on them,' I pointed out.

'Who said anything about spying?' he demanded, feigning surprise and not a little indignation. 'All I want is the stuff they're going to release anyway, just a bit early.'

'That *is* spying,' I told him.

'Bollocks,' Morris said, his voice now quite sharp. 'Come on, Amber, how long have I known you? Shit, I can remember you running around your Dad's garden in a little pink romper suit. You're going to turn old Morris out in favour of some fat pikey bitch just because she gave you a good spanking, are you?'

'It's not that, Morris,' I protested, going abruptly pink at the realisation that he *did* know that I'd been punished, 'I . . . I just don't want to get involved, that's all, not that way. Besides, if you know so much about what happened the other day surely you can get your information from whoever told you?'

'It doesn't work like that,' he insisted. 'OK, I'll come clean. I know you visited and I know you got your bum smacked because it's hardly a secret. The clowns looked in on you and they told everyone else. Now it's the main topic on their website forum.'

'There weren't any pictures, were there?' I asked, now blushing furiously.

'No,' he answered me. 'But I hear you got it good!'

'With a hairbrush?' Melody put in.

'Yes, with a hairbrush,' I admitted, now red-faced to the roots of my hair. 'And yes, she was pretty thorough.'

'Bare-bottom?' Harmony asked.

I nodded.

'And you took your own boobs out?' Melody added.

'No!' I protested. 'I did not!'

'Told you so,' Melody addressed her sister. 'Not our Amber. She needs it done for her.'

'Who said I did that?' I demanded.

'Some guy on the forum,' Harmony replied. 'The one who watched you, I think. He said a lot more too, like how you let Fat Hannah frig you off and you were begging for more.'

'I . . . I only let her spank me, that's all, because she thought I might have been sent by the council or somebody,' I said, stumbling over my words and praying that my furious blushes wouldn't make it too obvious I was lying, only for Kay to burst into giggles.

'You did it, girl!' Melody laughed, pointing at me in open delight. 'She did it, didn't she, Kay? She did it!'

'I didn't say anything!' Kay retorted. But Melody just laughed all the harder and even Annabelle was trying not to giggle, making the bottle quiver in her bloated sex.

'OK, she made me come,' I admitted. 'I . . . I couldn't stop myself.'

'You are really something,' Melody laughed. 'Ten minutes you'd known her and you're bare over her knee and begging to be rubbed off. You are one dirty slut, Amber Oakley.'

'It wasn't like that,' I protested feebly, leaving both sisters in fits of laughter.

'Girls, girls,' Morris cut in, lifting his hands in a soothing gesture but struggling not to smile himself. 'I'm sure Amber just got a little carried away, that's all.

You know she gets embarrassed about taking spankings, but there's no need to tease her. So, Amber, are you going to be sensible about this and pass a bit of info on to me, or what?'

I shrugged, too flustered to answer easily. Possibly there was an implied threat in what he was saying, possibly not. I took another mouthful of beef and a swallow of wine to let my embarrassment die down a little, then spoke.

'Morris, it simply isn't fair to ask me to pass on information that Hannah doesn't want given out, and she probably wouldn't tell me anyway. But yes, obviously I don't mind giving you a call when the venues and times are first released. OK?'

'That's all I'm asking,' he responded, spreading his hands in resignation. 'No more than that.'

I came away from Morris's feeling rather pleased with myself. The revelation that my spanking had become common knowledge was deeply embarrassing, but without pictures it was really no more than a rumour. I'd expected Morris to be far more demanding as well and at the least to have had to surrender Kay to Mel for a spanking – or even to have been forced to let her lick the other woman. Had Morris really decided to be a bastard about it I knew I might have ended up over Mel's knee myself – or his – or have been asked to participate in one of his private parties. As it was I'd ended up pleasantly drunk and horny but with my dignity intact and Kay unmolested.

In fact I was so pleased with myself that I made Kay stop the car on the way back and took her deep into the woods for a little attention to her bottom and a lick for me, with her kneeling at my feet, her dress pulled up and her knickers well down as she tongued me to ecstasy. We walked back to the car hand in hand, laughing, to the bemusement of a dodgy-looking individual in a long grey overcoat. He might well have been a flasher but if so was clearly too intimidated by us to do anything.

On the Monday morning I left Kay in charge of the shop and retired to my workroom to start on Hannah Riley's order. There was another club in two weeks and I wanted at least two of the large pieces of equipment finished by then, along with most of the implements and restraints. She'd left the design entirely to me and didn't seem to mind paying a little above the odds, if not exactly the highest prices. I was determined to give her her money's worth and used the best-quality leather, thick cowhide lined with fine pigskin and sewn at the edges, while all the fittings I used were chromed steel and were either cast or welded rather than simply bent into shape.

By the weekend I had the pillory done, along with four sets of restraints and a dozen implements, all of them finished to a high standard. That allowed me to slow down a little the following week despite having promised to deliver everything on the Saturday afternoon. I finished with time to spare and didn't even have to bother about informing Morris since the venue had been advertised on the Carnival Bizarre website the day after I'd visited.

The circus had moved on from Harrow to Barnet and had been pitched on an open space near the Scratchwood Services, while the club was to be held in a large pub on the Great North Road. That made it easy to get to and so we were taking our time on the Saturday morning, with me minding the shop and Kay still wandering around in just a top and a pair of knickers. I had a fair number of customers in the store, mainly locals after tack for the gymkhana at Essendon on Sunday, so it was a little awkward when a slender black girl in leather trousers and a scarlet top marked with the word *Bitch* walked in and kissed me full on my lips.

'Angel, nice to see you,' I managed. 'Kay's in the kitchen if you want to go through.'

'Great,' she answered. 'See you in a sec, yeah?'

She came round behind the counter just as I turned to speak to another customer, Mrs Mattlin-Jones from the local riding school, so that I could do nothing to avoid the friendly swat that Angel applied to the seat of my jeans. Mrs Mattlin-Jones gave me a distinctly odd look but said nothing as she paid for the box of pink rosettes she wanted, and I was left blushing as she left the shop.

Nobody else needed serving right then and I went back into the house. Kay had just put the kettle on and Angel was seated at the kitchen table with her chair rocked back on its hind legs.

'Not in front of my customers, please, Angel,' I said immediately. 'They think I'm a pillar of the local community.'

'Relax,' she answered me. 'The old bag would probably like to give you a few herself.'

Kay laughed.

'What happened?'

'Angel smacked my bottom in front of Mrs Mattlin-Jones,' I told her. 'Seriously, Angel, the locals don't know anything about what I do in private and I want it to stay that way.'

'Whatever,' she said, dismissing the incident. 'Mel says you two are going to Carnival Bizarre tonight. Can I come with you?'

'We're going, yes,' I admitted cautiously, 'and you can come if you like. But what's Mel going to say?'

'I don't give a fuck,' she answered. 'Yeah, sure, I love Mel to bits, but I'm sick of always being in her shadow. I want somewhere I can do my thing without being Mel's new recruit.'

'That's fair enough,' I admitted. I was about to take my coffee from Kay when the shop bell went.

'If you're coming with us,' I told Angel, 'you can help Kay load the car.'

She nodded, apparently indifferent to my minor gesture of dominance and I went back out·to the shop, taking my coffee with me. It was Mrs Mattlin-Jones again, already at the counter with a look of mild irritation on her face. She wanted to change her rosettes for a mixed box, which meant getting boxes down from the top shelf and sorting them out individually. She waited with every evidence of impatience or as if I was intent on cheating her in some way. I didn't even bother to adjust the price because I knew full well that she'd argue and it simply wasn't worth the trouble. When she'd finally left I went back indoors to find Kay and Angel exactly as I'd left them, sipping coffee around the kitchen table.

'I thought you were going to load the car?' I said.

'No rush,' Kay answered.

If ever there was a moment to assert my right to give her domestic discipline it was now. I walked straight up to her, removed her coffee cup from her hand and took a firm hold on her wrist. Kay gave a single squeak of surprise as I pulled her after me towards one of the chairs but went over my lap meekly enough as I sat down. Her knickers showed under the hem of her top and I tugged them down without any preamble, baring her bottom.

Angel quickly moved her own chair to get a better view as I began to spank, delivering fifty firm smacks to Kay's cheeks – which were already flushed pink from the hairbrush spanking that I'd given her earlier. Kay was soon kicking and wriggling on my lap but she didn't complain, merely standing to rub her sore bottom when I'd finished with her. She gave me a single self-pitying look over her shoulder as she went to stand in the corner without even having to be told, with her knickers still down so that her bottom was exposed to the room.

'You keep her well disciplined,' Angel remarked.

'She needs it,' I answered, wondering if I should attempt to give Angel the same treatment but deciding against it. 'We'd better get moving. Come on, Kay, at least go and get dressed.'

She'd only just put her hands on her head, and really should have stayed that way for at least five minutes by the kitchen clock. Yet she was at least doing what she was told, and immediately scampered from the room, one hand clutching her lowered panties to stop herself tripping over them. Angel chuckled.

'She's sweet, your Kay.'

I didn't answer, knowing full well that she fancied Kay. I went back to my coffee. Kay was soon back down, dressed now in jeans and a jumper. I went back to the shop while she and Angel loaded the car, locking up the premises with a few minutes still to go before noon. We found the venue easily enough but Mrs Riley wasn't there so we had to deliver my goods to the various carnival hands who were setting up. It all seemed to be very badly organised: none of them had been given any money to pay me even though Hannah had promised cash on delivery.

They were at least helpful with carrying the merchandise. Two grinning men, Mick and Sean, detached themselves from putting up black drapes to unload the car for us. I didn't recognise them but they seemed to know who we were, for which there could be only one explanation, a very embarrassing one. They knew about my spanking.

Fortunately they were nice about it and didn't say anything, content merely with letting their stares feast on my chest and the seat of Kay's jeans as she bent to get things out of the car. They seemed to be somewhat cautious of Angel, though. That was more or less what I'd have expected of ordinary men when faced with women who they know were going to be attending a fetish club, so I put up with it.

We quickly had everything transferred into the venue, a vaulted cellar presumably dating from when the pub had been a coaching house for the Great North Road. The walls were blank – worn brick that was white-washed in places and discoloured by the torn remnants of posters for past events, including ones dating from the raves of the late 1980s and even before.

All this was being covered up with the black drapes but not before I'd noticed the heavy iron brackets set high around the walls, presumably originally for long-vanished oil lamps but perfect now for attaching the chains of my wrist cuffs. I put up all four sets in a row along the wall opposite the stairs, with the pillory in front of them and a range of implements laid out on a small table covered in black cloth. The result was quite pleasing: it was a great deal more atmospheric than the huge warehouses that Morris normally used for his club.

With everything set up and the carnival hands starting to get a bit overfamiliar, particularly with Kay, we went upstairs and shared a bottle of wine. It was a long while since I'd been to a club and I felt surprisingly nervous, despite knowing that none of my usual bug-bears were likely to be there. And I hadn't volunteered to do anything whatsoever, either.

We were still sipping our wine when Mrs Riley appeared, blocking the light as she paused in the doorway. She was dressed in an immense floral dress of some man-made fabric, about as unsuitable for a fetish club as could be imagined, and despite our recent and intimate acquaintance her sheer bulk still had me fighting not to stare. As she started towards us Maggie appeared behind her. Angel spoke quickly and in an undertone.

'Don't tell her that I know Morris.'

There was no time for me to respond, and I found myself getting to my feet before I could remind myself that there was no reason for me to show any deference

44

to the big woman. Hannah motioned for me to sit down as if it was the most natural thing in the world that I should stand for her, and lowered her bulk into the seat opposite me and next to Angel.

'All ready?' she asked.

'Everything's downstairs and set up,' I told her. 'You've met Kay, and this is my friend Angel. Angel, this is Mrs Hannah Riley, who runs the club.'

'Hannah'll do nicely, sweetheart,' the big woman answered, turning an appraising glance on Angel.

'She's safe,' I assured her, and immediately wished that I hadn't. Watching Angel forced to take a spanking to prove that she was the real thing would have been immensely satisfying. I dug in my bag.

'Here's my invoice . . .'

'I'll sort that later, darling,' Hannah interrupted, 'when I've got a few punters through the gates. I've got no cash right now. Maggie, go downstairs and make sure the boys have got it all done.'

Maggie had been hovering in the background and promptly obeyed, disappearing down the stairs in a cloud of cigarette smoke.

'Oh, OK,' I said to Hannah.

'Speaking of punters,' she went on, 'it's fifteen quid each.'

'Sorry – I didn't realise we had to pay,' I responded as she held out one fat hand.

'*Everybody* has to pay,' she told me. 'Unless you want to be part of the act, that is.'

'Sounds good,' Angel responded immediately.

'What does it involve?' I asked.

'You know,' Hannah said. 'Getting the boys going, putting on a bit of a show, flashing a bit of tit, maybe.'

'Kay and I don't really have much to do with men,' I pointed out. 'But –'

'I'm up for it,' Angel cut in. 'Go for it, Amber: we can dom Kay together, yeah?'

'I'm not sure,' I began, glancing at Kay, 'maybe if . . .'

'I don't mind,' Kay said, 'as long as the audience are kept back. And I might not want to go bare.'

'You won't go bare?' Hannah sneered. 'What's the problem? You let your knickers down in front of me quick enough.'

'There will be men watching,' I said. I would have gone on to explain that Kay would be fine with going bare as long as she was given a chance to come to terms with what was going to happen to her first, but Fat Hannah interrupted me, speaking to Kay.

'The punters want to see your tits and arse, darling – that's what it's all about.'

'I need to think about it,' Kay said.

'That's not necessarily true,' I pointed out, eager to defend Kay despite being a firm believer in every spanked girl needing her knickers pulled down. 'In fact, submission and domination is more a case of psychology and doesn't really need to involve nudity at all. What matters . . .'

I stopped. Hannah had turned around, taking no notice of me whatsoever as she clicked her fingers at the girl reading a magazine behind the bar.

'A pint of Guinness, darling.'

The girl ducked down to get a glass and Fat Hannah went on, talking to us now.

'You wants to get in free, you gives us a show, plain and simple. And that means tits and arse – all three of you.'

'But I'll be dominating men,' Angel pointed out. 'I need to keep my clothes or I lose my authority.'

'Bollocks,' Hannah answered. 'You want in for free, you do it topless.'

Angel hesitated, but only for a moment.

'OK,' she said. 'If that's how you like to play it, I'll go topless.'

'Good girl,' Hannah said and turned to me.

'So?'

'I can't really make a commitment,' I began, realising that for all her expertise as a spanker she clearly had either no idea of or no respect for the ordinary ethics of SM. 'Kay isn't particularly happy performing in front of men, and at the very least she needs to be free to make her decision in her own time, while I agree with Angel that a dominant women should be fully covered.'

'Come on, Amber,' Angel urged. 'It's not like you haven't done it before.'

'No, but . . .' I began, then stopped. 'I think I'll just pay my entrance fee for now. You can take the fifteen pounds off my invoice, Hannah.'

'Thirty,' she corrected me, 'if your tart isn't getting her tits out. And I'd prefer it if you paid me up front or the takings will get in a muddle.'

I handed over thirty pounds, not without a little reluctance and promising myself that I would add the same amount to her final bill. Hannah's Guinness arrived and she didn't pay for that either, telling the girl to add it to the night's tab despite having my three ten-pound notes in her hand. It was about time that Kay and I got changed, I reckoned, so I swallowed the rest of my wine and stood up.

'Is there somewhere we could get ready?' I asked Hannah.

She shrugged.

'In the Ladies, I suppose, darling.'

It was more or less what I'd expected, and it was obviously pointless to argue. Our things were in the car and we went to fetch them, leaving Hannah talking to Angel. I was feeling more than a little put-upon and I was worried about getting paid for all the work I'd done. But there's also a stubborn streak in me and I was determined to enjoy the club in my own way.

I'd chosen one of my favourite looks: full riding gear, with a tailored black jacket, a white blouse, cream-coloured jodhpurs and highly polished riding boots. I also carried a horn-handled crop to keep Kay and any others in order and my hair was worn up to make my face look as severe as is possible with curly blonde hair. By the time I was ready so was Kay who looked absolutely demure and yet shockingly sexual in an old-fashioned Girl Guides uniform complete with a yellow neck scarf fastened with a woggle, smart black shoes, knee-length white socks and a skirt about half the length of the original but still far from indecent. She'd put her hair into bunches.

One glance was enough to make me want to get her over my knee – as she knew full well, giggling and making a run for the door as I snatched for her arm. She escaped and I followed, to find that the club had begun to fill up. Maggie was on the desk at the bottom of the stairs, taking the money before people were allowed through a black drape curtain, while the sleazy security guard we'd met at the circus site had taken on the role of bouncer, alongside a beefy balding individual who looked like a comedy strongman. Hannah was behind Maggie, a half-full pint glass in her hand.

Mick, Sean and two other carnival hands were at a table drinking beer and watching people come in. But to my relief that was the full complement of circus staff – there was no sign of the ghastly clowns. Otherwise, there was a barman from the pub, a handful of single men and three couples standing about chatting or simply looking hopeful. Angel sat on a high stool next to my pillory with her top off to show her pert black breasts, a whip trailing negligently from her hand. One man was already kneeling at her feet, his head bowed low, and she was sipping a drink that no doubt had been bought by him. We walked over to her.

'Get my friends a drink, Dipshit. Red wine,' she ordered, kicking the man with her toe as we joined her. 'Looking good, you two, but you should have gone for this. Free drinks all night has to be worth a flash of your tits, yeah?'

I shrugged, not wanting to argue the point. Kay came close to me, cuddling into the crook of my arm, evidently nervous. I gave her bottom a reassuring pat.

'This is not bad,' Angel went on. 'Small, but not bad. So, what – you going to play?'

'Maybe,' I told her. 'But later, if the atmosphere's right.'

I wasn't sure if it would be or not, because so far the men outnumbered the women by at least five to one. But shortly after Angel's slave had brought our drinks over a new group arrived, all female – and presumably circus staff since they didn't pay to get in but greeted Hannah and Maggie with smiles and kisses. All four looked exceptionally fit and not dissimilar to each other: tall and muscular, with long elegant legs and full chests, but not so full as to make them look awkward. When they emerged from the Ladies they'd stripped down to high heels and minuscule pussy pelmets made of glittering material in an assortment of colours, their boobs showing bare and unashamed. They at once began to mingle with the men, presumably on Hannah's orders.

As the place began to fill up my confidence grew. I recognised quite a few faces from Morris's clubs, although fortunately the appalling Protheroe was not among them. There was only Gavin Bulmer from among the regulars I'd been hoping to avoid, and he was pretty well unavoidable anyway since his paintball club owned the land next to my house. As he had discovered what I was into by spying on me and was also a male chauvinist pig to end all male chauvinist pigs he wasn't somebody I particularly wanted to talk to. But he seemed more intent on chatting up one of Fat Hannah's circus girls in any case.

More couples arrived, including some who'd bought things from me in past. Whatever the attitude of Fat

Hannah and her staff, the single men were generally deferential or at least understood the rules. Several approached me and asked me to dominate them, making no objection when I politely passed them on to Angel, who had to line them up along one wall so that they didn't get in our way. My equipment was soon in use: Angel flogged a man in the pillory and then gave way to a couple.

The woman was the submissive, small and pretty with nothing on but a tiny leather dress which had quickly been pulled up to expose an enticingly meaty bottom. The man used a thonged leather whip on her, making her count the strokes as she was flogged. He paused occasionally to expose her breasts and torment her nipples, to ease his fingers into her vagina and make her lick up her own juices from them, to slip a finger between her by then well-reddened cheeks to tickle and probe at her anus until she was wriggling in the pillory.

By the time he let her out of the restraints I was about ready to punish Kay. I was certainly aroused enough and was pretty sure that the crowd would behave themselves. Angel had asked if she could help and it seemed only fair to let her so long as I remained firmly in control. She was at the bar, seated on one man's back with her boots resting on the buttocks of another who lay prostrate on the floor, so I took hold of Kay's hand and led her over.

'Are you going to?' Kay asked at once, recognising my mood.

'Yes,' I told her. 'Unless you say no now.'

She merely shook her head, but I could feel the faint trembling of her hand as I stopped beside Angel.

'You said you might like to help me with Kay?' I suggested.

'Would I just!' Angel answered, jumping up immediately and provoking a grunt of pain from the man she'd been resting her boots on. 'You shits can fuck off – this is not for your eyes. One look and I'll thrash you senseless.'

Both men scurried off, along with her various other hangers-on, but only out of our immediate vicinity.

'Fuck *off*!' Angel yelled, and smacked the riding crop she was carrying against her boot top. 'Yes, that's right, face the wall. And if I catch you peeking ...'

They went, at least most of them, but Angel had already lost interest, her eyes shining as she looked down at Kay, who was blushing faintly, with her eyes raised to us, wide with excitement and apprehension.

'Yum,' Angel pronounced, deliberately smacking her lips. 'I'm going to enjoy this.'

'My panties stay up for now, OK?' Kay said faintly.

'OK,' I promised.

'Pity,' Angel responded, pulling a chair over with her foot. 'Knees together?'

'Perfect,' I agreed and pulled up a chair of my own.

Kay stayed as she was, watching us as we adjusted ourselves to make a lap for her with our chairs pulled close and facing each other so that our legs interlocked. As soon as I was ready I patted my thigh, looking up.

'Come on, Kay – over you go.'

A lot of people were watching, including some of the men that Angel had sent away although the majority still had their faces pressed obediently to the wall. I could see the excitement and envy in the onlookers' faces as Kay bent down across our linked legs, inspiring both my own arousal and a lot of pride. Kay was not only the prettiest girl in the club, she had the most spankable bottom. And she was mine to spank.

I wanted to take her knickers down very badly indeed but contented myself with gently lifting her Guides skirt to show them off. They were white cotton, full cut, and in her ignominious position they were absolutely bulging with cheeky bottom, ripe for spanking. How anyone could resist such a sight has always been beyond me and Angel clearly agreed, giving a little growl deep in her throat as Kay's bum came on display.

'Be my guest,' I offered. I took hold of one cheek myself, cupping the bulge where Kay's panties curved down between her thighs to leave a crescent of smooth pink flesh pushing out beneath the hem.

Angel didn't hesitate, first lifting Kay's skirt a little higher to leave the full expanse of the big white panties on show, then laying a hand on the taut cotton to stroke the ripe curves beneath with something approaching reverence. I could heartily agree with such an emotion, always astonished and delighted myself by how full and firm Kay's bottom was for such a slender girl and never tiring of exploring her.

Kay's own emotions wouldn't have been hard to guess from her heavy breathing and sobs from the moment her panties came on show, even if I hadn't known exactly what was going through her head. She needed it, badly, but that did nothing to weaken the intensity of her shame and sense of exposure as we caressed the seat of her panties – just the opposite. I could feel her trembling growing more violent and I knew she'd be getting warm – and wet – between her thighs.

'Spankies time,' I announced once I had taken a long lingering feel of her bottom.

Kay gave a tiny gasp and I felt her body stiffen in anticipation. I lifted my hand, deliberately holding back to watch her bottom cheeks twitch in her panties as she waited. Angel had done the same, and we shared a wicked grin before she spoke.

'One . . . two . . . three . . .'

We brought our hands down at the same time to plant a firm double smack on Kay's upturned bottom, making her flesh quiver under the tight white cotton and drawing a louder gasp from her throat. I felt a familiar tightening between my thighs at her reaction, and as

Angel and I set up a rhythm on Kay's bottom I was promising myself that I'd be sitting on her pretty face with her tongue well up my bottom-hole before the end of the evening, just as soon as we were in the privacy of my house.

For now what I most wanted to do was to get Kay's knickers down, to humiliate her properly and let everyone in the crowd and particularly Angel enjoy the view of her pretty fanny and the rude dark star of her bumhole. I began to spank harder, provoking the first tiny kicks from Kay's legs as my smacks started to sting. She was getting red, the flesh poking out around the leg holes of her knickers already flushed, a beautiful sight that made my fanny tighten again. Her bottom was so lovely, and so good to spank, while the little kicking motions she had started to make were almost painfully sweet. Her smart, square-toed shoes began to drum on the floor as her pain grew.

'Harder?' Angel suggested.

'Harder,' I confirmed. 'She's shy, but she can take quite a lot. Let's try turn and turn about, OK?'

Angel nodded and stopped spanking, allowing me to plant a firm swat full across the seat of Kay's panties instead of on just one cheek. The result was a satisfying squeal and one leg kicked up and a little aside to show off the soft bulge of cotton where the gusset of her knickers was pulled against her sex lips. Angel smacked in turn and again Kay squealed and kicked, and again as we established the new rhythm, now spanking her much harder with heavy swats delivered one at a time and full across her bottom.

As we smacked harder still Kay really began to kick, her legs all over the place, sometimes thumping on the floor, sometimes splayed to show off the bulge of her sex, sometimes pumping frantically up and down. She was panting for breath too, in between ever louder squeals and little heartfelt cries, all of which only served to encourage Angel and me as we spanked the juicy panty-clad ball of her bottom. The crowd were well pleased too, staring in open delight. More than one of the men in the couples was fondling his girlfriend as they watched.

I stopped suddenly, signalling to Angel as I once more began to explore Kay's bottom. She stayed down, limp and gasping across our laps, the exposed flesh of her cheeks now a rich red and hot to the touch. I could feel the warmth of her smacked skin even through her panties. I slipped a hand down between her thighs and proved that her sex was just as hot – and wet, too, with a damp patch starting to grow in the groove between her lips.

'Bad girl,' I told her. 'You're getting excited, aren't you?'

Kay's answer was a sob as I began to stroke her fanny through her panties, deliberately rubbing the wet cotton into her crease and against her clitty. She was soaking wet and obviously ready, though maybe not ready to have it all put on show to a good twenty gawping men and women. I took my hand away, running one finger slowly up the crease of her bottom to push her panties down into the warm deep valley. I continued higher until I reached the waistband, which I took hold of between finger and thumb.

'Well,' I asked, 'has my little Girl Guide been bad enough to need her knickers taken down? Has she?'

'Oh, I think she has,' Angel put in, her voice rich with excitement.

She too took hold of Kay's waistband, lifting just a little so that we could see down under the big white panties to where the crease of her bottom began to open out. Kay gave another sob, louder than before, and bitter, full of very real emotion. Her hair was dangling onto the floor but I could see her face. Her eyes were shut tight, and I knew she'd be fantasising, perhaps imagining herself as a real Girl Guide, spanked by her troop leader as her friends watched and about to have her panties pulled down to complete her humiliation.

'Well, Kay?' I repeated, more firmly. 'Do you or do you not need your panties pulled down?'

'She does,' Angel stated. 'All bad girls should have their panties pulled down when they're spanked, and Girl Guides are no exception.'

'Very true,' I agreed. 'And if she won't answer me, then I think they'd better come down anyway, don't you?'

'No,' Angel replied. 'I think she should be made to say it. Well, Kay, do Girl Guides need their panties pulled down? Do they?'

Kay's answer was an odd gulping noise, something close to the sound a girl makes when she's crying and can't speak properly. I looked down at Kay, ready to stop if she shook her head. But she gave no reaction other than to open her mouth a little.

'Do they?' Angel demanded, planting a firm smack on Kay's bottom with her free hand, then more, one smack to each word. 'Do . . . Girl . . . Guides' . . . panties . . . have . . . to . . . come . . . down . . . for . . . spanking?'

She ended with a full-power slap, jamming Kay forward across our knees and drawing a gasp of shock and pain from her. Suddenly Kay was babbling.

'Yes, they do . . . do it, please . . . pull down my panties, go on, pull them down, right down . . .'

'I thought they might,' Angel chuckled. And we began to pull.

Unveiling Kay was always a delight, all the more so when it was done in front of other people. Every single man and woman in the crowd had their stares fixed on her bulbous quivering bottom as she was slowly laid bare. The big white panties were eased down to show first the neat V where her crease began, then the gentle rise and flare of her cheeks, the deep shadowed valley between them hiding her anus, the full chubby swell where they tucked under to her thighs and, as we inverted the voluminous knickers into a tangle of white cotton, the sweetly pouted lips of her newly shaved fanny. She was wet and puffy, the wrinkled flesh of her inner lips moist and glistening, her hole clogged with white juice.

'What a little tart!' Angel crowed as she saw the wondrous sight. 'You dirty, dirty tart, Kay. Imagine getting all excited because your botty's been smacked! Imagine that!'

'Disgusting,' I agreed as Kay whimpered her response.

We went back to spanking her, no longer to a rhythm but applying firm smacks all over her bare quivering bottom to make her kick and wriggle on our laps, showing off her fanny. As we beat harder and her reaction became more pained, her bottom-hole, deep between her cheeks, brown and rude, was exposed. She knew it too, sobbing and gasping in her emotion and her pain as her bum bounced and reddened. She'd begun to cry as well, with tears running from her tightly closed eyes and spittle from around her open mouth.

'Shall we?' Angel asked, extending her middle finger and glancing down at Kay's now flaming bottom. 'You spank, I'll rub.'

'No,' I answered as Kay immediately began to shake her head. 'Not here. Come on.'

'Get up, you, you're going in the loos,' Angel ordered before I could say more.

It wasn't really what I wanted to do. But I *did* want to come, badly, while Kay was showing the full emotion of her bare-bottom spanking. I quickly tucked her Guides skirt up into its own waistband so that her red bottom showed as Angel and I led her across the room, hobbling in her lowered panties, which had fallen down around her ankles. We reached the Ladies, only to find that it was packed with people: women trying to get changed, a pair of transvestites adjusting their make-up in the mirror, a line waiting for the cubicles, even Gavin Bulmer who was now fucking the circus girl he'd been talking to, pressing her up against the wall.

Angel and I exchanged a single glance and shook our heads. Retreating, we made for the tiny cloakroom and retrieved our things, Angel slipping her top on over her bare breasts and Kay simply pulling her knickers up and dropping her skirt down to its 'proper' level. Outside the air was pleasantly cool as we made a dash for the car, ignoring the astonished faces of passers-by. All three of use were laughing as I started the engine, and Angel quickly flashed her tits at a group of lads pouring out of an Indian restaurant. Their shouted demands for us to come back faded as I pulled out into the evening traffic.

It was closing time, and busy, but clear enough once I got out onto the motorway. Angel and Kay were both in the back, kissing and giggling, with Angel's top up again and Kay exploring the girl's pert black breasts. I put my foot down, eager to get home and promising myself that Kay wouldn't be the only one with a hot bottom before the night was over. By the time I got there they were in a tangle, Kay with her Guide's blouse open and her bra up as she sucked on Angel's nipples, her thighs spread wide to let a hand down her panties.

I parked in the yard and we tumbled out together, laughing and groping at each other as we went in and straight up to the bedroom. Both of the other two were far too excited to mind what was done to them and I spanked them together as they knelt side by side on the bed, kissing each other as I stripped their bottoms. I used my hairbrush on the bare cheeks, pausing only to take an occasional swallow from the bottle of wine that I'd brought up from the fridge.

To see them like that, kneeling together with their bare bottoms lifted, was too much for me. Kay with her

Guide skirt up and her big white panties pulled down, Angel with her trousers around her knees and her bright red thong with them was an unbearably exciting vision. Before I'd given them more than a dozen smacks each I lost control, burying my face between Kay's cheeks to lick at her sex and easing a finger in up Angel's fanny.

From then on it was just raw urgent sex. We stripped each other, kissing and licking at breasts and bellies, bottoms and fannies as we became bare until all three of us were stark naked. I sat on Kay's face, making her lick my anus as Angel watched in giggling delight and then began to spank me. Too far gone to care who was dominating whom, I just stuck my bottom out, enjoying both the stinging slaps and the feel of Kay's tongue in my hole. I was red behind before I came, under my own fingers. The experience left all three of us hot-bottomed and feeling utterly uninhibited. We rolled together on the bed, kissing and licking and fingering, sucking and stroking and smacking, until we'd all come several times. We finally collapsed in sheer exhaustion.

Three

My first sensation on waking was of being oddly stiff, my second of satisfaction as I realised that the reason for my discomfort was that both Kay and Angel were snuggled up against me. They were both fast asleep and stark naked, with the covers in a tangled mess on the floor along with our clothes. Angel was sucking her thumb in her sleep, which made me smile as I gently detached myself from her embrace.

It had been a good night, an excellent night in fact. The way Hannah Riley ran the club might have left something to be desired, but by and large they were getting a good crowd. I had been able to do as I pleased without interference, giving Kay a spanking the memory of which still made me tingle and which had led to a delicious aftermath. Even Mick and Sean had been in the crowd watching us, and neither of them had tried to touch nor had they even made any inappropriate remarks.

Only as I was making the coffee did I remember that in my haste to get home and into bed with the girls I'd completely forgotten to collect my money. But that could no doubt be sorted out soon enough. Meanwhile, Angel was in bed with Kay and me and even considering all we'd done the night before that was something I intended to take full advantage of.

We spent most of the day together, only coming up for air occasionally between sessions of pleasantly naughty sex and cuddling. As always with Angel and me there was the occasional tussle for who was going to be in control, but we managed well enough, taking turns to be nice to the other. I even let her sit on my face, enjoying the feel of her firm little bottom cheeks spread open against me with my tongue pushed well in up the tight black bud of her bottom-hole as Kay watched in giggling delight.

Angel didn't leave until after dark, kissing Kay and me goodbye at the station in a way that drew more than one surprised look from her fellow travellers. Apart from a brief raid on the fridge Kay and I hadn't eaten, so we continued on to the Beehive for dinner. I only remembered the gymkhana when it was too late, arriving just as it was breaking up. The pub was already packed, with every table taken both outside and in, so when Mrs Mattlin-Jones beckoned to us to join her group we could hardly refuse.

It was quite amusing, chatting about the gymkhana and local gossip when just an hour before I'd had my tongue up a third friend's bottom. Mrs Mattlin-Jones and her friends were all so deeply respectable, with their Barbours and tweeds, pearl necklaces and gemstone rings. Aside from a bit of petty snobbery and the air of mild disapproval that they reserved for their juniors, they treated me very much as one of their own. I was sure there was the occasional remark made in my absence because I was living in an openly lesbian relationship, but in true English fashion nothing was ever said when I was in earshot.

The women also provided me with my main source of income, particularly Mrs Mattlin-Jones who invariably steered the girls from her riding school towards me for tack and clothing, so I was obliged to put up with her occasional airs and graces. Now, as she berated me gently for not attending the gymkhana, at least I had an excuse.

'I had a friend staying,' I explained. 'It's not really her sort of thing.'

'Ah, yes,' she replied, lifting her impressive beak of a nose a little bit more. 'Your coloured friend. Wherever do you meet these people?'

'She's very nice,' I said, determined to defend Angel despite knowing full well that at times she could be a complete bitch and probably had all the characteristics Mrs Mattlin-Jones would have regarded as faults with a few more to spare.

Mrs Mattlin-Jones's eyebrows rose a fraction, in doubt if not open disbelief.

'We met at a dinner party,' I lied. 'She, er . . . works for a property developer.'

That was true enough, given that Morris was a property developer and that Angel was a regular at his private parties, helping Mel to spank the girls for a couple of hundred pounds and occasionally taking it herself for considerably more.

'I see,' Mrs Mattlin-Jones replied. To my relief she then changed the subject. 'I was wondering: if you have a little time next week and the weather's dry, I would very much like my jumps repainted. Would that be possible at all?'

'Certainly,' I answered, not wanting to lose the work despite the amount of time that I was going to have to put in on finishing the order for Carnival Bizarre.

'That's very kind of you,' she responded and went on to tell me in unnecessarily minute detail exactly what she wanted.

My scallops had arrived, giving me an excuse not to make conversation as I ate. I was nearly finished when to my alarm Gavin Bulmer came in, along with two of his friends, the weasel-like Jeff Jones and the overweight and bearded Jeff Bellbird. All three were dressed in the drab green pseudo-military outfits that they wore to play paintball. Both Jeffs were spattered with dye. To my relief the landlord asked them to eat outside, only for Gavin to answer him back.

'I'm clean! Do you see any hits? I do not see any hits. But yeah, these two losers had better go outside. Money, Jeff – the drinks are on you.'

The landlord responded with his typical surly grunt as Gavin clicked his fingers at Jeff Jones, who handed over a ten-pound note. I was hoping that they wouldn't see me. The two Jeffs trooped quickly out but Gavin began to look around as he waited to get served. Too late, I tried to move my chair so that the largest of Mrs Mattlin-Jones's friends would block his view. He was already pointing at me.

'Hey, Amber, Kay! How's it going? You were smoking last night, really s–m–okin'!'

I managed a wan smile as my cheeks coloured up. He'd been in the audience at the beginning of Kay's punishment but had gone off with the circus girl before we'd finished, presumably turned on by the show. I knew he wouldn't say anything openly, but unlike me he had no reputation to keep up with the locals and was quite capable of making suggestive remarks. Sure enough.

'I didn't know you'd been in the Girl Guides, Kay?' he said as he sauntered up, adding a painfully obvious wink.

'The Girl Guides?' Mrs Mattlin-Jones enquired politely, looking between Kay and me.

'There was a, um . . . reunion last night,' I said, and immediately realised that I'd put my foot in it, as Bulmer would hardly have been invited. 'Not a proper reunion, that is, just drinks with a few old friends.'

'Did you two meet in the Guides?' she asked.

Kay and I answered at the same instant, yes and no, leaving me desperately trying to dig myself out of a hole.

'That is, we were in the Guides at the same time, but not in the same troop.'

'We met at a summer camp,' Kay added helpfully.

'How nice,' Mrs Mattlin-Jones answered, beaming. 'You must come round to one of my own little reunions. I'll be sure to invite you.'

Gavin moved away to collect his drinks, grinning and leaving me feeling badly flustered. Mrs Mattlin-Jones continued to talk about her Girl Guide reunions until I managed to change the subject back to horses, eager to avoid potentially awkward questions. I was furious with Bulmer and left the table as soon as I reasonably could, pretending to go to the loo but nipping out into the beer garden when nobody was looking.

The three men were seated on the grass with pints of beer and plates of food. Gavin had his back to me and his pint on the ground at his side. I resisted with difficulty the temptation to pour it over his head as I joined them.

'Hey, Amber,' Jeff Jones greeted me. Jeff Bellbird contented himself with a grunt through his mouthful of cod and chips.

Gavin Bulmer turned his head as I squatted down next to him.

'For goodness sake!' I hissed. 'Could you watch what you're saying in front of my neighbours!?'

'What?' he asked, all innocence. 'I didn't say anything.'

'You know perfectly well what I mean,' I insisted.

'So what?' he sniggered. 'You don't want Mrs Rattling-Bones to know you spank little Kay's bot-bot?'

'No, I do *not*!' I hissed. 'What do you think!?'

'What's it worth?' he quipped. 'How about a nice slow blow job?'

Jeff Jones cut in before I could find a suitably vicious retort, his voice full of envy.

'Amber, Gavin says you went home with that black girl Angel last night – and Kay and all? What, did you do the dirty?'

'Mind your own business,' I snapped. 'Look, Gavin, please, just be a little discreet.'

'Don't get your knickers in a twist,' he answered. 'All I did was make a crack about the Girl Guides. How's Rattling-Bones going to know that Kay was getting a spanking in the uniform?'

'Kay got a spanking in a Girl Guides uniform?' Jeff Jones broke in. 'Fuck me, I wish I'd seen that!'

'Will you shut *up*!?' I told him. I was angry, but also close to panic because he was barely making an effort to keep his voice down. There were both neighbours and customers of mine at the tables just a few yards away.

'Temper, temper,' Jones said and went back to his steak.

'Please, Gavin?' I repeated.

'OK, OK, be cool,' he answered. 'So how about a girl hunt this Saturday? I've got a great new idea, and –'

'I'm really not interested,' I told him.

'You can join the hunters, then,' he promised. 'Just as long as you bring some girlie-girls along.'

'That fat bit, Jade,' Jeff Bellbird suggested, spluttering batter down his beard in his eagerness to speak. 'Tits like fucking melons! And little blonde Sophie, and Penny, that dirty bitch you used to go out with.'

He smacked his lips in anticipation of the line-up of girls, spitting yet more batter from his mouth. I looked away in disgust, wondering how he had the nerve to call Jade Shelton fat when he had to weigh at least twice as much as she did. She was, just possibly, masochistic enough to want to be hunted through the woods by him. But I was in no mood to set anything up for them and was too busy anyway.

'Maybe,' I said, purely to placate them. 'Now, will you promise to be a bit more discreet, please?'

'Sure,' Bulmer responded. 'You got it.'

I spent Monday morning working on the equipment for Carnival Bizarre, an activity which reminded me constantly that I hadn't been paid. In the end I phoned Hannah but got Maggie instead, who was less than helpful. I did at least find out that the circus was still at Scratchwood and I decided to sort it out by driving down after lunch, leaving Kay to mind the shop. I was about to leave when Mrs Mattlin-Jones rang to ask why I hadn't come over to paint her jumps. I ended up promising to start the next day, though I'd been hoping to put her off for at least a week.

As I drove down towards the M25 I was feeling distinctly irritable, and stayed that way all the way to Scratchwood. The circus was laid out much as it had been in Harrow, set up in a field that formed the angle between the M1 and a railway. As before, the stalls were in a ring around the Big Top, with the caravans parked beyond. I was rehearsing what I intended to say as I approached, determined to be firm but not to cause offence.

Since this was a Monday afternoon there were very few customers around and hardly any children. Some of the stalls were already beginning to pack up. The two clowns were standing by their pillory in full costume but they were not performing, and unfortunately they saw me before I could avoid them. Baffo immediately jumped up and made an exaggerated bow towards me as I approached, so low that his scarlet hair touched the ground. I gave him a faint smile as he straightened up, not wanting to antagonise him, and he immediately stepped into my path.

'Welcome, Madam Boobfontaine! Have you come for another spanking?'

He almost shouted the crucial word, causing a number of heads to turn and my cheeks to flare to crimson in an instant. Buffo immediately jumped up and pushed his bottom out into a peppermint-striped ball, waggling it in a grotesque and obscene parody of a girl waiting for a smack. Baffo strutted forward, his cheeks puffed out with air, his chest thrust forward and his own bottom stuck out behind in what was presumably supposed to be an imitation of Fat Hannah. Then he bent, to apply the gentlest possible tap to the seat of Buffo's trousers. Buffo immediately pretended to burst into tears, rubbing at his eyes and blubbering, then clutching his buttocks and running in small circles as Baffo went into a wild, capering dance.

Blushing furiously, I took the opportunity to step past them. Over a dozen of the carnival hands were watching, most of them laughing and all of them aware that I really had been spanked by their boss. It was hideously embarrassing and came close to destroying my resolve to be firm about asking for my money. Only the prospect of the welcome shelter of the caravans allowed me to move on at all. But the guard's Alsatian dog was snapping at my feet the moment I'd passed between the first two vehicles.

'What do you want?' the lanky security man demanded, looking at me as if I'd been about to try and break into a caravan.

'I've come to see Hannah,' I told him, my voice sounding meek despite myself. 'Where is her caravan parked, please?'

He gave a grudging jerk of his thumb towards where the two thoroughfare embankments met beyond the caravans. As before, he came with me, the dog snarling occasionally, which left me feeling more uncomfortable than ever when I finally reached Fat Hannah's caravan. I knocked on the door, praying that she would actually be there after all my trouble. I was relieved when I heard her voice as Maggie opened the door.

'Who's that, then?'

'Amber,' I said, poking my head in as Maggie made way for me. 'Hello.'

'Come on in, love. What can I do you for?' she asked, her voice friendly – if anything, rather too friendly.

'I, er . . . I forgot to pick up my money on Saturday,' I told her. 'I hope it's not inconvenient, but –'

'Oh, right,' Hannah interrupted, her tone changing immediately. 'So you're after money. Always fucking money. What, don't you think I'll pay you?'

'No, no,' I assured her. 'Not at all.'

'Pair of thieving pikeys, that's what she thinks we are,' Maggie laughed.

'No, really,' I insisted. 'I just thought . . .'

'You thought what?' Hannah demanded.

'I just . . . that is, I . . . I thought . . .' I stammered, blushing pink.

'What?' she repeated.

I couldn't go on at first, too tongue-tied even to speak. What finally came out was very different indeed from the bold words that I'd rehearsed on the way over.

'Sorry,' I mumbled, looking down at my toes.

Maggie gave a grunt and went to sit down in the same chair she'd used before. Hannah also sat down, taking a cigarette from a packet on the table and lighting it. I looked up, fidgeting as I waited for her to say something. Finally she did, after taking a couple of long puffs on her cigarette and blowing out a cloud of evil-smelling smoke, all over me.

'So you're sorry, are you?'

'I really didn't mean any offence,' I assured her, although it was hard to put any real conviction into my voice when I was in fact guilty of exactly the attitude they were accusing me of.

'Really sorry?' she asked.

'Yes,' I assured her. 'I said sorry.'

'What do you think, Maggie?' Hannah went on. 'Is she sorry enough?'

I swallowed, because I had a nasty suspicion that I knew where the conversation was leading: straight to another spanking. Maggie blew a smoke ring before she replied.

'I think she ought to take another trip over your knee, that's what I think.'

'So do I,' Hannah replied. 'What do *you* reckon, Amber?'

I opened my mouth, intending to say that it wasn't fair, only to realise how utterly pathetic that would sound. Obviously she wanted to spank me. Equally obviously she had no intention of paying me unless she got to spank me first. I could demand my money, I could even threaten her with legal action. But I suspected she'd only laugh at me – and that would be the end of the rest my order, too.

Bitter humiliation rose up in my heart as I realised that I more or less had to go through with it. I was going to have my pants pulled down again. I was going to be spanked again. Maybe she'd even masturbate me, and if there was a tiny treacherous voice in the back of my head telling me that nothing could possibly be nicer, then it was very weak indeed next to my sense of raging shame and consternation.

'So?' Hannah demanded.

All I could manage was a weak nod of my head. Hannah chuckled and drew deep on her cigarette, blowing out the smoke to envelop me in a smelly cloud for a second time. I glanced at the nearest window, half expecting to see two horrible clown faces peering in. But there was nobody outside, only the deserted embankments with cars just visible as they sped by, fortunately too high and too fast to see in at the caravan windows. But there was still a chance that somebody would look in. While at least Kay wasn't there to witness my punishment I'd rather have had it done in front of her a thousand times than once when there was even a possibility of the carnival hands looking in on me.

'May I shut the curtains please?' I asked.

'Fussy, ain't you?' Hannah chuckled. 'Don't you like my boys seeing you get it?'

'Stuck-up, bitch,' Maggie added. 'Reckons she's too good for 'em, that's it.'

'No,' I protested. 'No, I . . . I just . . . sorry, but if I'm going to be spanked I don't want a load of men to see as well!'

'Temper, temper!' Hannah chuckled. 'Go on, then, if you're going to be prissy.'

A truly pathetic wave of relief flooded over me as I went quickly to the nearest window. I pulled the curtains shut, making absolutely sure that not the tiniest crack remained through which a peering eye might witness what was about to happen to me. I was shaking badly, and there was something especially awful about the way Hannah and Maggie just sat there smoking casually, as if having me surrender to a bare-bottom spanking wasn't really that important at all.

I knew it would be on the bare, too. It was ridiculous to hope for anything else. With all the windows closed and the interior of the caravan plunged into a rich pink glow from the sunlight coming in through the curtains I went to stand in front of Hannah. I bit my lip as I waited to be told to get across her knee, because I knew I couldn't just do it without an order. She nodded, then spoke.

'You do it, Maggie. I've had her over once – this time I'd like to watch.'

My mouth came open to protest. Then I shut it again, because I wasn't even sure why the idea of having my punishment given by the slatternly Maggie instead of by Fat Hannah was worse – unless it was that it put me one more rung lower down the ladder. I knew they'd only laugh at me anyway, but the tears were already beginning to sting my eyes as I turned.

Maggie was in jeans that encased her broad hips and heavy thighs, making a lap considerably smaller than Hannah's but a great deal bigger than mine. She also had a faded red T-shirt on, and from the way her huge breasts sagged beneath it and her nipples showed through she was quite clearly not wearing a bra. Her mouth twitched up into a cruel grin as she saw where I was looking. Then she spoke.

'Maybe I'll make you suck 'em when I'm done with you. How's that?'

I looked away quickly, blushing furiously and quite unable to answer. Her voice was harsh as she spoke again, reaching out to take hold of my wrist at the same instant.

'Not good enough for you, ain't I? Get over!'

Maggie was still speaking as I was jerked down across her knees. One arm took me firmly around my waist while the other pushed beneath me as she burrowed for the button to my own jeans.

'Snotty little cow! I bet you suck the titties of that little tart of yours all right, don't you? Don't you? What, too fat for you, am I, you snotty bitch? Well, let's get these down and see how fucking smart you look with your bare arse in the air!'

I was trying to deny what Maggie was saying as my jeans were popped open and hauled down off my hips, but my words came out broken and unintelligible. My clothes were coming down, the pink polka-dot panties I'd chosen that morning already on show and about to be pulled down, stripping my bottom. But that wasn't where her hands went as she settled me across her knee.

'Shall I get her tits out?' she asked as her arm slid up the back of my jumper.

'Yeah, why not?' Hannah replied. 'I'd like to see her tits – it'll do her good to have 'em showing.'

All I could do was screw my face up in abject humiliation as my bra was undone and my jumper hauled up, then my bra cups, flopping my breasts out to hang bare and heavy beneath my chest. Maggie didn't just leave me like that either, but began to fondle them,

70

taking each dangling globe in her hand in turn, hefting them and squeezing.

'I love the way a nice fat pair hangs down, don't you, Hannah?' Maggie remarked, bouncing one in her hand.

'Very nice,' Hannah agreed, her piggy eyes feasting on my breasts from among the rolls of fat on her face. 'She's a looker, our Amber – nice big nipples, too.'

'Yeah, and they go hard good and quick,' Maggie said, pinching one between finger and thumb, making me gasp and wriggle in her grip. 'Stay still, you little bitch.'

She continued to fondle me until I was choking on my own humiliation – and my knickers weren't even down. I was almost glad when she stopped, leaving my breasts feeling heavy and prominent under my chest and my nipples rock hard. She changed her grip, taking me firmly around the waist once more and laying a hand on the seat of my panties. For one moment I thought that she might be going to spare me the indignity of a bare bottom but she merely spent a moment stroking me through the cotton before taking a grip on my waistband.

'Knickers down, that's the way to do it,' Maggie chuckled. Then she'd done it.

I couldn't restrain a sob as my bottom was stripped, both full globes bared with one easy motion. Now I was showing behind, my cheeks big and pink and vulnerable in the dim light, exposed for punishment. She put a hand underneath, chuckling to herself as she wobbled my cheeks. Then she spoke.

'Fat, fat but firm. Love it.'

Maggie began to spank, not skilfully like Hannah but hard, a punishment spanking. It hurt. My resistance had broken in moments, my legs starting to kick and gasps and grunts escaping my mouth. As she set up a rhythm on my bum my boobs began to bounce in sympathy, making Hannah laugh and adding another layer to my already unbearable shame, at which point I burst into tears.

I just couldn't help it. It was too humiliating to lie bare-bottom across the awful woman's lap with my boobs bouncing stupidly under my chest as she spanked me and her ghastly boss looked on. I'd only asked for what was rightfully mine and I'd ended up getting a spanking, which was just so utterly unfair. She'd felt me up, too: she hadn't needed to get my breasts out, not if she only wanted to punish me, and she didn't have to laugh at me, or make fun of me for the size of my bottom, or spank me so very hard.

The tears were streaming from my eyes, my bottom and boobs were bouncing wildly, my hair was tossing and my legs were kicking about in my lowered panties to show myself off behind. A fine sight I looked and I knew it, bared for punishment, my fat bottom all rosy and wobbling, my face a mess of tears. And now mucus had begun to run from my nose. Still Maggie kept on, smack, smack, smack on my burning bottom, delivered full across my cheeks, each one sending a jolt to my fanny – with the inevitable shameful consequence.

I was getting turned on, aroused by my punishment, which made my feelings more bitter still. The tears flowed so thickly that I could no longer see, spattering from my eyes onto the floor of the caravan with each powerful smack of Maggie's hand on my bottom. She was laughing at me as she did it – so cruel to laugh at me as I lay blubbering over her lap, utterly surrendered to her, my fat bare bottom ablaze, my fanny juicing for her because I couldn't help myself.

'Enough,' Hannah said suddenly.

Relief and gratitude flooded through me. I blinked the tears from my eyes and wiped my bedraggled hair from my face to look at her. She hadn't ordered Maggie to stop because she felt I'd had enough. She wanted Maggie to stop because she was ready to be licked.

Hannah's vast thighs were apart and her dress was pulled up, exposing the tops of thick, badly wrinkled brown stockings held in place by suspender straps a good inch wide. Between those stupendous thighs the crotch of her knickers showed, greyish nylon edged with cheap lace, stained over the double ridges of her bulging fanny, with thick puffs of crinkly black hair pushing out at either side. She crooked a finger at me.

'Come here, little one, come to Mother Riley.'

I could only stare at her in horror for what I was expected to do.

'Crawling,' she added. Maggie laughed as she pushed me off her lap.

I wasn't expecting that and I sprawled on the ground, upside down with my legs open, making both of them laugh once again. A voice inside my head was screaming at me to stop, to pull up my knickers and run away. But it was too late. I'd been spanked hard, spanked bare, spanked to tears. My bottom was a hot ball behind me as I scrambled into a crawling position, and the need in my sex was too strong to be denied. I went to Fat Hannah like the slut that I am when I've been properly spanked, crawling on all fours with my boobs swinging under my chest and my fat red bottom showing behind. She was grinning as I approached. She knew. She understood.

'That's a good girl,' she chuckled. 'Now lick my cunt, you little tart, and don't you dare stop until I'm finished or I'll use my hairbrush on those fat tits of yours.'

All I could do was nod and move forward, wincing at the heavy tang of Hannah's scent, a mixture of the cheap perfume she wore and her natural odour. One fat hand went to the crotch of her panties, pulling them aside. I was faced with her bare, reeking cunt, a deep red gash between thickly haired lips, its centre smeared with white juice. Her clitoris was the biggest I'd ever seen, poking out from beneath its hood like an ugly little cock. I swallowed hard, not sure if I could do it, for all the state of grovelling submission that I'd been brought down to. Then her hand had closed in my hair and the choice had been taken away from me as my face was pulled in.

I closed my eyes and stuck my tongue out, lapping quickly. An acrid taste filled my mouth, making my stomach lurch as my face was rubbed in among Fat Hannah's rubbery, slippery folds. She gave a contented sigh and tightened her grip, pulling me in closer still as she spoke.

'Nice. That's my girl . . . that's right, lick it . . . put your tongue in, right up my hole.'

Hannah gave me little choice, forcing my head lower so that my lips were against the hole of her vagina. I stuck my tongue up it, as deep as I could, trying to tell myself that I had to obey and that I didn't really want to rub myself off as I was put through my ordeal. Again she sighed in pleasure and began to manipulate my head, using my nose to rub at her repulsive outsize clitoris. I felt my stomach lurch once more but I was fighting not to put my hand back down my lowered panties as she used me, an urge made harder still to resist by the thought of the view I'd be giving Maggie and of how she'd laugh at me for rubbing at my dirty little cunt while I was made to lick her boss. She was already laughing, maybe because my bottom cheeks had started to clench in my excitement. I was going to do it, I was going to stick my hand down my panties and rub and rub and rub . . .

'Now suck on my bump,' Hannah ordered suddenly, her voice thick with need.

She had pulled hard on my hair as she spoke, hurting me and breaking my sense of helpless arousal. My mouth was put against her hideous clitoris, and despite myself I pursed my lips around it and began to suck. It was like having the end of a fat worm in my mouth, a sensation at once so disgusting and so compelling that it started me crying again even as my hand began to slide back towards my fanny. I had to do it now, and as my fingers found the wet urgent groove between my sex lips I heard Maggie's cruel disdainful laughter from behind me.

'She's at her cunt, Hannah. What a tart!'

'Shut up,' Hannah growled in response. 'And you, suck my fucking bump and leave yourself alone.'

I barely heard. And I didn't stop, because whatever she could do to me it could hardly be worse than what she already had done and I knew full well what my reaction would be. She had me anyway, grovelling near-nude at her feet with her ugly clitoris sucked in between my lips, my bottom hot with spanking and my mouth full of the taste of her sex, well and truly abandoned. Now I was going to come.

'Stop that, you dirty bitch!' Maggie snapped from right behind me and then my hand was snatched away from between my legs. 'Do as you're fucking told, will you!?'

Maggie kept hold of me, filling me with a feeling of unbearable frustration and worse as she took a firm grip around my waist and began to spank me again. She was doing it not by hand now but with Hannah's hairbrush, hard and fast, stinging crazily, and all I could do was suck harder on the horrible thing between my lips and pray that they would take mercy on me when Hannah had come.

It took only a moment more, thankfully. Her fingers locked painfully hard in my hair, Hannah groaned and her thighs tightened on my face. Maggie realised what was happening, applying a crescendo of furious smacks to my helpless bottom as Hannah came against my nose and mouth. I couldn't breathe. I couldn't see. I couldn't control my rear body at all for the pain of the spanking. At the last instant a loud fart erupted from my

75

bottom-hole, bringing me an agonising stab of humiliation that would have tipped me over the edge to my own orgasm if only I'd been allowed to touch myself. If only . . .

Permission denied, I was left gasping for breath and clutching at my smacked bottom as they let go of me. I was dizzy with reaction and with pain, close to collapse, and the caravan was spinning around me through the haze of my tears. As Hannah settled back into her chair and Maggie stood up, the world swam slowly back into focus. I wondered if I was going to be made to lick Maggie too. If so, I was going to beg to be allowed to touch myself off while I did it. She was looking down on me, her fat face set in a cruel smile, and I felt sure that she was about to give me an order. But Hannah spoke first.

'Now fuck off. And next time you come here show a bit of respect.'

Maggie made to speak but quickly closed her mouth. I pulled myself to my feet, too confused to know what to say and not daring to ask Hannah to pay me. My head was still swimming as I pulled my knickers and jeans up and adjusted my bra to make myself decent. Hannah barely bothered to glance at me, lighting a cigarette and drawing deeply on it, while Maggie had sat down again. As I tugged my top down I was willing myself to say something, but when I turned to Hannah she looked up, meeting my gaze with a look so hard that the words died in my mouth.

'You still here?' she grated.

I shook my head and made for the door. Outside, the bright sunlight stung my eyes, adding to my confusion. I didn't know whether to run away in tears or find a quiet place to masturbate, and I had to lean against the side of another caravan before I'd gone ten paces because one of the muscles in my left thigh wouldn't stop twitching. When I looked up I realised that a man was looking at me from the door of the caravan opposite. It was Sean who had helped me at the club.

'You all right, Amber?' he asked. 'Hannah been giving you a hard time?'

I nodded, instantly flushed with relief at the sound of a friendly voice, even if it did belong to one of the carnival hands. He gave an understanding grin in response, then jerked his thumb at the open door of his caravan.

'You need a drink, love, that's what you need.'

I nodded again, and followed him up the steps. The interior of the caravan was shabby, and thick with a male smell and something else that I recognised but couldn't place. A curtain closed off the far end, leaving us in a gloomy space just a few feet square as Sean closed the door behind me. I sat down, barely aware of his friendly patter as he poured two large tumblers of Irish whiskey. As I took the glass I was shaking so hard that I nearly dropped it. I swallowed half the contents at a gulp, leaving a trail of fire down my throat.

'Did she spank you?' he asked. If there was a note of prurient interest in his voice then there was sympathy too.

'Maggie,' I answered. 'Maggie spanked me. In front of Hannah.'

'They love to spank the girls, them two,' he answered with a rueful shake of his head. 'But you mustn't take it bad – with a fine round backside like yours it's just what you're going to get.'

I nodded, knowing he was right, however outrageous his statement. The whiskey had begun to go to my head with astonishing speed, and Sean's friendly, casual attitude was just what I needed, short of a cuddle. Another swallow of whiskey, and suddenly the tears were coming to my eyes again. I'd been spanked and treated really harshly by the two women, when a punishment should always, always be followed by an embrace.

'Come on there, don't cry, love, it's not that bad, is it?' Sean said, seeing my tears.

He reached out, just to lay a friendly hand on my shoulder. But his touch was electric, bringing out my bruised feelings in a flood of tears.

'Hey there, don't take on so,' he said, his Irish lilt now soft and soothing. 'Come on with you – I thought you liked it?'

'I . . . I do,' I sobbed. Then I stopped, completely unable to explain my tangled emotions. 'Please, just hold me for a little.'

Sean responded immediately, squatting down to put his arms around me and cradling my head to his chest. I clung to him, trembling violently as I poured out my emotions in a flood of tears. He certainly wouldn't understand that I wanted to masturbate while he comforted me, but at least he was holding me, which was what Hannah and Maggie should have done.

With that thought my crying grew more bitter still. It was so unfair, to punish me and not make me better afterwards. Even being put to Maggie's teat would have been something, but no, they'd just kicked me out, and they hadn't even let me come. It was really too much, and I'd never needed so badly to be held after a punishment.

Sean was patient with me, stroking my hair and whispering into my ear, even after I'd stopped crying. When he began to kiss me, even on my lips, I didn't resist. I was just as powerless when he stood up to ease down his fly, pulling out a big dirty cock. I shook my head, but he pressed his prick to my lips, and before I could stop myself my mouth had opened and he'd fed it gently but firmly inside. I knew I was being taken advantage of, badly, but I was feeling too low to stop it. I started sucking immediately.

Sean was still stroking my hair as his cock swelled in my mouth, comforting me and continuing to comfort me even as he began to molest me. First he pulled up my top and flopped my boobs out of my bra, then he fondled them and rubbed his thumbs over my still-stiff nipples. Last he squatted lower and released his cock from my mouth to push it between my tits, squeezing both fat pink globes around his shaft as he began to rut in my cleavage. I thought he was going to come like that, because he was already grunting and gasping, but after a while he popped his cock back in my mouth. I realised I was in for a long haul.

I just let him use me, fucking me in my mouth and between my breasts alternately. Apparently he was in no hurry to come. Soon I was fighting my own feelings once more, and I had very quickly given in. Lifting my bottom from the chair I undid my jeans and eased them down over my hips. Sean saw and he gave a knowing chuckle, stepping back a bit. He guided me forward so that as I slipped my hand onto the front of my panties I was sucking cock while kneeling, the way a spanked girl should, giving oral sex to whoever has beaten her while her hot red bottom shows behind.

My bottom was indeed going to be bare in just a moment. As I reached back I was wishing that Sean had been the one to spank me, just as Maggie had done me, my boobs and bum out across the knee and then forced to give oral sex. But he would've cuddled me afterwards. My flesh still felt hot, even through the layer of cotton, and with my pleasure rising fast I began to show off for him hauling my panties up tight into my crease to expose my cheeks, fat and pink and naked to his gaze.

Sean grunted in appreciation and I gave him a wiggle in response, now feeling thoroughly dirty. As he took a grip on my hair and began to fuck my mouth I was pushing down my panties at the back to bare myself completely, and to stroke the hot skin of my cheeks – and between, tickling my sweaty slippery anus. That was too much. I had to come.

I pushed a hand down the front of my panties and then I was masturbating as Sean picked up his pace in my mouth. He changed his grip, holding me by the ears as he fucked my head. It hurt, but I wanted it to. My finger was up my bottom, wriggling in the hot slimy cavity of my open hole, and I was rubbing furiously right on my clitty, determined to come just as I was given a mouthful of thick salty spunk.

Sean got there first, grunting and jamming himself deep down my throat to erupt there. As my mouth filled with sperm I was tipped over the edge, my fanny contracting, my bottom-hole squeezing on my intruding finger as I started to come. I cried out in ecstasy as my head was jerked back hard, Sean's hand now in my hair once more, and he was milking himself in my face, jet after jet of thick white jism spurting into my open mouth and over my nose, spattering my hair and gunning up one eye. All the while I was jerking and squirming my way through my own orgasm, even after he'd finished and left me with my head still thrown back in ecstasy and his spunk slithering slowly down my well-soiled face.

Four

I had sucked cock, something that I'd told myself I would never do again – certainly it was not anything I was going to admit to Kay in a hurry. But I couldn't find it in myself to resent what Sean had done to me. Besides, I clearly needed allies in Carnival Bizarre and letting him fuck my mouth wasn't going to do any harm at all on that score.

We had talked for some time after our encounter, over another and slower glass of Irish whiskey, speaking with an openness and honesty that he would never have shown if I hadn't let him do what he had. Sean had explained to me that Fat Hannah saw paying her bills as a weakness rather than as an obligation, and that I'd be very lucky indeed to see a single penny of my money. After what I'd just been through in order to keep Hannah happy that was enough to make my blood boil, but what he said next made no sense to me at all. According to their contrary logic, apparently, if I did somehow manage to get Hannah to pay she would respect me for being wily or forceful, according to the means I employed. Sean seemed to think it made sense as well, so it wasn't just Fat Hannah being perverse.

By the time I left Sean's caravan I was too drunk to drive home immediately, so I rang Kay to tell her that I'd be late and stopped at a coffee bar near where I'd parked the car. As I sat brooding over a double espresso and a sticky bun my natural obstinacy gradually took command. I *was* going to get my money, by one means or another, and that was that. How to go about it was a different matter since Fat Hannah seemed to hold all the cards.

In a similar situation with Morris I'd have been able to arrange some sort of bet, putting my dignity on the line in exchange for whatever I wanted. Morris being Morris, I'd have won eventually, although quite possibly at very considerable cost. From Hannah's reputation I knew that she liked to gamble and would presumably take up any suggestion I made. Unfortunately I couldn't guarantee that she would pay up even if she lost – unless, of course, I insisted on my money being given to a neutral observer in advance. There were considerable drawbacks, such as losing and ending up back on my knees with my face stuffed into her big smelly fanny, but it was at least worth considering.

Meanwhile there was the question of what to do about the rest of her order. I'd already bought everything I needed, so I more or less had to finish off as planned. I could then withhold delivery until I'd been paid – in full – but I had a nasty suspicion that she'd find some way of getting around me and that I'd need both luck and determination to succeed. Alternatively I could sell everything I made to other people, either gradually at full price, or to Morris, who was sure to smell a rat and demand a high discount. That way I'd still be left without the money Hannah already owed me, which was less than satisfactory. I knew Kay's advice would be to walk away from the whole sorry mess. But I was far too stubborn for that.

It was nearly dark before I decided that I was sober enough to drive back, and the traffic on the motorway was heavy even for a Monday evening. When I eventually got home it was to find that Kay had made cottage pie for me and had it warming in the oven. That and half a bottle of red wine cheered me up considerably – at least, until I went to the bathroom on my way to bed and discovered what a mess Maggie had made of my bottom.

The tuck of my cheeks was one big bruise, presumably where she'd used the hairbrush on me while I brought Fat Hannah to orgasm because the rest of my bum was merely rosy. I was very tender as well as colourful and I had to put on a pair of my biggest panties with a long nightie on top so that Kay wouldn't notice. The moment I came into the bedroom she began to tease me, say that all I needed was a long white nightcap with a bobble on the end and an old-fashioned oil lamp to complete the picture.

I upended her across a pile of pillows, bared her, and gave her a couple of dozen strokes with my hairbrush. But with every smack of wood on flesh and every plaintive squeal I was thinking of how I'd reacted myself during my punishment by Maggie. It was worse as Kay licked me afterwards: images of how I'd crawled on the floor to Fat Hannah flickered in my mind until at last I was forced to think of how it had felt to suck Sean's cock while I masturbated. Only then I was able to retain at least some tiny vestige of dignity as I came.

There was at least no more urgency to complete the order for Carnival Bizarre, which meant I had plenty of time for the jumps that Mrs Mattlin-Jones wanted me to paint. She rang while Kay and I were still having breakfast to tell me that she wanted a particular brand of paint, which was apparently available at a good price in a shop in Potter's Bar.

It was the perfect day for painting, sunny with a faint breeze, and remarkably hot for mid-autumn. But my job would have been a great deal easier if the woman had left me alone instead of constantly interfering and criticising. I'd begun to wonder if she was trying to set me up for a trip across her knee. Not that it was very likely, but still.

The common perception, I suppose, is that people who are into what is seen as kinky sex will have a depraved or at least bohemian lifestyle. In reality it's just that people who can afford to be open about it are uninhibited. But for every girl working as a model in pornographic magazines or whatever who genuinely enjoys her spankings, there must be a dozen executives, a hundred secretaries and a thousand housewives who have to be more discreet. Kay and I run a tack shop, my ex is a senior lecturer at a university, Fat Hannah Riley runs a circus – all of us different, save in that we all like to spank or to be spanked. Why not Mrs Mattlin-Jones, then?

It had to be possible, maybe even probable to judge by the way she had behaved. Effectively, she had been bullying me. I went home in a distinctly odd mood, wondering how it would feel to be spanked by her, a prospect that made me at once excited and bitterly resentful.

Kay was in the kitchen, starting a pasta sauce, and when I came back downstairs from getting changed I was met with the smell of frying onions. As she French kissed me in greeting I took a moment to stroke her bottom, restoring something of my sexual confidence. I'd have gone further if she hadn't been busy but it had been a long hard day so I was hungrier for food than for sex. Giving her a last pat on each bum cheek, I went to pour myself a glass of the red wine she'd opened, only to discover that the bottle was nearly empty.

'Kay!' I complained. 'You're a greedy pig – look!'

I held up the bottle to show her how much she'd taken, but she shook her head.

'That wasn't me. Not all of it, anyway. Gavin came round to sort out Sunday.'

'What about Sunday?'

'You know, the turkey shoot.'

'Turkey shoot? Is this another of his games?'

'Yes, you said you'd get Jade and Penny and a few others up . . . didn't you?'

'No! I didn't say anything of the sort! The little bastard!'

'He seemed to think –'

'No, he didn't. He knew damn well I hadn't agreed to anything. Oh well, never mind – I'll ring him.'

I sat down and took a swallow of my wine, not at all happy about Bulmer's attempt to manipulate me. As if it wasn't bad enough with Fat Hannah Riley! The temptation to take my temper out on Kay's bottom was considerable but Bulmer had clearly lied to her so it wasn't really her fault at all.

Kay was concentrating on her cooking as I sipped my wine. She was mixing in tomato purée and beef mince to create a thick red sauce, the smell of which was making my mouth water. I pushed my chair back and closed my eyes, trying not to think about my difficulties as I let my tension slowly slip away. When Kay spoke there was a touch of hesitation in her voice.

'I, er . . . rang Jade anyway, but she wasn't up for it, and Penny's got the decorators in, apparently.'

I nodded vaguely as she went on.

'But then Mel rang, trying to get me to do a party as usual. She's up for it – as a hunter, of course – and she says she'll bring Annabelle and Sophie. Harmony's coming too, and Mel said she'd ring Angel.'

For a moment I could only stare at her. Kay turned to me, looking worried.

'Shouldn't I . . .' she began, and stopped.

I put my wineglass down, trying to think rationally instead of struggling to swallow the bubble of irritation that was growing in my throat. If Melody Rathwell wanted to play games with Razorback Paintball that was really none of my business. But Kay might have waited to consult me before inviting anyone, let alone

Mel. Where Mel went there would also be Morris, and quite possibly all sorts of even less desirable people. Inevitably everyone was going to want to change in my house, which meant a great deal of inconvenience at the least. Kay was likely to want to join in as well, unless the turkey shoot turned out to involve the risk of direct contact with men. If she did, with Mel as a hunter, I'd have to participate as well. I pushed my chair back a little further.

'Kay.'

'What?'

'Come here.'

I patted my lap. Kay's mouth began to work but I was in no mood for argument. Reaching out, I took her firmly by the wrist and dragged her towards me. She gave a single squeak of consternation and protest, but I was having no nonsense. I'd grabbed from her hand the spatula she'd been using even as I pulled her down across my knee. A slight lift of my leg and her bottom was sticking high in the air. A simple movement and her skirt was pulled up over her back. A single jerk and her knickers were down, baring her for a well-deserved punishment.

The spatula came down on Kay's bottom with a meaty smack, spattering pasta sauce everywhere. I didn't care. I was going to spank her and spank her well, taking out all my ill feeling on her bottom as I applied smack after smack after smack, a cheek at a time, covering her and myself with sauce as she kicked and wriggled over my knee. She was making more fuss than usual, protesting bitterly that it wasn't fair. But I took no notice, belabouring her bottom with the spatula until both bulbous bum cheeks were rosy as well as smeared with sauce and stopping only when I caught a whiff of burning from the cooker.

'That will do,' I told her. 'And you can keep your knickers down and your skirt turned up while you finish dinner. Clean up this mess like that, too. I'm going to change.'

Only my top was dirty so I put it in the laundry and went upstairs for another one, leaving Kay looking distinctly sorry for herself as she inspected her smacked bottom and stirred the sauce to stop it burning. It had felt good to spank her but it hadn't changed anything, except to turn me on even more than I had been before. When I came down again I brought a wet sponge and cleaned Kay's bottom for her as she cooked. This was simply the final stimulus to my mounting lust. Taking her gently away from the stove I set both the sauce and the pasta to simmer and put her down on her knees, baring my sex to her face so that she could lick me to ecstasy as she masturbated. We came together, a long lingering mutual orgasm that did far more to soothe my ruffled feathers than any amount of wine. When we'd both quite finished I made sure to give Kay a loving cuddle before we finally settled down to eat.

The rest of my week was spent painting for Mrs Mattlin-Jones and occasionally doing a little more work on the order for Carnival Bizarre. I'd decided that I might as well join in with Gavin Bulmer and Razorback Paintball for their ridiculous game, although I still had no idea what was going to happen. As a hunter I could at least be sure of preserving my dignity.

Gavin came on Saturday to explain things, parking the Razorback jeep in my yard and immediately going to the back of the vehicle. I followed, curious, to find him rooting in a box from which he lifted a pair of old-fashioned school knickers in bottle green. As he held them up, grinning proudly, I realised this was no simple male panty-fantasy but something altogether more perverse.

He had cut the seat out of the knickers so that the girl wearing them would have her bottom bare, while the

rear of the waistband, already thick, had been rein-
forced with a broad strip of black elastic, sewn on so
that it bulged up into a series of little bumps. His reason
for making a girl go bare-bottom needed no explanation, but the elastic was puzzling – until he opened
another box, which proved to be full of large feathers
marked with brown and white stripes. I recognised them
as from the tail of a turkey cock.

'Turkey tails,' Gavin said happily, pushing one of the
feathers into the elastic.

I watched as he put the feathers in, twelve in all, each
one poked in so that it would stand proud above the girl's
bottom when she was in the pants. A fan of feathers
would rise above her exposed bum cheeks to create an
absurd erotic parody of a real turkey's rear view. As I
stared at the thing I was trying to think if I had ever seen a
more ridiculous and humiliating garment, but I couldn't.

'We've got loads of different sizes,' he explained. 'So
if you change your mind and want to get hunted that's
no problem.'

'No, thank you,' I told him.

'Shame, you've got a great arse,' he answered, sensitive as ever. 'That's six hunters and five tarts, then.'

'Five *women*,' I corrected him. 'Who's the fifth?'

'My girlfriend Jilly,' he told me. 'You know, you saw
her down the club.'

'The girl from Carnival Bizarre?' I asked, surprised. 'I
thought they were only there to keep the men happy?'

'She kept *me* happy, all right!' he laughed. 'Watching
you slap up little Kay's arse got her well horny, and she
is one ace fuck.'

'So she's going out with you?' I queried. 'I thought
the circus people kept themselves to themselves, pretty
much?'

'Yeah,' he answered. 'That's carnies for you, all right
– Jilly's old lady would go apeshit if she knew, but she
doesn't, so that's cool.'

I nodded doubtfully but didn't reply, reasoning that if Gavin wanted to get himself in trouble with the 'carnies' then that was hardly my problem. He was now opening yet another box, this one black plastic with rounded corners. Inside, resting in a shaped depression, was a gun, sleek and black and evil-looking except for the fitting where a transparent canister full of scarlet paintballs was attached.

'Splat gun,' he said, taking the thing reverently from the case. 'Paintball for kids. Watch.'

'No . . .' I began, too late as Gavin lifted the gun and pulled the trigger, splashing scarlet dye all over my newly painted wall.

'It's only vegetable dye,' he said, breaking the barrel open as he turned to me. 'See this little nipple thing here? That breaks the paintball as it come out, so you get a burst of dye. It's only good up to about five metres, but you get a serious spread.'

'I see – like a fancy water pistol?' I replied, glad that however humiliating the game might be for the victims it would be less painful than usual. 'How does the game work?'

'Simple,' Gavin explained. 'Each tart – I mean young lady – has her turkey knickers on, with twelve arse feathers. We have a splat gun each and our own colour paint balls. The tarts . . . whatever, let's call them turkey-girls, get to run and after five minutes we come after them. Our targets are their bums, and anything inside the cut-out counts as a hit. When we get a hit we take a feather, and when the first turkey-girl has been fully plucked the hunter phones in and it's game over. The winner is the hunter with the most feathers, and he gets to do what he likes with the losing turkey.'

'He?' I queried. 'What makes you think it will be a man?'

Gavin just laughed, snapped the barrel of the gun closed and fired off three shots in quick succession, producing three perfectly spaced splats of dye on the wall.

'The hose is over there,' I told him. 'Come in for some lunch when you've cleaned up.'

I didn't actually expect to win. What mattered was that Kay shouldn't lose. She insisted on playing, but I knew very well that if she got fully plucked and found herself faced with the prospect of sucking one of the men's cocks – or worse – she would back out. And guess who was sure to end up in her place?

Fortunately she wasn't very likely to lose. She was small, agile and would do her best to make it hard for the hunters. Among the other turkey-girls Annabelle and Jilly were probably fitter and faster, but both were considerably taller. So they would find it harder to hide among the scrubby woodland at the back of our properties where the hunt would take place. Harmony was equally tall, more heavily built and less agile, with much the biggest bottom among the five of them, but she was still not the one I expected to lose. That was Sophie, who was also fairly well padded behind but, more importantly, wasn't going to mind being shot. Just the opposite, in fact. She would be keen to lose and be made to do whatever the winner wanted.

I had already decided to take the risk rather than spoil Kay's fun, and when Sunday dawned bright and fresh I actually found myself quite looking forward to it. We were up early and before we'd even had our coffee I put Kay across my knees on the bed for her twenty strokes of the hairbrush, which warmed her nicely and got me in the mood for play. I'd invited the others to come to me first and I was allowing my paddock to be included for the hunt, which made sure that we would be secure from prying eyes. The result was a game field shaped like an upside-down Y with a long tail, which looked like making for some interesting tactics.

The three Razorback boys were sure to work together, more or less, as were Morris and Melody, which left me on my own. To judge by previous games, the turkey-girls would simply flee down the tail of the Y and either hide and hope the hunters passed them, or end up trapped at the end. In that case they would be sitting ducks – or rather, sitting turkeys – and would have little choice but to run in circles until one or another had had all her feathers plucked.

I knew I wasn't fit enough to keep up with Gavin or Jeff Jones, but I could easily go faster than Morris, let alone Jeff Bellbird. Mel would be about the same as me, but if we stayed in groups I would be the fastest. The best bet therefore seemed to be to run down the length of the Y, hopefully with the turkey-girls fleeing ahead of me, and try to get as many shots on target as possible before the others caught up. With luck I might even get to choose my victim, in which case it would be Harmony. If so, I would make her sister watch as I first spanked her, then made her lick my bottom and fanny – a highly satisfying thought.

The Razorback boys were the first to arrive, all three of them in camouflage combat fatigues, brisk and efficient as they unloaded the equipment and spread it out on the big workbench that Kay and I had brought outside. Kay hadn't seen the altered school knickers and she threw me a worried look as she held them up for inspection. But she made no complaint, taking them upstairs along with a handful of turkey feathers.

Gavin had set out six splat guns: his own smart black model, a similar one with the turquoise paintballs that I recognised as Jeff Jones' personal colour and three cheaper models with balls of purple, pink and a vivid leaf green. The sixth gun was a huge thing like one of those sub-machine guns you see in old gangster movies, heavy and unwieldy, with a tank full of vivid yellow paintballs on top, at least five times as many as the rest of us had.

'The sprayer,' Fat Jeff said proudly as he saw me looking at it.

'Is that fair?' I queried, addressing my question to Gavin, who shrugged.

'Seems fair to me.'

I wasn't at all sure myself. But if Jeff was going to take advantage of his firepower he had to catch the girls first, and he was hardly built for speed. He was, however, their best shot, as I knew from bitter experience. Again, I congratulated myself on not letting them talk me into being hunted. I was also relieved that this time I was not going to end up on my knees with Fat Jeff's cock in my mouth and half my friends looking on as I sucked him off.

Choosing the purple paintballs for myself I spent a few minutes practising against the rear wall of the yard. Aim didn't really come into it because the paint came out in a wide gush although, as Gavin had said, it didn't travel very far. Obviously I'd have to get close before I fired, but any girl showing so much as the tiniest slice of bottom cheek was sure to be hit.

The sound of a car horn from the street signalled the arrival of Morris and I opened the gates to let him in. He had brought his new gold Rolls-Royce, around which all three of the Razorback boys immediately clustered admiringly. I seemed to be the only person who thought it ostentatiously vulgar. Melody climbed from the front passenger seat and came over to kiss me before walking to the table where the guns were spread out. Harmony, Annabelle and Sophie followed, chattering happily together and dissolving in giggles as they saw how they were to be dressed.

Kay leant out of the bedroom window and called to the three of them to come up, leaving Gavin explaining the game to Morris and Melody as the front doorbell sounded. I went inside, praying that it wasn't going to be Mrs Mattlin-Jones demanding that I work on a Sunday. I was relieved to find Jilly standing outside. I'd never spoken to her before but she greeted me with a friendly kiss, speaking as she moved quickly inside.

'Sorry if I'm late. I had to dodge out.'

'You're fine,' I assured her. 'The others are in the yard.'

She went through as I indicated the way, walking ahead of me so that I had a chance to take her in. I knew that she performed in the Big Top, and she certainly looked the part. As tall as me, she was well built and exceptionally muscular, with long legs and a full round bottom, a slender waist and heavy firm breasts. Her hair was dyed blonde and cut quite short and she was dressed in jeans and a sloppy T-shirt under her fleece.

Gavin greeted her with an open-mouthed kiss to which she responded without a trace of embarrassment. Like the others she found the ridiculous turkey-girl knickers amusing. As a circus girl she was presumably used to dressing up in outfits that left a lot of flesh, if not her bare bottom, showing, yet I was pleasantly surprised to find her taking to kinky behaviour so easily. As we talked I began to wonder if I might not have an ally in her. Certainly she wasn't in awe of Fat Hannah as the other carnies seemed to be.

Mel had chosen the pink paintballs, leaving Morris with green. Both were dressed casually, like myself, although Mel had gone so far as to put on a peaked cap with ear flaps as if she was an American deer hunter. Jilly was sent in to change and it wasn't long before she was out again, along with the other girls, all five of them giggling as they paraded themselves for us.

They did look sexy, although in that foolish and very British way that I can't help but hate when I'm the one dressed up like it. The cut-out school knickers were quite tight, the green material hugging the girls' bellies and the mounds of their fannies to show off every contour beneath. The full expanses of their bottom cheeks stuck out behind, bare and round beneath the ridiculous puffs of turkey feathers.

Aside from her target area each girl was different. Kay had very sensibly dressed in a thick sweatshirt and work boots with long woollen socks, so that only her upper legs and bottom were at risk of scratches as she pushed through the foliage. Sophie, as I'd expected, was the opposite, stark naked except for her turkey knickers and a pair of plimsolls, casually showing off her small round breasts as well as her bottom. Harmony and Jilly had both gone for something in between the two extremes, in a crop top and a bra respectively. Both were wearing trainers. Annabelle had obviously been given her instruction by Mel. She too was in trainers, was wearing long yellow-and-black-striped socks and like Sophie she was topless. But she had been put in an absurd bird mask with a long curved beak and a big red turkey wattle made of some jelly-like substance fixed above her nose.

'Very nice,' Morris remarked as the girls finished their parade and lined up against the wall.

'Very nice indeed,' Gavin agreed. 'Come on, girls – let's see those targets.'

The girls turned around, only Annabelle hesitating until Mel had nodded permission. They displayed their bottoms, four pink and one brown, some plump, some slim, but all delightfully round and feminine. Every one of them was well worth spanking, yet I felt sure that the great majority of bottom enthusiasts would have had Kay first. The way her hips flared from her tiny waist, the full, cheeky shape she made, so big for her figure yet so firm and high, the delightful way she tucked under, the whole exquisite ensemble of her rear view all made for an irresistible combination.

'Stick 'em out a bit, yeah?' Fat Jeff suggested, his voice full of longing.

'Yeah, show us those brown-eyes,' Gavin drawled, at which Jeff Jones gave a nasty snigger.

Sophie responded immediately, not merely sticking out her bottom but reaching back to pull her fleshy little cheeks apart and spread out the rich pink dimple of her anus. She looked back over her shoulder as she did it, with her tongue stuck out at the three boys. Jilly also responded quickly, not quite so brazenly but still sticking her bottom out enough to make her cheeks part and show off a dun-brown anal star between them. Harmony was slower and gave Gavin a dirty look as she stuck her bottom out, while Kay and Annabelle stayed as they were. I knew it was a bad move, as any display of reluctance on their part would only make the men more determined. But I still felt confident in Kay's ability to outwit the hunters.

'Are we ready, boys?' Gavin asked, including Mel and me in this characterisation.

'Ready,' Mel answered, adjusting her paintball gun and firing off a pink splat against my wall.

'Let's go, then,' Gavin went on. 'Take a pair of goggles each, girls, and off you go. We follow in five.'

The girls scampered for the goggles, all except Sophie who sauntered casually over to the table and waited for the others before choosing a pair of goggles for herself. She walked away twirling them around her finger, a mocking wiggle in her walk as she made for the gap in the hedges that led to the paddock.

'Cheeky cow,' Gavin remarked.

'Nice bum, though,' Fat Jeff added, adjusting his cock in his combat trousers.

'Cute, but too easy,' Jeff Jones put in. 'Now that Kay – she's a babe. I'd like to fuck her up the arse.'

I immediately felt myself bridle. But I held back the words that came to my lips. They would only start teasing me and become even more determined to have Kay lose. If they demanded too much of her she'd refuse, and while under no circumstances would I allow Jeff Jones to bugger me it would still be an awkward situation to handle.

Mel and I exchanged a look, both of us in agreement on our opinion of Jeff Jones whatever our other differences. Morris was looking at his watch and I found myself checking my own, despite not having the faintest idea what time it had been when the girls had left. The two Jeffs and Gavin clustered together, as I'd suspected they would, and I moved towards the gap, trying to seem casual.

'Time to go,' Gavin said suddenly, I ran.

The paddock was empty, as I'd expected it to be, and I crossed it and the long piece of land that led up towards the back of Gavin's property without bothering to search. As I reached where the trees shielded us from the railway I turned right, running parallel with the embankment. Nobody at all seemed to have followed, and I was grinning to myself as I caught a flash of movement ahead. It was Harmony, her yellow crop top hardly an attempt at camouflage even among the autumn foliage. She turned in surprise as she heard me coming, but not far enough – I was on her before she could face me to protect her bottom. I fired and saw the purple paint splash against her hip and one full black cheek. I had her.

'I didn't know you'd started!' she complained as I took a feather from the waistband of her knickers.

'Well, we have,' I told her. 'Am I supposed to give you a chance to get away now?'

'Search me,' she answered, but then quickly nipped away down the path.

I took a moment to get my breath back. Then I heard the calls that the Razorback boys used to communicate with each other. It seemed like they'd stopped, perhaps

96

for two of them to flush out their own property while the third guarded the junction. I could only hope the tactic didn't work, and pressed on. As each girl had twelve feathers we obviously had to shoot them all at least twice to win, while the loser would have to be hit twelve times. That meant Harmony was fair game if I could catch her, so I picked up my pace.

There was no sign of her, nor of anyone else. As I reached the halfway point nearly a mile from my house I stopped, wondering if I hadn't made a mistake and run past the turkey-girls as they hid among the bushes. Most of the trees were still in leaf, providing plenty of concealment, and I could have missed a couple of hundred of them, never mind five.

When I heard the pop of a splat gun from well behind me my doubts increased. It was a long way to the end of my land, and if I went all the way there and back without getting another hit I was going to look a fool. I was still trying to decide when Kay stepped out onto the path, just a few yards further along, looking the other way. Her bare bottom on full show.

She was too good a target to miss. I shot her, causing her to squeak and jump up in the air, clutching her now purple and slimy bottom as she came down.

'Amber!' she exclaimed as she turned to see me.

'Sorry,' I told her, 'I couldn't resist you. Can I have a feather, please?'

She plucked one out and handed it to me.

'Where are the others?' I asked, sticking the feather into my belt alongside Harmony's.

'Down towards the end,' Kay told me without hesitation. 'Except Sophie. She went the other way.'

'Then she's had it,' I told her, just as another pop sounded from behind us. 'Run along.'

I sent her on her way with a smack – a mistake, because my hand came away purple. Sophie was going to lose, as I'd predicted, but I still wanted to win. I ran on, resisting the temptation to shoot Kay again even though she was right in front of me. She'd soon ducked off to one side where a big holly bush hung low to the ground. Annabelle, Jilly and presumably Harmony were ahead of me and I slowed down, searching the greens and yellows and browns of the autumn foliage for any tell-tale hint of skin or clothing.

Not twenty yards on I saw Annabelle, her red wattle showing plainly in a clump of fern. She saw me at the same instant and ran, but not fast enough, her little pink bottom presenting a prime target as she darted down the track. She was grinning as she handed over her feather, obviously enjoying herself, and as with the others I let her run off before continuing my hunt.

More pops sounded behind me, but nearer now. I guessed that Sophie had made a break down the track and I hesitated, wondering whether to wait for her or go after Jilly. A series of pops and a gleeful shout from Fat Jeff decided me and I ran on – straight into Jilly. We went down together, full length in a puddle with me on top, the splat gun knocked from my hand. I apologised immediately and had begun to help her up as Sophie appeared at at run, nearly tripped over us and disappeared down the track. I heard Jeff before I saw him and called out a warning as I struggled to my knees, only to have Jilly grab me and pull me on top of her again. Jeff's laughter rang out directly behind me. I heard the stutter of the sprayer and felt the splash of dye on my back and bottom and legs, soaking me in an instant.

'Not me, you idiot!' I yelled, struggling to break free of Jilly's grip.

'Get out the fucking way, then!' Jeff laughed and let rip with the sprayer again, this time catching both of us.

Some of it went in Jilly's mouth, making her slacken her grip just long enough for me to wriggle free. She had recovered in an instant, squirming backwards in the mud so that she didn't present a target. I grabbed for my splat gun, not so much to shoot her, but meaning to get Fat Jeff. He rushed forward as Jilly jumped up, hurling himself into the bushes in an attempt to get her bottom from the side.

I stuck a foot out. Fat Jeff went down in the undergrowth with a crash and Jilly darted away, fast but not fast enough as I loosed off a shot, splattering her mud-soiled bottom with purple dye. She didn't stop but she'd lost several feathers in the tussle, one of which I took as I stood up. I was covered in yellow dye: it was in my hair, down my neck and, worse still, trickling down the back of my jeans to wet my panties and leave me feeling revoltingly sticky between my cheeks.

Jeff was getting up and I rounded on him, intending to give him a piece of my mind. But he was grinning and shaking with laughter, covered with twigs and leaves and mud. He extended a hand and I took it, shaking as he glanced at the feathers in my belt.

'Four? Nice going.'

'Thanks. And you?'

'I got two on Sophie, and Annabelle. That's it, so far.'

He was checking the sprayer as he spoke, and fired a burst into the undergrowth before giving me a ponderous salute and shambling off into the bushes. What I really wanted was a hot bath, but I was determined to finish the game. Sophie, Jilly, Annabelle and maybe Harmony were now ahead of me, Kay behind. It was in my best interests to lead the others further down the track, so I fired off a few shots to encourage them. Then I continued down the path, carefully now.

I was far from comfortable, what with the dye squelching in my panties at every step, and I wished I'd shot Fat Jeff after all. It wasn't so bad for the turkey-girls since they were bare and would soon dry, while all five of them would no doubt enjoy the wet sensation. I didn't, and after a hundred yards I'd decided that there was only one thing for it: I'd have to strip off, discard my wet panties and wipe my bottom dry with the clean part of my top.

Nipping in among the bushes, I chose what I hoped was a quiet enough place and began to strip, only to stop, frozen, with my jeans pushed halfway down off my bum as several people crashed past. I didn't see them but I heard Mel's voice, then the pop of a splat gun. A moment later they were gone and I continued to undress, now hurrying as it seemed that all or nearly all the hunters were beyond my position and closing in on the turkey-girls.

Naked now, I hung my soiled panties on a twig to be retrieved later and was just wiping my bottom when for a second time I heard voices, the snap of twigs and then laughter, unmistakably Sophie's. She was close and I ducked down, absolutely silent. I caught a glimpse of pale skin, then bottle-green cotton and then turkey feathers as she backed towards me, laughing at whoever was facing her and moving from side to side to deny him her target area.

I, on the other hand, had a prime shot, her round dye-spattered bottom in clear view. Raising my splat gun, I took careful aim and shot her, splashing her buttocks and legs and making her jump, trip and fall back, right at my feet. She looked up in surprise, just as Jeff Jones stepped out from the bushes. I found myself covering my breasts and sex by instinct as his gaze moved down my body.

'Nice,' he drawled. 'What are you doing stripped off? Up for some?'

'No, I am *not*!' I answered him. 'Fat Jeff hit me with the sprayer so now, if you *wouldn't* mind . . .'

As I spoke Jones's expression had changed from a mixture of amusement and lust to a crafty smirk. He dashed forward and, thinking he was going to grab me, I stepped to the side – only to have him go right past and snatch up my clothes, laughing in triumph.

'Hey, stop! That's not fair!' I shouted.

Jones paused – but only to wave goodbye with my panties. Then he was gone, leaving me stark naked. Sophie was giggling as she got up and held out a feather.

'You be careful, Sophie Cherwell,' I told her. 'You're already in trouble for luring Kay into the box with you at Morris's, and I am just in the mood to dish out a serious spanking.'

'I lured *Kay*?' she responded, completely unfazed by my threat and still with laughter in her voice. 'More like Kay lured *me*!'

'Well, she's already been punished – and so will you be in a minute,' I said, the only response I could think of. But it sounded distinctly lame when I was stark naked and partially yellow.

'Yes, please – but later,' she laughed, and ran off.

The only things Jeff Jones had left me were my socks and boots, which I put on while seething and plotting revenge. I felt more ridiculous than I had when I'd been totally naked, but there was altogether too much holly about to go barefoot so I was just going to have to put up with it. Telling myself that at least I didn't have to run around in cut-out school knickers with a spray of turkey feathers sticking up over my bum I made my way back to the track.

Popping noises from some way off indicated that the game was still going strong, with Fat Jeff using the sprayer by the sound of it, but I wasn't at all keen on exhibiting myself naked in front of the other hunters. Not that it made much difference. Unless I went straight back to the house they were bound to see me anyway, and Jeff Jones was sure to waste no time in telling the others what he'd done to me.

He'd taken my feathers too, all except the one that Sophie had given me. Still, my score was still five: maybe if I went the other way I could catch Kay and cheat a little, making her stand still while I took all but one of her feathers so that I'd have a good total and another girl would lose. It seemed the most sensible thing to do and I started back. But I couldn't find her at all.

I found Morris instead, sitting on a pile of old railway sleepers at the back of the Razorback property, one foot bare and his trouser leg rolled up as he massaged an ankle. I didn't mind him so much: he'd seen me naked so many times and in all sorts of situations. He was talking to somebody outside my range of vision and I assumed it was Mel, until I emerged from the bushes and saw that it wasn't. It was Hannah Riley.

She was seated on a log, her great brawny arms folded under her massive breasts, and she had already seen me.

'So there you are,' she said, her stare moving down my naked body and up again as I once more covered my breasts and fanny. 'Arsing around when you should be working on my order. There's no point covering yourself, love. I've seen it all, remember?'

I kept my hands firmly where they were as I turned to Morris for support.

'Might I borrow your jacket, please, Morris?'

'You're yellow,' he pointed out, 'and quite muddy too. Why are you naked, anyway?'

'It's a long story,' I told him. 'Please? The dye washes out.'

He shrugged and peeled off his jacket, which I put on gratefully. Not that it was a lot of use, because even when it was done up my breasts still bulged out, while my fanny showed between the flaps at the front and the tuck of my bottom was bare behind me. It was still better than being stark naked: I even managed to inject a little force into my voice as I addressed Hannah Riley.

'I have been working on your order, but I'm afraid I can't deliver anything more until you've paid for what you've already had.'

Morris laughed and Hannah shot him a dirty look.

'Can't pay for your goods, eh?' he said. 'Not going too well then, your club?'

'I can pay,' she answered him. 'In fact, the reason I come up was to give little Amber her money.'

'You did?' I asked.

'Sure I did,' she answered. 'I was just larking around before, eh?'

If what Hannah had done to me was just larking around then I didn't want to meet her when she was genuinely angry. I was still cautious and Morris was looking sceptical. But she had taken a bundle of notes from her bag, holding them up so that I could see them properly before she levered herself to her feet.

'In private,' she said, stepping towards me.

I edged back, half expecting to be whipped over her knee and spanked purple on some trumped-up excuse. But Hannah merely took my arm and led me towards the Razorback hut. Somewhat reluctantly, I went, not trusting her at all but hoping that for once she was being straightforward with me. Inside the hut she closed the door and divided the money into two equal-sized bundles, holding one out.

'Here's half,' she said and I took the money, quickly feeding it into the inside pocket of Morris's jacket.

'How about the other half?' I asked.

'You'll get that, ducks, you'll get that,' she assured me, 'But only after you've done old Hannah a little favour.'

'What's that?' I asked doubtfully, wondering what she could possibly want to bargain for when she had more or less forced me to lick her fanny.

'Just a bit of a laugh for the lads,' she said. 'You know, give 'em a bit of fun for all their hard work.'

'But what?' I demanded.

'Thing is, see,' Hannah went on, 'a lot of them reckon you're a bit stuck-up, like, so they want you to go in the pillory and that. Nothing nasty, just to show you're one of us.'

'In the pillory?' I echoed. 'At the club?'

'No, no, love, nothing like that,' she insisted. 'Just round the back of the caravans one day when we're closed, you know, just for the boys, just family.'

They were no family of mine, but I bit back the angry retort that came to my lips.

'What would you do to me, exactly?' I queried.

'You know, wet sponges and that,' Hannah said. 'Maybe a bit of spankies, but don't worry – I'll make sure the boys don't get too frisky.'

'You want to spank me in front of your men?' I said, astonished by what she was asking. 'Bare-bottom presumably?'

'Sure – it's not half the fun if you're not bare, now, is it?'

Hannah waggled the second wad of money at me as she spoke. Obviously she wanted me to do it, and I was sure there was more to her request than simply punishing me and putting me down for the satisfaction of the carnies. I was not going to do it, but as she had treated me so badly I didn't feel that I should show her any more consideration than she'd shown me. Perhaps I could turn the tables on her.

'Maybe,' I said cautiously. 'But only if you pay me the full amount, for everything.'

'What, even the stuff you haven't done yet?'

'Yes,' I insisted. 'You can rely on me to do it. I keep my word.'

'Meaning I don't?'

'Well, frankly . . .'

I'd been ready to bolt for the door if she made a grab for me, but to my surprise Hannah suddenly laughed.

'So you *have* got some guts, after all,' she said. 'OK then, love, have it your way. All the money, just as soon as you're out of the pillory.'

'In advance,' I replied, made bolder by her sudden change in attitude.

'Half and half,' she answered me, holding out the second bundle of notes.

'OK,' I told her. 'I'll bring the rest of the order, and you can pay me in full before I go in the pillory. How's that?'

'Done,' she said

Evidently what Sean had said was true. If I stood up to her she respected me, and as I took the second bundle of notes I was very glad I hadn't made a fuss when he'd tried to feed me his cock. Now all I had to do was avoid the pillory. That would be easy. I could take the money, then say I'd left something in the car, go back for it and simply drive off.

Hannah spat on her hand and stuck it out. Trying not to grimace, I took it and shook, telling myself that the agreement was no more valid than her original broken promise to pay me cash on delivery. I could hear people outside and I poked my head out of the door to find Gavin and Jeff Jones just emerging from the end of the track. Fat Jeff was behind them holding a lead made of bailer twine, the other end of which was lashed around Sophie's wrists.

My immediate reaction was delight that they hadn't caught Kay. Sophie's tail had been fully plucked, so she'd obviously lost, while with my mobile in the pocket of my stolen jeans I hadn't received the call to say that the game was over. My second reaction was irritation, because Jeff Jones didn't have my clothes.

'What have you done with my things?' I demanded.

'Shit, I forgot all about that!' he laughed, obviously lying. 'Never mind, babe, I'll fetch 'em for you when Fat Jeff's finished with Sophie.'

I made to remonstrate but thought better of it and went to sit down instead, on the railway sleepers beside Morris. He had now put his shoe and sock back on but was still rubbing his ankle.

'Tripped on a root,' he explained, ignoring the fact that Sophie had just been put on her knees a couple of feet in front of him.

Sophie still had her plimsolls on, and the cut-out school knickers. But otherwise she was naked, with her paint-spattered bottom stuck out and her eyes bright with excitement for what was about to happen to her. With her wrists tied she was helpless anyway, and I knew that Fat Jeff would make full use of her – a prospect that put a lump in my throat even though it wasn't me about to be put through my paces.

He didn't waste any time either, contenting himself with a brief and obscene victory dance that involved pushing down his combat trousers at the back and waggling his vast and hairy bottom at the audience. Hannah Riley had come out of the hut and for a moment even she looked horrified. But Fat Jeff ignored her, leaving Morris and me to explain why she was there as he waddled over to Sophie.

I wanted to watch and I turned back as quickly as I could, filled with a horrid fascination at seeing such a pretty girl made to serve as a sex toy for such a grotesque man. Fat Jeff wasn't even embarrassed for his pasty overblown body. Rather, he seemed to revel in it, deliberately pulling up his top to show off his great flabby beer gut before he pushed his combat trousers and the greyish underpants beneath to his ankles.

All that showed of his cock shaft was the tip, the wet red helmet already poking out from within an unpleasantly meaty foreskin. The underside of his balls, thick with coarse red hair, was also visible. Just the sight was enough to make me wince but as he lifted his great belly out of the way Sophie simply took him in her mouth, sucking with her eyes wide open as she looked up at his towering bulk.

It was good to see it done to her, especially when she was still in her cut-out school knickers and had her hands tied. I could feel her humiliation as Fat Jeff's cock stiffened to full erection in her mouth as she knelt in front of her friends, although I knew it would have been stronger for me had I been made to do the same, kneeling naked and ashamed as I sucked on his big ugly penis . . .

'Hi, Amber.'

Kay had returned. She kissed me and turned to show off, her turkey tail still high and proud above her bum, with ten of its twelve feathers in place and her flesh marked with my purple and with Gavin's scarlet. She obviously knew that I'd ended up nude because she didn't say anything, sitting down on my knee after just one curious glance towards Hannah.

'That's rude,' she sighed as Jeff took a grip on Sophie's pretty blonde hair and began to fuck her mouth.

I put my arm around Kay, stroking the curve of her bottom and where the material of her school knickers hugged her hip. Jeff's treatment of Sophie *was* rude, and it was turning me on – not because of Jeff in his own right but for what he was doing to the girl. I was sure he'd go further, too, because he wasn't going to waste his chance to get every last drop of pleasure out of her. Sure enough, no sooner was his cock stiff than he'd adjusted himself, tugging on his erection and feeding the full hairy bulk of his scrotum into her mouth instead. She could barely get it all in, pop-eyed and gagging as she struggled to cope, with spittle dribbling down her chin.

Mel and Annabelle returned, sitting down next to me on the sleepers. Like Kay they showed no surprise at me being near-naked, Mel contenting herself with an amused look. I stuck my tongue out and went back to fondling Kay's bottom. By now I was thoroughly aroused and eager to watch as Fat Jeff grew increasingly excited, red-faced and puffing.

I really thought he was going to spunk in Sophie's hair and leave it at that, but he wasn't finished. Pulling out, he shuffled across to the steps of the hut and sat down, his knees spread wide to show off the mass of his cock and balls, obscene in arousal and wet with Sophie's spit. She came after him, awkward with her tied hands, and immediately took his cock in her mouth again.

Fat Jeff let her suck – but only for a moment before taking her by the hair and pulling her away from his cock, only to push her lower. Even Sophie, dirty submissive Sophie, whimpered as she realised what she had to do. But she did it anyway, poking out her tongue to lick his anus, her face buried in the deep hairy cleft below his balls. Although I couldn't see in detail, the expression of bliss on his face told me that she was really doing it, her tongue pushed in deep, right up his hole.

I felt my fanny tighten and Kay made a little noise deep in her throat. Sophie was not only licking Fat Jeff's bottom – her own infinitely prettier rear view was exposed to us all, her dirty bum cheeks spread wide to show off the soft pink dimple of her bumhole and her puffy swollen fanny lips, only half covered by her cut-out school pants. She looked as though Fat Jeff had already had his fingers up her, in both holes, making me wonder just how far he was going to take her.

Sure enough, he'd no sooner had his fill of her tongue up his bottom than he was lifting Sophie and turning her to bury his face between her cheeks in turn. Her eyes were glazed with pleasure as her fanny and bumhole were prepared, and Fat Jeff was nursing his erection as he licked, ready for her holes. He soon had her wet enough and made her straddle him, her bottom open to us as he fed his cock in up her fanny hole – although I was sure this was only a preliminary to buggering her.

As Sophie rode him I could see everything: the taut pink ring of her penetrated hole pulling in and out as they fucked, her anus stretched taut above. My own bottom-hole was twitching at the thought of where Fat Jeff's cock was going next, and I didn't have long to wait. Out it came, slippery with her juice. He adjusted himself, pressing his cock's great bulbous head to her tiny bumhole as she deliberately impaled herself, her ring opening to take him and like her vagina, pulling in and out as he gradually forced himself deep inside her.

Kay was trembling in my arms as we watched Sophie being buggered. We listened to the soft squelchy noises of her bumhole being used and to the grunts of pleasure and reaction from both of them. I wanted it myself – not Fat Jeff's cock up my bottom, of course, but something equally rude, something to make me come in a welter of uninhibited ecstasy.

There was no resistance as I slipped a hand under Kay's bottom and eased a finger up into her sex. She merely sighed and stuck her quim out a little, letting me get deeper in. As I began to finger Kay the couple were getting increasingly urgent, Fat Jeff clutching Sophie under her bottom and bouncing her up and down on his cock, until he suddenly gave a louder grunt and jammed himself deep into her. He'd come, and Sophie cried out as he pumped spunk into her rectum, wriggling on his cock in a vain effort to get friction to her own sex.

It didn't work. She was whimpering with frustrated passion as he eased her off his prick to leave her bumhole gaping wide, spunk and vaginal slime oozing out over his balls as he sat her down on his lap. I heard Mel give a single sharp order, and as Fat Jeff took Sophie in his arms Annabelle was scrambling forward to bury her face between Sophie's spread bottom cheeks, lapping up the sperm and girl juice, swallowing it and then licking again. In just moments we saw Sophie's bottom go tight and she was crying out in ecstasy as she came in Annabelle's face.

That was too much for me – and too much for just about everybody else. Mel had Morris's cock out, tugging at it, and the moment that Sophie was finished she bent down to take it in her mouth. Kay went down on me without having to be told to and I spread my thighs to let her lick, too eager for my climax to worry about anything else. Jeff Jones and Gavin were staring, faces heavy with envy, and I deliberately pulled my jacket open, and took my breasts in my hands, squeezing them gently and holding them up as Kay licked me, my orgasm already building in my head.

Kay was masturbating as she licked me, her bare bottom on show to everyone beneath the ruff of her turkey tail, her fanny too, with her fingers working down her cut-out school knickers. Just to know that felt almost as good as what her tongue was doing to my clitty, and it was all the better for knowing that Fat Hannah Riley was watching, watching me with my Kay kneeling in front of me, watching me get what she had earlier made me do to her while right now she had nothing . . .

I was coming, and as I saw that Harmony was going to take pity on Jeff Jones I closed my eyes, sure now that I was safe. My thighs tightened on Kay's head as the orgasm hit me and I cried out, wriggling myself into her face and squeezing my breasts as I came, pinching at my nipples and rubbing my bare bottom against the hard wood beneath me. It was long and glorious so I never even realised that anything was wrong until I opened my eyes to find that Hannah Riley had got to her feet, her fat face twisted into an angry scowl as she fronted up to the girl who had just stepped out from the bushes – Jilly.

Five

Watching Jilly spanked was quite an experience. She went meekly enough in response to a single crooked finger, despite wearing a petulant scowl as she walked across to where Fat Hannah was standing. Gavin Bulmer was just as ineffectual as I'd have expected, opening his mouth to protest as he realised that his girlfriend was about to be given a public spanking but quickly thinking better of it. He settled down to watch the show like the rest of us.

For me there was not only the pleasure of seeing a pretty girl spanked – despite feeling some guilt about the circumstances – but also deep relief that for once it wasn't me being put over the big woman's knee. I got the best possible view as well, with Jilly bottom-on to me as she was put in spanking position but with her face still visible as she looked back. Her bottom was already fully bare, as much target as Fat Hannah could possibly have wanted on display through the hole of the cut-out school knickers, but they were pulled down anyway after her feathers had been plucked out.

Jilly's face was a picture, her lower lip pushing out into an increasingly sulky pout as her pants were taken down only for her expression to break into shock and pain as the first smack landed full across her seat. I knew I'd been spanked to turn me on more than to hurt me and now I was actually glad of it as I saw the way that Hannah laid into Jilly's bottom, using the full force of her brawny arm and even swinging her shoulder into the blows.

Under the same treatment I'd have been howling my head off, probably in tears and definitely kicking in my panties, but not Jilly. Jilly was either tough or used to it, her face working with reaction but her body unmoving, while no sound escaped her lips at all. Only after maybe fifty spanks, her big muscular bum now a rich rosy pink where it wasn't purple with dye or brown with mud, did she finally break.

Fat Hannah paused in the spanking to jerk Jilly's bra up and flop out two heavy breasts, which immediately began to bounce and wobble as the punishment started again. Having her breasts stripped did something to Jilly's spirit. First she began to making little snivelling noises, then abruptly she burst into tears. As the tears began to flow, so she surrendered her attempt to maintain her dignity. Her legs began to kick and scissor in increasingly ridiculous postures as the spanking grew harder still, until her cheeks were spread to show off the tight pucker of her anus between them.

I knew I'd looked just the same, only even more undignified, so that pity was mixed with my excitement as I watched. None of the others seemed bothered in the least, watching with quiet pleasure or open excitement – even Gavin, who I felt might at least have spoken up for his girlfriend. He didn't, and to judge by the size of the bulge in his combat trousers and the fatuous smirk on his face he was in no hurry to have the spanking stop.

At last it was over, with Fat Hannah delivering a last furious salvo that left poor Jilly lying limp and gasping, her legs splayed wide apart too far gone to care about the display she was making of herself. Her bottom was a fine sight, pink and purple and brown save for the pale pink of her crease and the dun-coloured star of her anus, while for all her very real humiliation and distress her fanny was puffy with arousal and distinctly wet.

Fat Hannah didn't wait around, taking Jilly by the ear and hauling her off to where the BMW was parked just inside the gates. At that Gavin finally found his courage, indifferent to his girlfriend getting a public spanking but not wanting to risk having a near-naked and obviously freshly spanked girl seen on his land. Fat Hannah simply told him to fuck off, without even turning around, and there was nothing Gavin could do but open the gates and let her out as quickly as possible.

I retreated myself, worried that somebody might try to look in. After sending Jeff Jones to fetch my clothes and a brief clean-up for everyone in the Razorback hut we went back to my house. Most of the talk was about Fat Hannah's behaviour, which had somewhat over-shadowed the turkey shoot, and for all the general disapproval there was an undercurrent of excitement at having witnessed Jilly's punishment. Kay in particular was strongly affected, fidgeting and nervous for the rest of the day, and when the others had left it took a vigorous session with my hairbrush to quieten her down.

In the calm of the following day, as I painted red stripes on Mrs Mattlin-Jones's jump poles, my plan for retrieving my money and cheating Fat Hannah of the chance to amuse herself by putting me in the pillory seemed less sensible. Not that there was anything wrong with the way it worked, but it was hard to see her accepting the outcome. She could easily make life difficult for me at no risk to herself, and to judge by her previous behaviour she would have no compunction whatsoever about doing so.

It took me all week to admit to myself that the best thing to do was to go through with it: it was really the only sensible choice. That way the slate could be wiped clean and if that meant a few sponges in my face and a smacked bottom in public, then I would just have to put up with it. Not that it was an easy decision, especially the thought of having to go bare for punishment in front of Fat Hannah's carnies. The two odious clowns would be the worst of all.

My pride rebelled against the idea that somehow my background, or being stuck-up as Hannah had called it, made it amusing and appropriate for me to be spanked and humiliated in front of them. Not that I had any illusions. Ever since a couple of unpleasant incidents at school I'd known that people like that resent anybody who they feel looks down on them, even when it's not true. Personally, I'd been completely indifferent to their existence until they'd forced their attentions onto me, so it was hardly fair to call me stuck-up.

Yet I knew that I could cope, especially as there was a tiny part of me that actually wanted it to happen – as there always is with me in that sort of situation. Not that it made much difference because it was really a choice between that or walking away with only one quarter of what I'd been promised and be left with a considerable stock of goods that might take months to shift.

What I was going to need was some support afterwards. Sean would provide that, a cuddle and a glass of whiskey, and if he made me take him in my mouth, well, I'd done it before. I could do it again, but despite the fact that I was in a sense willing that knowledge only fuelled my resentment – not of Sean but of Hannah. Sean was a man, and no saint. Inevitably he was going to try and take an opportunity to have his cock sucked. Hannah, on the other hand, had repeatedly and deliberately manipulated me.

Despite telling myself that is was the only sensible option, I found it very hard indeed to accept the idea of going into the circus pillory. I had completed the order and arranged for it to be delivered on the Saturday, but as I drove up towards where the circus was pitched near Welwyn Garden City my stomach felt so weak that I had to stop at a pub to visit the Ladies.

I knew full well that part of the reason Hannah had asked me in advance was to make me feel apprehensive. But that knowledge only made it worse, fuelling both my fear and my resentment. Yes, I could cope. I'd done worse for Morris, far worse, and in front of a crowd, but this wasn't just any old crowd. These were Fat Hannah's carnies, which drew on a personal insecurity that went right back to my childhood. I didn't trust them either, which was why I'd made careful arrangements to protect myself.

First there was Sean: my association with him would protect me from the other male carnies and allow me to satisfy my private feelings with my fingers without making an utter disgrace of myself or getting gang-banged in public. I understood my own sexuality well enough to know that I'd be turned on afterwards and would have to make arrangements to ensure that things didn't get out of control.

Second, there were Jeff Bellbird and his friend Monty. They were meeting me at the station and each of them had his task. Jeff was to stay in my car and leave as soon as I'd given him the money, coming back to pick me up after the carnies had finished with me. Monty would remain hidden, to hold the money while Jeff collected me and to be ready to call the police if anything really went wrong.

Hopefully it would all be unnecessary. With luck I would simply be put in the pillory, have a few sponges thrown at me, get my bottom spanked and that would be that. If that really was all, I knew full well that I'd leave with as much disappointment as relief, and yet had it not been for the presence of Jeff and Monty I think I'd have turned back.

I didn't, though, and found myself in a pub just down the road from where the circus was set up, a triple gin and tonic in one shaking hand as Jeff and Monty drank pints of real ale. Both of them were enjoying themselves, Jeff especially. He was even in his camouflage gear and was treating the whole thing like a military operation, which I found more worrying than reassuring. Neither of them seemed to have the faintest idea just how nasty carnies could be, either. But possibly that was just as well.

We left the pub after my second drink, Jeff now driving and Monty staying put. The circus was only just beginning to break up and the field was crowded with cars. I looked around for Sean among the carnies who were directing traffic, but there was no sign of him nor of anyone else I knew. Leaving Jeff with the car, I started around the edge of the stalls to avoid being seen by the clowns, both of whom were capering up and down beside their ridiculous plastic pillory while children threw paint-soaked sponges at some unfortunate man with his head trapped in it.

I winced. It wouldn't be long before I would be in the same sorry position myself, presumably in my own pillory but with an audience of jeering carnies to throw the sponges and Fat Hannah Riley to spank my bottom. It was hard not to pout as I walked on, in resentment for what was about to be done to me, for the way I'd been manipulated, and for the involuntary sticky feeling down my panties.

As before, the security guard managed to intercept me. But this time he clearly knew what was going on, his usual surly manner replaced by a lewd grin as he conducted me to Fat Hannah's caravan. As I climbed the steps his stare was fixed firmly on the seat of my jeans, leaving me blushing even as Maggie opened the door to my knock.

'You're early,' Hannah addressed me. 'What, fancy having your bum tickled up first, do we?'

'No, thank you,' I answered, grimacing. 'I just wanted to make sure that everything was sorted out.'

'Shame,' she answered, much more affably than I'd expected. 'Still, best to have you fresh at the start. Have you got my gear, then?'

'Yes, everything. It's in the car. Could you spare somebody to help me unload – Sean, perhaps?'

'Sean's at work, love.'

'His friend Mick?'

'Mick's at work, too. When Sean's at work, Mick's at work.'

'Oh. Never mind, then. I've brought a friend who'll help. Where shall I put things?'

'In the club trailer. Gerry'll show you.'

Gerry turned out to be the security guard, who did as he was told but didn't lift a finger to help with the unloading. By the time Jeff and I had everything in the trailer I was feeling hot and bothered, yet with that done I was one step nearer my fate, leaving me more nervous than ever. I was even a bit sorry when Hannah handed over the full amout of money without arguing, because now I had no excuse to back out.

'See you later,' I told Jeff as I handed him the thick brown envelope.

'Ain't you staying to watch the fun?' Hannah asked.

'Been there, done that,' Jeff answered casually, bringing a blush to my face once again. 'See you, Amber.'

He went, rolling off in the direction of the car, and I was on my own. It was a relief to find that they hadn't minded Jeff watching, as that surely meant they didn't have anything too horrible planned for me. I was still desperately nervous as we walked back in among the caravans, although Hannah was friendlier that she'd ever been before, doing her best to soothe my feelings as we walked.

'Don't be scared, darling – this is just a bit of fun, just a laugh. How about a nice drink?'

I was already slightly drunk, but I accepted, allowing her to pour me a generous measure of whiskey in the caravan. The circus was beginning to break up for the day and Maggie was back, smoking with her feet up as I sipped at my drink. Both of them were looking at me, sizing me up as if I was a piece of prime meat.

'So what we going to dress her in?' Maggie asked after a while.

'Something posh,' Hannah answered. 'Maybe –'

'I, er . . . I thought I'd just be as I am.' I interrupted. 'These are old clothes, and I have a change in the car.'

'No, no, won't do at all,' Hannah answered, shaking her head.

'You can tell she's no showgirl,' Maggie agreed. 'You got to have a bit of style, love, a bit of class.'

'What did you have in mind, then?' I asked.

'Let's look at you,' Hannah replied. 'Give us a twirl.'

I turned around with as much elegance as I could muster.

'Catwalk model?' Maggie suggested. 'I'd love to see one of those stuck-up bitches get it.'

'Nah,' Hannah replied. 'She got the height, but too much tit and arse. I don't see her on a catwalk. In a porno mag, maybe, but there's no kick in it if she starts off looking like a tart.'

'What do you have?' I asked, hoping to steer the decision so that the experience wouldn't be any more humiliating than I knew it was already going to be.

'All sorts, love,' she told me.

'I often ride,' I said cautiously.

'Ooh, she rides,' Maggie echoed, imitating my accent.

'Shut up, Maggie – give the poor girl a chance,' Hannah responded. 'She's playing our game, ain't she?'

'Only 'cause she has to,' Maggie grumbled. But Hannah ignored her, speaking to me again.

'We could do you some riding gear, jodhpurs and boots, nice smart black coat, top hat. Yeah, why not?'

She hauled herself to her feet and I allowed myself to draw a carefully concealed sigh of relief. When I'd first realised that I was to be dressed up I'd had visions of being put in a circus costume, maybe even a clown suit, which would have made my ordeal far, far worse than being in riding gear.

'Come with me, love,' Hannah said, beckoning.

I followed her from her caravan to another one, bigger but a great deal less smart. It was a communal changing room and wardrobe, with racks of costumes at one end and crude dressing tables at the other. The smells of cheap perfume and sweat hung thick in the air. There was also something else, which I recognised from my visit to Sean's caravan and could now identify: greasepaint.

Hannah went to the end of the caravan and began to rummage among the costumes. She'd soon found a jacket, which she held up against me, nodding in satisfaction.

'This ought to do. There's jodhpurs here, and boots in that rack, blouses and all. Take what you like – but make it smart, like you was going out on your horse.'

I nodded and she retreated to a chair, lighting a cigarette as she watched me undress. Curiously, I felt far less self-conscious than I had when changing in front of Mrs Mattlin-Jones, but then Hannah had already had me bare and had made me come under her fingers. She knew my secrets and had already stripped me of both my clothes and my dignity, exposing everything I might have liked to keep private, both mental and physical. The same was not true of the carnies. They knew, but they hadn't seen. Now they were going to, and the lump in my throat was growing bigger as I dressed.

None of the jodhpurs quite fitted. The pair that came closest were distinctly tight over my bottom and thighs so that the shape of my sex was clearly outlined. I told myself that they were going to see it all anyway and continued to dress, finding a reasonable blouse and a comfortable pair of boots. The jacket was a little loose if anything, and once I'd put my hair up and added a black top hat with a broad ribbon I really did look as if I might be about to go riding. Hannah was impressed too but insisted that I add a little make-up, mascara and red lipstick, to which I agreed but kept it sensible.

'My, but you do look a pretty picture!' she said when I'd finished. 'We *are* going to have some fun with you, ain't we?'

It wasn't really a question, it was more a statement of fact, and I didn't answer. Still, I managed a weak smile. She was evidently enjoying herself enormously, making me bold enough to ask the question that I'd intended to put to Sean.

'You *will* look after me, won't you, Hannah? I mean, your men . . .'

She laughed, cutting me off.

'Don't you go worrying yourself about my boys, love,' she assured me. 'You're mine, and they know better than to let their greasy little mitts stray where they're not wanted, not without my say-so.'

As Hannah spoke she patted my bottom and I found myself blushing and swallowing. Now it looked as if I was likely to end up on my knees in front of her after my ordeal, a thought that made my already muddled feelings even harder to cope with. One thing was especially important.

'If . . . if you want to do that to me,' I said, 'please could you hold me afterwards?'

It felt deeply pathetic to be asking, after all the antagonism there'd been between us. But I knew I would need it, and when Hannah was being friendly there was no denying her attraction as somebody who could spank me and spank me well, bringing out my rare submissive feelings as few others could.

Hannah nodded, casually accepting my need, and as we left the caravan she took hold of my arm. The last of the light was fading from the sky but the carnival music was still blaring out, while powerful lights had been turned on, their beams mixing with the dimmer ones from the caravans to create strange patterns on the muddy ground. Ahead was a brighter area and as we came into it I realised that it was the place where I was to be pilloried.

Some caravans had been arranged into a rough square with only narrow gaps between them, ensuring that there would be no prying eyes to witness what went on. More lights had been set up, brilliant spots mounted on high supports to cast a brilliant white illumination over the central space and throw everything else into black shadow. A few chairs had been set out and a table on which several cases of beer had been stacked, but nobody else was there. Nor was there any sign of my pillory.

'We'll be waiting until the punters are out,' Hannah told me. 'Sit down for a bit.'

I did as I was told, feeling numb as I lowered myself into the nearest chair. Hannah walked over to the table and pulled two beers from their plastic wrappings, smiling as she handed one to me. I took it gratefully, despite the gin and whiskey I'd already put away, because I knew it would be so much easier if I was drunk. At least I felt secure in her protection. She spoke again after taking a hearty swallow of her own can.

'Like our Sean, do you?'

'He seems nice,' I answered, uncertain how much she knew.

'He's a laugh, is Sean,' she went on. 'Always was. So, what, you all right with him doing the sponges and that?'

'Yes, I suppose so,' I agreed.

'And Mick?'

'Maybe – if there *have* to be two people.'

'Come on, love, you can't have Sean without Mick.'

'All right then, I suppose so.'

'Good girl. So how far do they get to go, then? I mean, they both fancy you rotten, and Mick's well pissed that you gave Sean a blow that time.'

I didn't answer. I blushed furiously, not only because Sean had obviously made what had happened between us common knowledge but because I seemed to be being treated as common property.

'I can hardly be expected to –' I began, only to be interrupted. Hannah's voice now revealed something of her temper.

'Don't give me that crap, darling,' she said. 'We both know what you are.'

'What?' I demanded, although I knew perfectly well what she meant.

'A slut,' she confirmed. 'Or you wouldn't be here, would you, now?'

'That's . . . that's not reasonable at all!' I protested. 'Just because I'm in touch with my sexuality and reject conventional social mores about what is and is not appropriate for a woman does not mean I am available for sex to all men – or to all women, for that matter. You have to realise, Hannah, that just because I have chosen to empower myself in the context of third-generation feminism does not mean –'

'You don't half talk a load of bollocks,' Hannah laughed, cutting me off again. 'You did Sean, so how about Mick? I mean, it ain't exactly as if Sean's your old man now, is it?'

'No, of course not, but I . . . I really don't like to have to agree to something like that in advance,' I managed. 'I don't know, maybe . . . maybe if I feel right at the time . . .'

'All right, all right,' she broke in. 'So you like it taken out of your hands, is that it? Like you need an excuse to get off on going over my knee?'

'I . . . I suppose so, in a way . . .'

'So you need an excuse to suck dick?'

'Maybe.'

Hannah was going to reply but then Gerry appeared, now with his dog, to say that the last of the paying customers had gone and the field gate was locked. I felt my stomach tighten. Hannah hauled herself to her feet and lumbered off towards a group of carnies as they came in at the far side of the square, turning to me as she went.

'I'll make sure you get your excuse, darling. Now just you be a good girl.'

'No, look . . .' I managed, then shut up.

I knew she ruled the group with a rod of iron, but it seemed absurd for her to be dictating to me who I could and couldn't have sex with, or whether I should do so at all for that matter. Yet what if Mick and Sean took me into a caravan afterwards, both expecting to have their cocks attended to? Would I resist? Would I want to?

It was nearly too much – too exciting and too humiliating – to be used as their sex toy, to be spanked and made to suck cock, to be deliberately shamed in public. With the crowd now gathering, it wasn't going to be long before things kicked off. I tried to tell myself that I had no choice and that it would be nice, a really exciting experience. But I could already feel the tears gathering in my eyes. They all seemed to be watching me, men and women both, drinking beer and smoking, laughing together, each and every one of them out to enjoy the show.

I stood up, shaking so badly that I nearly fell. Just yards away the black opening between two caravans beckoned, a tempting escape route, only for Gerry to appear once more and favour me with a dirty leer as he propped himself against the side of one of the caravans. I forced a smile and turned to look as I caught a movement across the square. Two carnies were dragging something between them. It was the pillory, only not my beautiful wood and leather creation but the ridiculous plastic thing that the clowns used. I sighed heavily.

Others followed, with buckets, sponges and other bits and pieces, not all of which I was able to see. The pillory was set up at the very centre of the square, in the full glare of the lights, while the spectators arranged themselves beside one of the largest caravans. There was no sign of either Sean or Mick and I waited, trying to look calm and ignoring the audience's attention, wisecracks and muffled sniggers. Hannah had been talking to a group of men by the large caravan but now came back, once more all smiles as she approached me.

'Don't you worry about a thing, darling,' she said, patting my bottom. 'Just remember, Ma Riley's here to look after you.'

I nodded, despite thinking that putting me in a pillory for the amusement of her bunch of carnies was a pretty strange way to look after me. Turning away from me, she held up her hands, at which the noise of the crowd changed from open, easy banter to something more tense, with many of them looking towards the largest of the gaps between the caravans. I looked too, just in time to see the two clowns emerge. Baffo performed a series of impressive somersaults, which Buffo attempted to imitate only to trip over himself and sprawl in the mud.

The response was laughter, somewhat forced, from everybody except me. I was staring at the pair of buffoons as a nasty suspicion began to dawn. Hannah was now behind me, whispering in my ear as the two clowns turned with all too obvious intent towards where I was standing.

'Run,' she hissed. 'Try to get away from them.'

I didn't really need to be told. My heart had sunk into my boots as the truth dawned on me and I was already close to panic. They were coming for me, both of them crouched low like wrestlers only in ludicrous exaggeration, with their bottoms thrust out and their arms spread as wide as they could possibly go. Hannah's hand touched the middle of my back and shoved, and then I was running, darting between the two clowns.

Baffo gave a crow of laughter, Buffo a great groan of dismay as he immediately tripped up. Around me the crowd had closed ranks, blocking any possible escape as Baffo began to chase me around the pillory, coming behind in great leaps and bounds, now drawing real laughter and shouts of encouragement from the crowd. He wasn't going to catch me – but Buffo was, rushing in from the side and hurling himself forward in a flying tackle.

Actually, he missed completely, once more sprawling in the mud, but I knew the clowns were only playing cat and mouse with me. I darted back the other way, missing Buffo's hand by an inch as he snatched at my ankle, and dodging Baffo only to slip in the muddy grass and go down. Both of them were on me in an instant, grabbing my legs and lifting me head down, so that my hat fell off and my head trailed in the wet grass as they dragged me towards the pillory.

I was gasping for breath and could do nothing as I was turned over and had my head and arms forced down into the pillory. Then the top was closed and I was trapped, helpless, my bottom stuck out behind, a position both vulnerable and ludicrous. Already the crowd was cheering and clapping, even before I'd had anything done to me. I closed my eyes, trying to bring my feelings under control before the clowns started to torment me but there wasn't to be even a moment's peace.

Buffo was behind me, sniggering loudly as he made a great display of lifting the tails of my smart black coat and examining my bottom from just inches away. I'd

125

begun to shake, expecting my jodhpurs to be pulled down at any moment and my panties to follow. Nothing happened. Baffo strode pompously back and slapped Buffo's wrist before leading him out to the front. They stood together, at arm's length from each other, and performed a sweeping bow. Then they straightened up and Baffo addressed the crowd.

'My Lords, Ladies and Gentlemen, may I present to you the disgrace of Madame Boobfontaine! This busty young scallywag has been caught exhibiting her airs and graces to the good folk of the Carnival Bizarre, and for this she must pay the price: a thorough trumping until she learns the error of her ways and a little respect! Buffo, to the sponges!'

Baffo bowed again as Buffo went forward to collect two large plastic buckets, one red, one green, both bulging with large sponges soaked in liquid of the same vivid colours. I waited as they had a quick fight over who was going to have which bucket, and closed my eyes as they raised their sponges.

One missed but the other caught me full in the face, hard. A cheer went up from the crowd. I stifled a sob, already close to tears because of the utter lack of sympathy, with every single person there, male and female, thoroughly enjoying watching my public humiliation. The next two sponges both hit me, one in my face again and the other on my back, and then came more, a barrage of the things, heavy and wet, with the clowns capering and calling out encouragement to each other as they soiled me. The crowd laughed with ever greater glee.

I didn't dare open my eyes but I knew they were getting closer. Their voices were louder, the smack of the sponges in my face harder than before. Then I felt a hand in my hair: my head had been pulled up and one of the clowns was smearing a paint-soaked sponge directly into my face, leaving me with water bubbling out of my nose. I was gasping for breath. Instantly another sponge was shoved against my face, filling my open mouth with foul-tasting water to the delight of both clowns and the crowd.

They never even gave me a chance to catch my breath, sticking a second sponge into my mouth as I was still spluttering out the contents of the first. Another was squeezed over my head, water dripping from my already bedraggled hair and running down my neck. One of them pinched my nose, trying to force the sponge into my mouth again so that I was forced to bite a piece off. I was spitting out bits of it as he finally let go, to renewed laughter and applause from the crowd.

Suddenly it stopped and I risked opening one eye to see both clowns dancing back, only to come forward again. My relief vanished as they ducked down beneath me, both peering up to where my breasts hung in my blouse. I struggled not to show my emotions as Baffo reached up to take hold of one dangling globe and squeezed. But it was impossible. As Buffo took hold of my other breast I'd begun to pout, and more so as they began to wobble me, and to speak.

'Big,' Baffo remarked.

'Very big,' Buffo agreed.

'Fat,' Baffo continued.

'Very fat,' Buffo added.

'Wobbly.'

'Very wobbly.'

'A fine pair indeed. But the question is, should they be bare?'

'That is indeed the question. Should they be bare?'

The crowd caught on, yelling as one for me to be stripped. A bubble of bitter humiliation was growing in my throat as the clowns continued to fondle me. It burst as both of them cried out in unison.

'Of course they should be bare!'

Even as they spoke their hands gripped my blouse. Before I could do more than squeak in surprise it had been torn open, flopping out my breasts, which were immediately grabbed and my bra cups jerked up to leave me with both my boobs swinging nude under my chest as the carnies roared with laughter. My sudden stripping left me gasping with reaction, but once more I was given no time to pull myself together. Both my breasts were taken in hand again, to be groped and slapped and tickled, my nipples pulled and pinched. Then the sponges were applied, slapped hard against me to soil my ruined blouse and my bra, both tits too, until I had coloured water dripping from my nipples, green on one side and red on the other as yet again the two clowns broke away into a mad capering dance.

They were soon back, and by now I was choking with sobs as they went behind me, carrying their buckets. Again they went through their humiliating little routine, commenting on the size of my bottom as they had a good feel of my bum cheeks, then asking the spectators if I should be stripped. Again the crowd roared for me to get it, only this time it wasn't done fast. It was done slowly, my jodhpurs peeled slowly down off my bum to reveal my panties and left around my thighs. The clowns began to molest me, their fingers everywhere, pulling out my waistband to let the elastic snap back against my flesh. Then they were pinching my cheeks where they stuck out below the leg holes, pushing the thin cotton into my crease and tickling my quim until I'd begun to wriggle and squirm in helpless response, and pressing their knuckles to the swell of my fanny to rub me up. Despite myself I'd soon begun to whimper in pleasure.

When the clowns finally stopped I thought my panties were going to come down. But no. They merely took a grip on my waistband, pulling it out so that they could see down the back. After a moment spent inspecting my bare bottom two water-laden sponges were dropped down my knickers and the elastic left to snap shut. I gasped as I felt the water, first on my bum cheeks and then between them, wetting my anus and trickling into the open hole of my fanny, cold and uncomfortable. Water had quickly begun to soak into my panties, and more followed as the clowns gave the sponges a purposeful squeeze.

Even then they didn't strip me, just left me with the two big sponges bulging obscenely in my panty pouch and the water trickling down my legs and dripping from the crotch of my knickers. I'd given in, dizzy with reaction, my body trembling and the tears pouring down my face, my dignity surrendered along with my decency. They were going to spank me, and I was beginning to want it. Hannah Riley was right: I was a slut.

Baffo came around to my head, puffing his chest out as he stood over me and spoke.

'Well, Madame Boobfontaine, I trust you are beginning to learn your lesson?'

I nodded weakly, unable to deny it, not in the middle of punishment.

'She is learning her lesson, she says!' he called out to the crowd. 'But is she really, or is she lying? Shall we see?'

There was a note of horrid glee in Baffo's voice and I tried to look back. Buffo was behind me and he'd taken hold of the waistband on my knickers. Baffo looked down at me and spoke.

'Shall we bare your bottom?'

They weren't merely going to strip me and spank me – they were going to make me ask for it.

'Yes,' I managed, my voice little more than a croak.

Baffo immediately ducked down, one hand cupped to his ear as he called out: 'I can't hear you!'

'Yes,' I repeated, forcing myself to speak clearly despite all the humiliation it brought. 'Bare my bottom.'

'Once again,' he demanded.

'Yes!' I shouted. 'Bare my bottom! Strip me, spank me, you bastard, Sean, you utter bastard!' I could no longer pretend to myself that I did not know Baffo's real identity.

I'd burst into tears, really bawling, but I got no sympathy. Baffo stood up again, his chest puffed out as far as it would go, and he raised his arm in command as he spoke.

'Down with her panties!'

Buffo responded immediately, jerking my knickers down to spill the sponges out onto the grass and leave me bare. My bottom stuck out in the full glare of the lights, fat and pink, with streaks of red and green where the coloured water was running down my skin. My fanny was showing, too, the lips protruding between my thighs like a plump fleshy fig so overripe that it had split.

The crowd roared with delight at my exposure, clapping and cheering, calling to Baffo to do as I had asked and spank me. But he raised his hands for silence and called out again.

'She wants a choice, she says,' he called in his most pompous voice, 'because she's not sure if she wants to suck our cocks. Perhaps she thinks we're not good enough to have our cocks sucked by her?'

I looked up in fresh horror. Hannah hadn't been talking about what I was expected to do *after* the show at all. She'd meant what I was supposed to do *during* it. My mouth came open in a feeble protest, completely drowned out by the crowd, every one of whom was calling for me to be made to do it anyway, the girls as loudly as the boys, but Sean a.k.a. Baffo once again raised his hands for quiet.

'No, no,' he said, 'Madame Boobfontaine wants a choice, so she shall have a choice. The choice is this. She may have her bottom spanked – or she may suck my penis.'

I hung my head, unable to make the choice between pain and shame, part of me angrily rejecting both choices, another part wanting both, and at the same time. It was hard to think. But my panties were already down, my bottom was bare and soiled with paint, and a spanking would make me warm and eager, and would take away so many of my bad feelings.

'Spank me,' I said weakly. Then I yelled out before he could add to my suffering by making me repeat it. 'Spank me! I told you to spank me!'

'Ah, yes,' Baffo replied, his voice suddenly lawyerly as he put a hand to his chin. 'But that was before I gave you the chance of sucking on my great big cock instead.'

'Spank me,' I repeated. 'Just spank me, please . . .'

I trailed off, barely able to speak for my emotions, but he merely began to strut up and down in front of me. Behind, Buffo had begun to fondle my bottom, greatly to the amusement of that part of the audience which could see. I couldn't help but respond, pushing myself out to draw ribald laughter from the crowd as Sean in his Baffo mode spoke.

'Oh, very well. If the little tart wants spanking, then spank her.'

He turned his back on me, sticking his nose in the air as Buffo set to work on my bottom, ducking down behind me as he began to smack on my cheeks as if they were a pair of tom-toms, making the crowd howl with laughter. However ridiculous it was to have my bottom played like a musical instrument it still got to me, the sharp stinging smacks quickly bringing the blood to the surface of my skin until I was panting and gasping in excitement. He slapped faster, setting up a furious rhythm on my bum cheeks, making my boobs swing and my feet tread in the wet grass. At last Sean turned, to look down on me from his ridiculous clown's face. Immediately Buffo stopped spanking me.

'So?' Sean demanded, pushing his hips forward. 'Do you want to suck?'

'Later,' I begged, forcing myself to keep my voice down. 'Later, in your caravan. I'll do –'

'Spank!' he ordered, and it had begun again, Buffo or Mick, as I knew it must be – beating out a rhythm on my bottom, then changing abruptly.

Now I was getting a proper spanking: full, firm swats across the width of my cheeks, aimed low, right on my sweet spot, so that every slap sent a jolt to my fanny. I knew I couldn't cope. My arousal soared immediately, the thought of what was being done to me burning in my head – spanked and molested in front of a crowd of rowdy carnies, every one of them eager to see my mouth filled with penis, my face soiled with spunk . . .

The spanking stopped. I looked back between my dangling boobs and my open legs, just as Mick/Buffo pushed his thumbs between my bottom cheeks to spread them wide, inspecting my anus from a distance of mere inches. Fresh sobs burst from my throat at this new indignity, followed by a gasp of dismay as he touched me, probing my slippery, sweaty anal ring with the tip of a finger making my muscles twitch and my bottom cheeks tighten.

'Do behave yourself, Buffo,' Sean said. But the finger continued to work its way up my bottom, until it was pushed in deep and began to wiggle around.

'Please,' I managed, looking up only to break off in another gasp as Buffo's thumb was pushed into my vagina. 'Oh God, no . . .'

Buffo began to masturbate me and spank me at the same time, manipulating my bumhole and fanny as he rained smacks on my already hot bottom. It wasn't going to make me come but it really brought my feelings to the boil – so much shame and so much pleasure that I simply couldn't take any more. I began to babble.

'Oh God . . . OK, OK, you pig . . . I'll suck your cock while he spanks me . . . go on, do it . . . do it to me, you bastard!'

'Ah ha!' Sean/Baffo called out. 'I knew she wanted it really! Get out of her, Buffo – you're spoiling her concentration.'

Buffo gave an exaggerated sniff to express sadness. But he stopped spanking me and his fingers eased out of my body, leaving me open and vulnerable behind. I struggled to regain my composure, but I knew I was lost, staring bleary-eyed at Baffo as his fingers went to the huge buttons on the front of his costume. He undid them, one after another, and allowed the front to fall open slowly. His scrawny chest came into view, then his belly, lean but disgustingly hairy, then the thick bush of his pubic hair, and at last his cock, fat, turgid – and thickly coated with greasepaint.

His balls were red, his shaft was white, and the fat helmet already half out of his foreskin was also red. The colours were smeared together where they'd touched. The crowd roared approval as they saw, and Baffo gave another crow of gleeful laughter as he saw the expression on my face.

'You can't really expect . . .' I began. Then I broke off, squeaking as Baffo stepped forward and pinched my nose, hard.

My head was forced up, lifted by my nose, my mouth came open to gasp in air – and then he'd done it. He'd fed me his cock. A roar of approval went up from the crowd as they saw I was doing it, then came jeers and clapping and laughter as Baffo began to fuck my mouth, pushing his fat greasy rubbery shaft in and out between my lips. I was gagging, my mouth full of foul slimy greasepaint and the taste of unwashed cock, but he wouldn't let go of my nose and I knew that, whether I co-operated or not, I was going to get my face fucked.

133

I was going to get my bottom smacked, too. Buffo once more applied his hands to my cheeks, now using firm slaps planted right across my meat, each one jamming my head onto Baffo's rapidly swelling penis. With that I gave in, sucking and slurping at the foul-tasting mess in my mouth, again and again, struggling to clean Baffo's cock as my bottom bounced to the slaps.

'Gobble-gobble, Madame Boobfontaine!' Baffo yelled, and another roar of delight went up from the crowd.

They had me, their dirty cocksucking little slut, trapped and helpless maybe, but working eagerly on the big penis in my mouth and waggling my hot bottom for more attention from behind. I got it: harder spanks and a finger up my fanny, opening me as I caught the meaty slapping noise of Buffo bringing his cock to erection. He was going to fuck me. I didn't even try to protest but braced my legs to take him as the crowd began to chant.

'Spit-roast! Spit-roast! Spit-roast!' they yelled louder and louder as I felt the rounded head of Buffo's cock press against my sex, and in.

As I was penetrated the crowd screamed out their delight once again. It was done. I'd been made into a spit-roast, that awful, degrading phrase, my body used by the clowns, a cock in each end, fanny and mouth, and in public. Buffo was still spanking me too, slapping at my bottom cheeks even as the two of them rocked my body back and forth in the pillory.

Deep down I was still trying to tell myself that I had no choice, that I was trapped and was just being used. It was a lie. I *was* being used, yes, but I was enjoying it. Had I not been trapped my fingers would have been busy with my fanny, to bring the final disgrace upon myself by coming in front of the entire jeering crowd of carnies as I was spitted on the clowns' erections.

But I couldn't reach my quim and when Buffo pulled his cock out of my fanny I felt only disappointed that it

134

was nearly over. He gave me his spunk on my bottom, across both cheeks and between them, dribbling hot and sticky over my anus as the crowd roared their approval. I was still sucking, urgently now, and praying that Buffo would bring me off to add the final touch to my humiliation.

He didn't, and when Sean finally pulled out of my mouth I was left gaping for more. What I got was his spunk, full in my mouth and across my already filthy features as he jerked himself off in my face. A thick pool of it splattered my tongue, two fat worms of it dangled from my lips and another from my nose. But before I could swallow or lick it up Sean had slapped his hand into my face, smearing the filthy mixture of come and greasepaint and lipstick and spittle and snot all over me.

A few touches and I'd have come. I was mumbling brokenly, begging for it, but nobody paid the least attention. The clowns just left me like that, tumbling around me in a series of cartwheels and playing leapfrog as their come dribbled slowly down my face and bottom. I wanted to be rubbed off, to be spanked harder, to be made to suck cock again, to be fucked – buggered, even.

All I got was Gerry, grinning evilly as he approached me. He had a bucket and I wondered if my ordeal was going to begin all over again. But it was only water, cold water, which he threw in my face before sponging off the worst of Sean's mess and opening the pillory. I stood up clumsily, my muscles aching, so dizzy that I immediately sat down on the grass, my head spinning as I massaged my wrists and neck.

I knew, dimly, that it wasn't over. Hannah would come for me, maybe Maggie too, and I'd be put through my paces in their caravan. I wanted it, wanted to grovel on my knees as I licked them and brought myself to wanton ecstasy under my fingers. They had me, well and truly, wanting to pleasure them and be punished by them despite all they'd done to me. Deep down I could feel a spark of self-pity for the state I was in. But it wasn't going to stop me.

The spotlights had gone off, leaving me in dim light from the caravan windows. As two bulky forms loomed out of the shadows I realised that I was probably going to be done then and there. Only it wasn't Hannah and Maggie. It was Jeff and Monty. They helped me up, even adjusting my clothes, and guided me away between the caravans to my car.

Monty drove, out to some dark lay-by in the countryside where he stopped. I knew what they wanted and I was happy to give it, still in a haze of drunken, submissive ecstasy yet curiously triumphant at having cheated Hannah and Maggie of their pleasure. I stripped off for the two men, stark naked in the back of the car as they watched me by the interior light. I took them in my hands, wanking them as best I could in the confined space. I took them in my mouth, sucking turn and turn about.

They took me outside and had me over the bonnet, fucked me deep and hard – Jeff first, then Monty, both of them coming all over my bottom as I played with myself. As Monty took his turn I was near orgasm, imagining myself back in the pillory, trapped helpless with my jodhpurs pulled down in front of a jeering crowd, stripped and soiled and spanked, made to suck cock and fucked and spunked on, in my face and over my bottom, my bare, spanked bottom.

As Monty ejaculated all over my bum cheeks I was coming myself, crying out in ecstasy as the hot spunk spattered my still-glowing bum flesh. My fingers worked in my sopping fanny and even as I began to come down my mind was still full of images of how I'd been abused.

Six

The sensible thing to do was to wash Fat Hannah Riley and everything associated with her right out of my life. I had provided their equipment, I had been paid, and they had had their fun with me. Obviously I'd been wrong in thinking that Carnival Bizarre might be somewhere I could express my sexuality without being interfered with, but with hindsight that seemed inevitable. There is something about me that seems to bring out the worst in dominant men – and women, too – and while I have to confess that I do need that sort of attention occasionally, it is something that I prefer to keep firmly under my own control. Fat Hannah and her carnies were well out of my control, dangerously so, and they had to go.

Unfortunately it wasn't so easy. I'd told Kay that I'd had to go in the pillory but I left out the more lurid details. She seemed to really quite like the carnies while I found them at once threatening and fascinating. Kay wanted to go to the next Carnival Bizarre, which was being held in Enfield, less than a twenty-minute drive away. To make matters worse, Angel also wanted to come, the idea being to play a little at the club and then go to bed together as we had before.

I was still trying to find a convincing excuse on the Wednesday when to my dismay I saw Hannah's BMW pull up directly outside the shop window. Kay was in

137

the shop, helping me stocktake as it was a quiet day. She immediately ran to the door, holding it open as Hannah waddled through closely followed by Maggie with her ever-present cigarette hanging from one side of her lip.

'Hi,' I managed, grateful that none of my respectable neighbours were around. 'Um ... why don't you come through to the kitchen? Kay, could you look after the shop?'

'I'll be able to hear the bell,' Kay protested.

'Got your clothes, Amber,' Hannah said. 'You left them behind.'

'I know ... thanks,' I answered her. 'I've washed what I was wearing. I'll get it.'

'Don't worry about it,' she said. 'You can keep it. Wear it another time.'

'Um ... thanks, er ... ,' I stammered, thinking of myself back in the pillory. 'Come in, please.'

I opened the door at the back and led them through into the kitchen, Kay as well. Hannah and Maggie sat down, the mere sight of their laps enough to set my fingers trembling as I put the kettle on.

'Wondered what had happened to you, we did,' Hannah went on. 'Thought some of the boys might have taken you into a caravan for a bit of the other. Made Gerry go right round, I did.'

'Sorry,' I answered, immediately wondering why I was apologising. 'It was nothing like that. My friends picked me up a bit earlier than I'd expected, that's all.'

'Thought you were going to come back to the caravan, we did,' Maggie put in. 'Thought you might be in need of satisfying – and I never did get mine.'

'Do you take sugar?' I asked, frantically trying to change the subject as the blood rushed to my face.

Kay gave me a questioning glance but said nothing. I turned back to the work surface in an attempt to hide my embarrassment as Hannah replied to my question.

'Three, please, love.'

'Four for me,' Maggie added, putting down the bag with my clothes in it on the table. 'Weren't that a laugh, though, specially when Sean –'

'So, what's the venue like for the next club?' I said quickly, blushing hotter still at the thought of Kay discovering that I'd been made to suck cock, to say nothing of my having been so stupid as not to realise that Baffo and Buffo were actually Sean and Mick.

'Got a great place,' Hannah told me. 'An old school. Still got desks and stuff, it has, so we want everyone to go in uniform. That was Angel's idea, that was. We've got our big Christmas party lined up too, at a big club in Hackney. Here, have a look at the flyer. Maggie?'

Maggie took a flyer from her bag and held it out, a garish thing showing Jilly in a red bikini trimmed with white fluff. She was holding a cane and had thigh boots on, but it would have been a better picture if she'd looked stern instead of merely sulky.

'When's it on?' I asked.

'The twenty-third, Friday,' she told me.

'That's the same night as Morris's club,' Kay pointed out.

Hannah shrugged.

'Best night, ain't it?' she said. 'Friday before Christmas.'

'Aren't you worried you won't get many people?' Kay asked.

'Nah,' Hannah answered. 'We're five quid cheaper on the door, and we're going to have the girls in their little outfits going round with mince pies, and mulled wine for free, and more tits and arse than Morris an' all. Put on a bit of a show, and you two can come in free. Same goes for this Saturday.'

'Yes, please,' Kay answered immediately, giggling. 'You can spank me in my uniform, Amber.'

'I'm not sure . . . ,' I began.

'Please, Amber,' Kay broke in. 'Don't be such an old maid! It'll be fun.'

'We'll look after you, if Amber wants to be a stick-in-the-mud,' Maggie offered.

'I'll come, of course,' I said quickly. 'I'll put a teacher's outfit together.'

'What?' Hannah queried. 'A pretty thing like you? You want to be in school uniform, you do.'

'I don't think so . . . ,' I began, only to be interrupted again.

'Why not?' Kay agreed. 'You could be a prefect.'

'We'll see,' I said, not wanting to argue but promising myself I'd be a teacher.

'You make a great prefect,' Kay went on happily, first to me, then to Hannah. 'We were playing with Sophie once – she's the blonde girl who lost the turkey shoot – at a school thing that Morris did. Amber made her wet herself, then spanked her for it, with her soggy panties in her mouth. How mean is that?'

She was laughing, and I saw Hannah's eyes widen a little, in surprise or even shock.

'I'm sure Hannah doesn't want to hear about that sort of thing,' I said, desperately trying to signal to Kay.

Her back was to me and she took no notice whatsoever as she went on.

'Another good one she does is to pin the spanked girls' skirts up at the back and make them leave their knickers down so that their red bums are showing all the time. And when our friend Jade wouldn't stop sucking her pen during a class scene, Amber put her over, spanked her, then stuck the pen right in up her bum and made her suck it afterwards!'

'You dirty bitch,' Maggie remarked, looking up at me. But Hannah merely nodded, which was a great deal worse.

'Here's your coffee,' I said, once again trying to change the subject.

'A dose of your own medicine, that's what *you* need,' Maggie said as she took the mug, and for once there was no laughter in her voice.

'You've given me one,' I pointed out as my stomach tightened at the prospect of a spanking.

'Not like that I haven't,' she answered me. 'What do you reckon, Hannah? Shall we teach the dirty bitch a lesson?'

'No, please . . .' I began, already backing away with a rising sense of panic as Maggie began to get up.

'Leave her, Maggie,' Hannah laughed, to my vast relief and the usual treacherous stab of disappointment.

Maggie sat back down. My heart was hammering and my hand was shaking badly as I picked up my coffee cup. She'd have done it, I knew, if Hannah hadn't stopped her, by force if necessary. She'd have spanked me in my own kitchen, undoubtedly on the bare and possibly with some added humiliation, and all in front of Kay. Worse, I knew full well that I'd have enjoyed it – and if I'd been ordered to lick afterwards, I'd have licked.

The two of them were dangerous, worse than Melody, because at least she wasn't strong enough to put me across her knee unless I surrendered. Both Hannah and Maggie could do it with ease: if I'd gone willingly twice that didn't mean they weren't perfectly capable of taking me unwillingly a third time.

'It would be good if the two of you could come early,' Hannah was saying. 'To help set up and that, seeing as you're getting in for nothing.'

'Of course – we'd love to,' Kay answered before I'd had a chance to speak.

'There's not much we can do, is there?' I tried. 'Not if it's all school.'

'We're having a dungeon, too,' Hannah told me. 'Make it about three o'clock. And I'll have another dozen of your school canes, if you'll give me a decent discount, so that there's plenty to go around.'

I had more than a dozen canes ready in the work-room because they take so long to make and there is always a demand. But I wasn't going to say anything until Hannah dug in her handbag and began to count out notes onto the table. Evidently she'd had her fun with me when it came to withholding payment, either that or she'd decided she could punish me when she liked anyway.

'A dozen for fifty?' she suggested.

'They're normally twelve pounds each,' I pointed out. 'Shall we say a hundred?'

'Sixty,' Hannah countered.

'That's not really –'

'Eighty – and I get to put one across your backside on Saturday.'

'Sixty will do, then,' I said hastily, telling myself it still meant nearly four hundred per cent profit.

I went to fetch the canes, selecting the less good ones as she was paying so little, tying them in a bundles and wrapping them up to disguise them. I was sure they would think nothing of walking out of my shop with a dozen very obvious school canes on plain show. Maggie took them and I put Hannah's money on the side as she drained the last of her coffee.

'Better get going,' she said. 'You can't leave the men to run the circus for five minutes, you know.'

We showed them out, and as the BMW drove off I could feeling my tension draining away. I'd come within an ace of another spanking, possibly a worse one than the first two, a spanking that would have been entirely Kay's fault. She'd gone back behind the counter, chattering happily about nothing in particular as I crossed to the stand of whips and riding crops. Then an even more deliciously wicked idea struck me and I continued to the display of boots. Beside the polish was a stack of big heavy boot brushes, with long rounded wooden handles. I picked one up and smacked it thoughtfully on my palm. It would do very nicely.

I slipped a can of Eldridge and Thwaite's rich mahogany polish into my pocket. Then I went to the door, twisted the key in the lock, slid the bolts home and turned the sign to *Closed*.

'What are you doing?' Kay asked, looking up. 'We don't close for . . .'

She went quiet as she saw the boot brush.

'Not with that!' she squeaked. 'No, Amber, not with that!'

'I'm not going to spank you,' I told her.

'What, then?' she asked, obviously far from reassured. 'What have I done, anyway?'

'What have you *done*?' I echoed. 'You very nearly got me spanked by Maggie, that's what! Get in the back – now!'

'That wasn't my fault!' Kay wailed as I took her by the wrist and pulled her after me into the kitchen. 'I didn't know she'd start on you, did I? How could I?'

'I don't care,' I told her. 'And even if you didn't know, then you should know better than to say things like that in front of those two. You'll give them ideas. Now get over my knee, you little brat.'

'You said you weren't going to spank me!' she howled. 'Amber!'

I'd got her over, her bottom well up, just the way I wanted it.

'I'm *not* going to spank you,' I repeated. 'Now lift your hips so I can get your tights down.'

Kay had turned her face up to me, pouting furiously. But she obeyed, going up on her toes to let me tug her tights and panties down under her skirt. I took them right off, along with her shoes, and turned her skirt up into its own waistband, leaving her whole lower body nude. Her bum was very tempting indeed, the meaty cheeks wobbling slightly in her apprehension, and I couldn't resist giving her a couple of gentle pats.

'You said you wouldn't –' she began pitifully, breaking off with a squeal as I gave her a harder slap.

'I'm not,' I said, taking out the tin of polish, 'I'm going to black up your bum.'

'What?' she demanded, twisting around to try and look.

'I'm going to black up your bum,' I repeated. 'With boot polish – Eldridge and Thwaite's rich mahogany, to be precise, so I suppose it should really be *brown* up your bum.'

'Amber, no,' Kay protested. 'I don't want to be dirty!'

'Shut up – you've earned this,' I told her, taking a firm grip on her waist as she began to wriggle.

I'd got the lid off the can and I dug my fingers into the slippery polish, which cracked under the pressure, allowing me to scoop up a big piece. Kay gave a gasp of disgust as I slapped it onto her bottom and began to rub it in, smearing the thick brown paste liberally over first one chubby cheek and then the other. It was immensely satisfying to see her bottom go gradually brown, and it went a long way to soothe my feelings about the enforced spanking that I'd escaped so narrowly.

She'd stopped fighting as soon as she was dirty and she lay limp and submissive as I dealt with her, covering the full cheeky globes of her bottom with boot polish, all over both buttocks and in between. Only when I pushed a lump into the tight brown cross of her anus did she react, and then only with a sob of disgust. It was a different matter when I took the brush and began to rub the polish in, using the bristly side for once, although to judge from the sudden tumult of squeals and pleas for mercy it must have hurt almost as much as being spanked with the flat.

I took no notice, giving Kay's whole rear end a vigorous scrub-down before I was finished. Her entire bottom was now a glossy brown ball, the polish rubbed well into her skin. It was something she wasn't going to forget in a hurry if only because it was going to take ages to get out. I chuckled to myself as I gave her a final rub under her cheeks, then reversed the brush in my hand.

'This really isn't fair, Amber,' she whined.

'Not at all,' I told her. 'It's very fair. *This*, maybe, isn't fair.'

As I spoke I'd cocked my leg up and pushed my knee between Kay's thighs, forcing her to spread her bottom cheeks and show off the dirty brown spot of her anus, with the piece of boot polish I'd pushed in still stuck in the centre. She gasped in shock as I put the rounded tip of the brush handle to her hole, and again as her well-lubricated ring began to open to the pressure.

'Amber, no, not up my bum!' she wailed, squeezing her cheeks together in a desperate and futile effort to keep her ring closed.

'Just relax,' I told her. 'That way it won't hurt – and it's going up anyway.'

Kay did as she was told, but gave a long plaintive moan of disgust as the full length of the boot-brush handle slid in up her bumhole. Her ring closed on the narrower part of the shaft, holding the brush well in with just the bristly bit sticking out, a fine sight that had me chuckling to myself. She pouted more furiously than ever as I let her up and told her to go and inspect herself in the hall mirror. She looked a real picture with her bottom all brown and glossy, as if she'd soiled herself and rubbed it in, while it was quite obvious that the big boot brush sticking out between the dirty bum cheeks was jammed in up her rectum.

'You do look comic,' I told her. 'Now, come on – down on your knees.'

'You're so mean,' she told me as she got carefully down on all fours, crawling to me.

I went back into the kitchen, forcing Kay to follow. But instead of seating myself I pushed my jeans and knickers a little way down and made myself comfortable over the table, propped up on one elbow so that I could watch her.

'I think you know what to do,' I told her. 'And don't neglect my bottom.'

Kay gave a nod and came close. I closed my eyes as her hands touched my hips, holding me gently. Her lips touched my bum, kissing the turn of one cheek, then the other. I felt her tongue flick out, licking me, warm and moist against the skin of my cheeks as she sought for her courage and then between them as she found it, lapping in my crease and at last on my anus, just the lightest of touches.

'That's a good girl,' I sighed. 'Lick my bumhole clean – right inside, too.'

Kay's face pushed more firmly in between my cheeks and her hands moved to spread them, allowing her to lap at my bottom-hole, then to probe deep, her tongue-tip wriggling in my anus until I was moaning and clutching the table in ecstasy. She let go of my cheeks but kept her face well smothered and her tongue well in up my hole. I heard a faint wet noise and I knew that she'd begun to masturbate, but I let her carry on, thinking of her stroking her dirty brown bottom and working the boot brush in her own bumhole as she licked mine.

It felt perfect, so soothing and so good, to have my darling's tongue up my bottom while she masturbated. Perhaps I was in prime spanking position myself, bent over a table with my jeans and panties pulled down, but for once I wasn't being beaten. I was being licked: Kay's tongue burrowed in up my anus as deep as it would go as she revelled in the punishment that I'd given her. She could finish, I decided, and when she had come I would add to her punishment for daring to do it first, which would make my own climax more satisfying still. For now I would help, talking to her to bring out her feelings.

'That's right,' I told her. 'Lick it, Kay, lick my bottom-hole. Get your tongue well in, taste me while you rub yourself. You're to fuck your bottom with the brush, too. Go on, shove it in, good and hard . . . pull it in and out . . . bugger yourself with it, Kay, bugger your dirty bottom while you lick my bumhole clean . . .'

I felt her go tight against me and then she was coming, whimpering out her ecstasy between my bum cheeks with her tongue stuck so deep up my bottom that she'd opened me completely. For a moment I thought of how Buffo the clown had stuck his finger up that same rude hole, making me equally juicy but in very different circumstances. But I pushed the thought away. I was not going to think of how it had felt to have my anus fingered in public while my girlfriend was tonguing me.

'Are you finished?' I asked when she'd finally stopped shivering. Her face was still pressed firmly between my cheeks.

Kay nodded, not even taking her tongue out of my bottom-hole.

'And what did you do wrong?' I demanded. 'You were very selfish, weren't you? You came first, didn't you?'

Again she nodded. I reached back, gently shifting her face from between my cheeks. Her mouth was wet, her eyes half-focused. I turned around to seat myself on the corner of the table. She looked up at me in expectation and her tongue flicked out to add a little more moisture to her already glistening lips.

'You like to lick me, don't you?' I asked. She nodded at once. 'You like to lick my bottom clean, don't you? You like to taste me, don't you, you filthy girl?'

Again Kay nodded, more urgently now. I smiled and pushed my clothes down further to allow me to open my thighs properly. She started forward as my hand went to my sex, but I wagged a finger at her.

'Uh-uh, Kay – no fanny for you, not today. I have something different for you. Take the brush out of your bum.'

Her eyes went wide but there was no hint of disobedience in them. Reaching back, she eased the boot-brush handle out of her bottom-hole. I began to rub myself, my excitement rising at what I was going to make her do and at the wonderful expressions on her pretty face as they flickered between consternation and lust, shame and excitement.

'Put it in your mouth,' I ordered. 'Suck it, Kay, suck it clean, so I can see.'

She hesitated, her face working with emotion, but only for a moment. Her mouth came open and she pushed in the handle of the brush, the handle that she'd pulled out of her own bumhole just moments before. She began to suck it. I was rubbing hard, my eyes fixed on her face as I masturbated, watching the thick wooden shaft slide in and out between her lips, with her beautiful big eyes full of self-pity as she sucked up the taste of her own bottom.

My climax hit me, setting my entire body tight as I ran through in my head what I'd done to Kay, over and over: stripped her pretty bottom . . . stripped her pretty bottom and boot-blacked her bum cheeks . . . stripped her pretty bottom, boot-blacked her bum cheeks and buggered her with the brush . . . stripped her pretty bottom, boot-blacked her bum cheeks, buggered her with the brush and made her lick my bottom clean as she came . . . stripped her pretty bottom, boot-blacked her bum cheeks, buggered her with the brush, made her lick my bottom clean, and last . . . last, made her suck the brush handle she had just had wedged in up her bottom-hole.

I cried out her name as I came, telling her that I loved her and that she was a dirty bitch at the same time. Then I was reduced to incoherent moans and babbling as wave after wave of ecstasy swept through me. When it finally stopped Kay was just as before, holding the brush in her mouth so that I wouldn't be robbed of an instant of pleasure.

'You can take that out now,' I managed after a moment. 'That was lovely.'

'Naughty, Amber,' she said, and smiled. Then she stood and came into my arms.

We clung together for a long time, Kay shivering in my embrace. She wanted to kiss too, and I let her, as to deny her need would have been an unthinkable betrayal. I'd done it to her, so for all my dominance it was only right that I should share. At last she let go and I sent her upstairs to have a shower.

After a brief visit to the downstairs loo I made for the shop, picking up Hannah Riley's money as I passed through the kitchen. Only then did I realise that she'd paid me not sixty pounds, but eighty.

If Hannah Riley thought she was going to cane me at a club she could think again. Maybe she could take me over her knee for impromptu spankings – we both knew that my resistance would be weak – but a public caning was a very different matter. It wasn't acceptable and that was that, something which I intended to make very plain.

Given how manipulative Hannah was being, it was with no little satisfaction that I rang Morris to tell him the details of her Christmas party. He already knew, which took the wind out of my sails somewhat, but he thanked me anyway. Angel and Sophie were there too, getting ready for one of his paid spanking parties, and they confirmed that they were coming on the Saturday.

Hannah had said three o'clock. Kay was eager to go, anxious to show off in her tiny red tartan miniskirt and white panties. She'd also put her hair up in bunches, making herself look almost indecently young, an impression heightened by her long white socks and badly knotted tie. We ended up leaving only an hour after we'd locked up the shop.

It was no distance at all, and we found the place immediately, an old Victorian red-brick school building in a quiet side street at the back of Enfield Town. I had to admit that it was perfect: high walls protected us from prying eyes and created a brooding atmosphere that made me feel as if I was about ten. Not that my own school, Bridestowe Ladies' College, had been even remotely like it, but some things don't change, even between the best and the worst extremes of education. The smell, for instance, which still lingered years after the place had last been used for its original function.

There was another edge to the atmosphere, too. Just as I'd always detested carnies for their vulgar behaviour and nasty habits, so I had always been made to feel defensive, even frightened, by common girls from comprehensive schools. The mere thought of the sort of school I was now in had been enough to put my hackles up, and something of that still lingered, making me think of nasty little urchins always ready to tease or throw mud or pull hair.

Not that I let it show as I strode confidently across the yard with Kay trailing behind me. Her uniform was concealed by her coat, a necessity when her skirt failed to cover her knickers behind – to say nothing of the weather. I hadn't bothered with a coat and I'd made a point of ignoring Hannah's instructions to go in uniform, to Kay's dismay until she'd actually seen me. Instead I had chosen a long black hobble skirt, black high-heeled shoes and a white blouse with a slight ruffle at the front and a black ribbon tie. I also carried a gown, mortarboard and cane as accessories.

The combination of the atmosphere and the prospect of Hannah's reaction to what I knew she would see as disobedience had me increasingly nervous as we entered.

first to an ante-room into which the stairs came down, then to what had obviously been the assembly hall, both rooms painted in magnolia and maroon. Nobody was about but I could hear noises from deeper inside the building. We followed the sounds, across the hall and up another flight of stairs to a lone corridor flanked by classrooms.

'Somebody's getting it.' Kay remarked as we caught the unmistakable *thwack* of a cane applied to girl-flesh.

A squeal of pain followed as we reached the right door and both of us peered in through the glass inspection panel. Inside, the room had been made up much as it might have been thirty or more years before, with lines of sit-up-and-beg desks facing a larger desk and a blackboard, while the walls were decorated with maps and charts – including a poster exhorting girls to good behaviour on penalty of dire retribution.

That was the least of it. Somebody was getting her retribution from Angel, who was standing cane in hand, dressed as a schoolgirl herself but with a prefect's badge pinned to her blouse. Her was face set in combined amusement and contempt as she inspected her victim's bottom. Her victim was Sophie Cherwell, as pretty as a picture as she bent over one of the desks in the front row, her green tartan uniform skirt pinned up to her blouse, her big bottle-green knickers down around her ankles. Her full pink bottom was lifted to receive the strokes of Angel's cane, which had already laid four dark welts across the rosy skin. Sophie's face was looking out from beneath her dishevelled blonde hair, full of pain and self-pity, right at a camera.

It was a video camera, an expensive one by the look of it, mounted on a tripod. Sean was operating it while Hannah stood beside him, watching Sophie's caning with a critical eye. Mick was standing to one side, with a second camera, this one hand-held to allow a different and ruder view of Sophie's bottom. I could see at a glance that she'd been spanked first, her cheeks flushed an even rose-pink around the livid welts from the cane. She was playing up, too: the misery and consternation in her expression was very different from her usual reaction, and when Angel's cane bit into her bottom one more time she screamed and stamped her feet on the floor as if she genuinely hated what was being done to her.

'Are they making a commercial video, do you think?' Kay whispered.

'They must be,' I agreed.

There were now five welts decorating Sophie's pretty bottom, and as we watched Angel added a sixth, harder still. Sophie screamed and jumped up, clutching her hurt bottom and making frantic little treading motions with her feet. Angel stayed as she was, the cane trailing from her hand, her expression smug and cruel, which was probably a genuine reflection of her emotions.

'Cut,' Hannah ordered when Sophie had finally calmed down. 'Well done, girls.'

Sophie immediately burst into giggles and ran over to Angel, first to kiss her, then to nuzzle her face and neck. Angel responded with a hug and looked up as I pushed the door open.

'Hi – we're a bit early, I'm afraid. That was a great scene, you two.'

'Thanks,' Sophie answered. 'You look good, both of you. I could eat you right now, Kay.'

'Me too,' Angel agreed, stepping forward to greet us.

'Leave that till later,' Hannah warned as Sophie grovelled down to kiss my shoes in welcome. 'We've got to finish this.'

'Sorry,' Sophie said quickly. 'Just the corner scene, then?'

'It won't take a minute,' Angel said, moving back to where she'd been standing before.'

Kay and I stood back against the wall to watch as Sophie was told off, given a last couple of smacks and made to stand in the corner of the room with her nose pressed into the angle of the walls and her red bottom showing to the room. Mick took the final shot, squatting down directly behind her and zooming in for a close-up of her welted bottom. I was smiling to myself as he did it, partly for the pleasure of seeing Sophie as she was and partly because I couldn't help but notice how many of her clothing details Hannah had borrowed. The big bottle-green knickers had been lifted from Gavin and the pinned-up school skirt from me, and there were very likely more.

As they began to pack away the video equipment I extracted a twenty-pound note from my purse and went over to Hannah.

'I think you overpaid me for the canes. We said sixty, didn't we?'

She gave a sour chuckle but didn't take the note.

'I'm not being caned,' I told her firmly.

'I see,' she said, glancing down at the dark brown malacca trailing from my hand. 'You like to dish it out but you can't take it, is that it?'

'I can take it,' I assured her. 'But I don't want to take it in public or in front of any men, and I definitely don't take it from anyone who won't take the same from me.'

'Prissy, ain't we?' Hannah answered me, and took the note. 'I see the boys didn't manage to teach you your lesson in the stocks after all.'

'It was a pillory, not a stocks,' I insisted. 'And no, actually – they didn't do anything that I wasn't prepared to accept, as it happens.'

'Didn't they?' she asked and turned away with a chuckle that I didn't like at all.

'How do you mean?' I said, puzzled, only to realise that Kay was altogether too close for comfort when the conversation looked likely to come round

153

to cocksucking. 'No, never mind. Where would you like me to set up the dungeon?'

'Any room on this floor,' Hannah told me. 'Except this one, and next door, which is the detention room, where naughty girls and boys are going to get taken for their whackings. Seeing as you're dressed up like that, you can take a class and all.'

I agreed, and left the room rather pleased with myself despite a nagging doubt over what she'd said about my ordeal in the pillory. She'd seen everything, and she knew full well that I'd been willing, even if it had taken a lot to get me there. By the end I'd been begging for it. Possibly she didn't realise that I'd been pushed into the same wanton state before . . .

Hannah had at least given up her idea of caning me, which was a considerable victory. It was bad enough to be spanked, but at least over her knee I could console myself that she was strong enough to force me to take it. With a caning I'd have to pose, holding a thoroughly humiliating position of my own accord. Then there would be the stinging pain, under which I invariably lose control, and the welts to keep me reminded for a week or more of what had been done to me. It had also been a very long time since it had last happened, and I intended to keep it that way.

The next couple of hours were spent helping to set up the school. I had no intention of getting sweaty and dirty but I was having considerable trouble getting the carnies to do as I wanted. The idea that after seeing me brought low in the pillory they would accept me was plainly ludicrous: if anything, they were less respectful than before, some of them even demanding blow jobs in payment if they helped. In the end I had to get Maggie to back me up, which worked, even though there were a few sneers from her for my lack of command.

Once everything was ready, Kay, Angel, Sophie and I went out to eat at a local Chinese. Sophie hadn't bothered with a coat but stayed in her indecently short schoolgirl outfit so that as she helped herself from the all-you-can-eat buffet the other diners could see not only her knickers but the flushed skin from her spanking where her cheeks bulged out from the leg holes, along with a hint of her two lowest welts.

She didn't care in the slightest, egging on Kay and Angel to take their coats off too and merely laughing when I threatened her with serious retribution at the club if she didn't behave. Afterwards she was worse, first doing cartwheels in the street to show off her knickers, then trying to pull Kay's down. I had to put a stop to her naughtiness by taking a firm hold on her ear and pulling her away. As luck would have it, that was the exact moment a police car was passing: it stopped beside us and I was the person who was warned to mind her behaviour.

Sophie was helpless with laughter as the police drove away, while I was feeling deeply embarrassed. The temptation to take her across my knee then and there was almost irresistible, but I could just see the police car going round the block and catching me as it came back. I held my peace, but then I saw that there was a late-night convenience store ahead, Turkish or Greek, with trays of fruit and vegetables outside. This gave me a still more satisfying idea. I told the girls that I wanted to get a bottle of water and that I'd catch them up, then nipped inside the shop where I bought not only the water but the largest piece of ginger root that I could find.

I needed a small knife too, and managed to find one at a newsagent's further up the road. Then I returned to the old school. People had already begun to arrive and it took me a moment to get through the door, as neither Gerry nor the two carnies would believe that I had free entry. When I did get in it was to find the main hall already quite crowded, with more people than there had been at the club in Barnet. Evidently word was getting around.

There was a higher proportion of men too, and fewer people whom I knew. Gavin had been banned, and Jilly was wandering around looking morose in full uniform, with the same style of green tartan miniskirt as Sophie's. The other circus girls were dressed the same, with white blouses and red-and-black-striped ties too – bottle-green knickers, as I discovered when I went upstairs to look at the detention room. There I found one of them being caned by Maggie in front of an audience composed mainly of gloating men.

Kay and the others weren't there, nor were they in the schoolroom. In fact, they were in the bar, one of the larger rooms in which a line of beer cases was stacked up and with what seemed to be half the circus staff helping to serve the contents. They were also helping to drink it, and my appearance was greeted with jeers and catcalls, demands to get my breasts out and my knickers down, and even one or two threats to fuck me or make me suck cock.

'What a bunch of pigs!' Kay said as I pulled the three girls hastily out of the room. 'As if you'd let them do anything like that!'

'I told you they were like that,' I replied, taking the bottle of beer that Angel had bought me. 'I don't suppose they have any glasses?'

'No,' Angel confirmed. 'Sod them – they're a bunch of wankers. Are we going to do this class, then?'

'In a while,' I told her. 'I think Hannah's going to announce it.'

I was right – she did so as soon as she'd found us. We went up and I put the three girls in the front row, hoping we'd get some more participants and not just the men dressed as schoolboys who made up such a large proportion of the people there. Soon Jilly and the other three girls who'd been at the previous club, all looking very sweet in their identical uniforms and all with prefects' badges on, joined us. They were followed by eight men, which filled every classroom seat, while the walls were soon lined with watchers, more of whom had gathered at the door.

With all the maps on the walls it seemed best to give a geography lesson, although I had no intention of actually teaching – at least, not for more than a few minutes. The pupils began to misbehave from the start, throwing paper darts and passing notes between each other the moment my back was turned. Sophie was among the ringleaders, inevitably, but she was sneaky too, so that every time I turned to face them she was sitting quite still, her face set in an angelic smile.

The men were less subtle, obviously wanting to be caught. I enjoyed myself caning a few of them, not sexually so much – as their hairy lumpish buttocks did little or nothing for me – but it was still satisfying, even if I would have preferred to do it to the carnies. Angel and Kay were about the only ones being good, neither of them wanting the indignity of a public punishment, albeit for different reasons, while the circus girls were enjoying themselves teasing the men. When I caught one flashing her tits I finally had a chance to punish a girl. I rounded on her immediately.

'What is your name?' I demanded.

'Siobhan,' she answered in a soft Irish lilt with a sulky undertone that sealed her fate.

'Siobhan what?' I demanded. 'And you will address me as *Miss*.'

'Siobhan Riley, Miss,' she said.

I gave a thoughtful nod, disguising my surprise and delight. Possibly she was Fat Hannah's daughter, in which case caning her would be especially satisfying. It was also a dangerous game and I decided on a different course of action.

'Do do normally show your breasts to boys?' I asked.

'No, Miss,' she said.

'Oh yes she does!' one of her friends put in, causing a ripple of laughter.

'Quiet!' I snapped. 'What's *your* name?'

'Little Hannah,' she answered.

'You don't look very little to *me*,' I responded, glancing down her bulging blouse. 'Right: as you two seem to think it's so funny to show your breasts to boys, you can take your tops off, both of you – your bras, too. Right now!'

I smacked my cane down on the desk as I spoke, and after an exchange of glances they obeyed. Both of them had been in the audience when I was pilloried, no doubt laughing and cheering along with the rest of them as I was abused and degraded. It was immensely satisfying to watch them unbutton their blouses and peel them off and to see them open their bra catches and pull the cups off to expose full firm breasts. Siobhan's were somewhat smaller than Little Hannah's, but both girls' tits were a good size. Unfortunately, neither of them seemed to be particularly embarrassed. But that might very well change before the lesson was over.

With the two circus girls sitting topless I grew bolder. Evidently they wanted to play, either that or Fat Hannah had ordered them to participate. That seemed odd, disturbing even, if any of them really were her daughters, but I put it from my mind as I went on with the lesson. All four were grown girls and could presumably make their own choices in life, the way Fat Hannah had handled Jilly notwithstanding.

No sooner had I turned back to the board than they were misbehaving again. This time I waited, determined to catch Sophie in the act. Sure enough, after maybe a minute I heard Kay's distinctive squeal and spun around to find Sophie pulling her hair.

'Leave her alone, Cherwell!' I snapped. 'One more piece of mischief from you and you really *are* in trouble, believe me!'

I'd meant to pick fault with her anyway, but she spared me the trouble by immediately sticking her tongue out.

'Get up here – *now!*' I yelled. I made sure she obeyed by grabbing her by the ear and hauling her up to my desk, and over it.

Sophie was squealing like anything as I forced her into position for the cane, making a fine show of herself for the audience too, with her bum wiggling in her panties as I lifted her skirt and fastened it up with the safety pin that was still attached to the hem. I was fairly sure that she'd be making a fuss for real in a moment but I was in no hurry. I took my time about stripping her bottom, standing beside her so that everybody could see as I peeled the big green knickers down off her bum cheeks to the level of her thighs.

'I see you've already been punished this evening,' I remarked, running a finger along one of her welts where Angel's cane had made twin tramlines of puffy reddened flesh.

'Yes, Miss,' she answered, snivelling slightly over her words. 'By Angel, Miss.'

'No doubt you deserved it,' I told her. 'And you know what happens to girls who have to be punished twice in one day, don't you?'

Sophie looked round, genuinely puzzled, just as I took the big piece of ginger root from my bag along with the knife. It took her a moment to realise what it was, and then her eyes went slowly round. I was waiting for her to use her stop word, but she merely swallowed.

'Hold still, Sophie,' I told her as she began to wriggle again, but this time for real.

Most of my audience had no idea what I was doing as I took the knife and began to whittle at the ginger

159

root. Angel did, though, and her eyes brightened with sadistic glee. Kay was biting her lip and was no doubt extremely grateful that she wasn't in Sophie's place. Only as I cut away more ginger to create a plug shape did the others realise what was going on. This led to laughter and shocked gasps, while the four circus girls began to look seriously worried.

'She is to be figged and caned,' I announced when I had finished. 'This is a fig, which as some of you clearly know is a plug of ginger root designed to be inserted in a girl's anus during punishment, both to make it harder for her to clench her cheeks and to add to her humiliation. Sophie, pull your cheeks apart.'

Sophie gave me a single wild look as she reached back. But she obeyed, spreading her buttocks to expose the soft pink dimple of her anus for all to see. I knew she'd had a good many cocks pushed in up her bottom and as a result was quite loose, but the fig was as wide as all but the biggest penises. It was also pointed, helping me first to penetrate her ring and then push it in deep. She had began to pant with reaction even as her bottom-hole spread, opening to a taut pink ring of flesh as she struggled to accommodate the fat fig and closing softly on the neck as I gave a last firm push.

'There we are,' I told her, stepping back. 'Now, maybe being like that will teach you not to pull other girls' hair?'

Sophie's response was a whimper. I'd done it so that everybody could see the fig go up, and even as she let go of her cheeks the base was clearly visible in her straining anus. The muscles around her fanny had began to pulse and twitch to the heat of the ginger, which I knew would be rising rapidly towards a burning sensation scarcely endurable even for a girl of her experience and high pain threshhold.

'Now I shall cane you,' I told her. 'Six of the best, which you will count. You will also thank me for each stroke.'

I had picked up my malacca and now I tapped it on her bottom, taking careful aim across her twitching cheeks. Sophie was getting in a fine state, which was turning me on, and I took my time, tapping her again before lifting the cane and holding it high above her waiting bottom. She clutched at the desk and began to kick one foot up and down in her distress.

'We shall begin,' I told her. I brought the cane down hard across her bottom, making her cry out and kick quite violently before she managed to recover herself enough to speak.

'One, thank you, Miss . . . thank you.'

'Good girl,' I told her. I brought the cane down again, harder than before.

Again she screamed and bucked, this time shaking her head and thumping one fist on the desk before she could thank me.

'Two . . . two, thank you, . . . thank you, Miss,' she managed, her words broken between gasps for air. 'Ooh, it *hurts*!'

'The fig, or your welts?' I asked.

'Both! Ow! Ow! Ow!'

I allowed myself a chuckle before giving Sophie a third stroke, lower this time, across the meatiest part of her bum, jamming the fig in up her bottom-hole as she screamed out her pain. Once more she thumped the desk in her emotion before she could speak.

'Three, thank you, Miss.'

'And four,' I said, lashing the cane down to catch her in exactly the same spot. Again the stroke set her dancing and waggling her hurt bottom in a futile effort to dull the pain.

'Four, thank you, Miss,' she managed.

'Good,' I told her. 'Now five.'

I caught her a little high, setting a welt into as yet unmarked flesh, just a half-inch below where her bottom crease opened out. This must have hurt even more to judge by her piglike squeals and the frantic stamping fuss she made with her feet.

'Six . . . I mean five . . . five, thank you, Miss,' Sophie sobbed, looking back at me with moist eyes as I lifted the cane for the final stroke.

'Yes, five,' I told her. 'Learn to count, you stupid girl. *This* is six.'

Even as I spoke I brought the cane down, full across the fattest part of Sophie's cheeks, on already welted skin, wringing a loud double scream from her throat and leaving her hopping on one foot and gasping for breath. I knew she could take it. I knew she wanted it, yet I still felt a touch of guilt for the state of her bottom as she reached back to touch herself, ruefully inspecting the damage and wincing as she prodded the fig in her anus. I also felt aroused, though, far too much to let the guilt affect me.

'Leave it in,' I ordered her. 'You can stay like that for the rest of the lesson. Your skirt stays up and your knickers stay down. Now go back to your seat.'

Sophie obeyed instantly, scurrying back to place her bare bottom on the hard wooden seat. I turned to the class, flexing my cane as I tried to compose myself Figging Sophie and caning her had turned me on badly, leaving my fanny feeling urgent and sticky in my panties. The entire class was staring at me, the audience too, with low murmurs of excitement running among them as they waited to see what I would do next. It took me just a moment to decide, with all thoughts of justice, possible retribution from Fa Hannah or who might want what pushed aside in my arousal. This was for me.

'I'm sick of this behaviour,' I announced. 'I migh expect it of boys, but not of you girls, who are supposed to be young ladies. Evidently you are not, and if you ar going to behave like little brats then I shall treat you lik little brats. Spankings for all of you, bare-bottom. Forn a line, all six of you. Angel, you will pin up their skirts and take down their knickers.'

I'd seen the worry on her face as I spoke, but it turned to delight as I finished. The box of safety pins was still on the side and she fetched it as I pulled out two chairs and the six girls climbed reluctantly to their feet.

'You first, Sophie,' I ordered, patting my lap. 'Kay, go to Angel.'

Sophie came to me eagerly, draping herself over my lap and sticking up her already bare bottom, legs wide to show off her fanny and the fig in her anus to the men in the class and to the audience. Her whole bottom was a mess of welts, neatly applied, but her skin was so badly marked with the puffy flesh of her tramlines that I was reluctant to do more than give her a few firm pats under her cheeks. As Sophie took it, Angel was dealing with Kay, first pulling down her panties under her school skirt and then pinning the skirt up to leave her bottom bare and ready for spanking. This time there was no fuss about going bare.

I released Sophie, ordering her to stand in the corner, and took Kay over my lap. Merely the sight of her lifted bottom was enough to send a powerful jolt to my sex. Unlike Sophie she was pristine, her cheeks smooth and full, so round, so juicy, so *spankable*. I had a quick feel before spanking her, not hard, but hard enough to have her gasping as her cheeks bounced to the slaps. I finished with a final humiliation I knew would be strong for her, pulling her bottom open to show off her sex and the tight brown knot of her bumhole.

Kay went to stand by the wall and I took Jilly across my knee as Angel sent her my way with a slap. As with the others Jilly's skirt was pinned up and her panties well down, but she came to me reluctantly, scowling at me as I tipped her up and raised a knee to get her muscular bottom nice and high. I spanked her as Angel prepared Siobhan, and again finished by pulling her cheeks apart to show the audience her anal charms before she joined the others against the wall.

Siobhan came next in what was by now an efficient production line. Her bottom was spanked and her anus inspected before she went to the wall, by which time Little Hannah was ready. She too went over, got spanked, had her anus shown to the assembly and was sent to the wall. The last of the four circus girls followed and then I had a line of six standing against the wall, each with her skirt pinned up to show off her rosy rear view. I was nearly finished.

'Come here,' I told Angel, patting my lap. 'Let's get you bare, then over you go.'

She looked completely horror-struck, but I wasn't giving in. I patted my lap again, more firmly.

'Are you going over, or do I have to get some of the girls whose knickers you've just pulled down to hold you?'

'But I'm a prefect, Miss,' Angel responded, glancing uneasily to the line of girls.

They could do it, easily, and to judge by the look that Jilly gave her they would be more than willing.

'So are some of the others,' I pointed out, 'and they're not complaining about their punishments. Now come here. Ten . . . nine . . .'

She came, her face wonderfully sulky, trembling violently as she passed me a safety pin, but nonetheless obedient. I love spanking girls, but I *adore* spanking dominant girls, and I was enjoying myself hugely as I pushed my hands up under her tiny skirt and took hold of her knickers. Down they came, to her knees, where I left them in a tangle of thick green cotton. I lifted Angel's skirt and then her pert black bum was bare, right in front of my face, so slim and so sweetly turned that I could see the jet-black lips of her shaved fanny between her thighs. The safety pin went in, set high to keep her buttocks completely bare, and she was ready.

I adjusted my chair a little as I took Angel across my knee, to make sure that as much of the audience as possible had a full view of her bottom as she was spanked. Her lips were pursed tight, her eyes blazing with consternation, and her pretty black bum was stuck high. With her, I didn't need to show off her bumhole: she was showing already, her cheeks too slim to hide herself, everything visible, and all the more so when I'd begun to spank her. I did it hard, deliberately slapping her cheeks to make them open, and after a while pulling up her blouse and bra to add her tits to the display. She was soon kicking and wriggling, and long before I'd finished with her the tight black knot of her bumhole had become too much of a temptation to ignore. I stopped spanking but tightened my grip on her waist and lifted one leg to force her bottom into greater prominence.

Angel was already sweaty, her ring a little loose, but I spat between her cheeks and rubbed the spittle in, drawing something between a groan and a sob from her lips as she realised she was not going to get away with a simple spanking but was going to have her anus penetrated in front of the class. Not that I was playing the teacher any more: teachers do not, as a rule, stick things up their pupils' bottoms. I did, unable to keep the grin off my face as I opened her bumhole and slid a finger inside, wiggling it in the hot slippery cavity of her rectum.

Angel was moaning and squirming on my lap as I fingered her bottom. By now I was lost to any impulse of decency. I pushed deep and slipped in a second finger, stretching her anus open so that as I pulled free it was left slippery and gaping, the bright pink interior visible beyond the ring of coal-black flesh. Something had to go up there but nothing seemed to be handy – until inspiration struck.

I peeled off her knickers, trying not to laugh as I wiped my fingers on them and pushed them back between her cheeks. She'd been looking behind her, wondering what I was up to, and as she realised she gave a gasp of dismay. It was already too late. I had pushed a good-sized pinch of panty material in up her anus, lodging it in well to the sound of her half-hearted protests and noises of disgust.

'There, you're done,' I told Angel, and gave her trim black bottom a last slap as she started to rise. 'Up against the wall with the others.'

The expression on her face as she turned to me was priceless, but she went, scampering over with her panties bobbing beneath her bum cheeks. All six other girls had put their hands on their heads, and she did the same, completing one of the most satisfying line-ups I had ever seen: seven girls, all with their skirts pinned up to the waistbands, all freshly spanked, two topless, one caned and with a fig up her bottom, six with their knickers down, one with her knickers right off and dangling from her anus.

I took a long moment to savour the view, then dismissed the class. By now I was not just ready for a climax but in urgent need of one. It had to be the three of them, all submissive to me, perhaps Sophie and Angel posing their bottoms as Kay licked me, perhaps all three of them made to lick me in turn, their tongues up my bumhole and on my fanny, three beautiful girls with their bottoms well spanked attending to me with their tongues . . .

First I needed somewhere private. As the class dispersed I was wondering where to go. I decided to explore the upper floors as I answered what seemed to be a never-ending stream of fatuous questions from the male students. The three girls stayed with me, as keen as I was, but as we were leaving the room Jilly came back. She hadn't been too happy about taking her spanking, but now she looked positively smug.

'Mum's after you, Amber,' she told me. 'She's going

to spank you in the main hall, so you'd better go down – right now.'

My immediate reaction was a flush, first of fear, then of righteous indignation that I could simply be summoned for punishment, and in front of so many people. But fortunately common sense took over before I started to speak.

'I suppose so,' I said, 'if she's going to do me anyway.'

'Oh she is, hard – for me, and Little Hannah, and Ellie, and Siobhan. Four times over.'

I nodded and bit my lip, feigning submission.

'Come on,' Jilly demanded.

'I . . . I just need to go to the loo,' I told her.

'Yeah,' Angel laughed. 'If it's really hard she might wet herself!'

I threw her a dirty look, but it was the perfect excuse.

'Come with me, please,' I said. We retreated towards the loos at the end of the passage.

Only when I reached the stairs did I run, knowing full well that the stairwell came out by the front door. I ran as fast as I could in my tight skirt. Jilly immediately realised that something was wrong and followed, yelling at me to come back. Unfortunately Sophie hadn't quite caught on, and as Kay and Angel and I crashed out the front door she was well behind. Angel had already reached my car when Sophie came out with Jilly right behind her, and we were forced to wait.

'Don't try it, Amber!' Jilly warned. 'You'd better learn to take it when you're told, you better –'

I grabbed her, pinning her arms behind her back and holding on as hard as I could while I babbled instructions.

'Help me, Angel! Tie her wrists, Sophie . . . with your tie! Kay, do something, anything!'

Jilly fought like crazy but there were four of us and Sophie quickly had Jilly's wrists lashed behind her back.

Just next to us were the old bike stands and we tied her hands to one, leaving her helpless but shouting for her sisters and the other carnies. She got her knickers pulled off and forced into her mouth for her pains. Angel secured them, using her own tie to create an impromptu gag. Then she tucked Jilly's skirt up, back and front, to leave her squirming frantically against the bike stand with her bum and fanny on show for whoever came out to rescue her.

We left, laughing together as we drove away, all four of us in the best possible mood, full of nervous excitement and the thrill of naughtiness at what we'd done. I knew we shouldn't have gone so far, I knew there would be retribution, but at that instant I wasn't going to show any misgiving. Kay and two of my best friends were in my car, all three of them with their bums hot down their panties and their fannies wet for me – who was full of mischief too.

All four of us were giggling as we tumbled into my house. We went straight upstairs, already fumbling at each other, and as I collapsed on the bed I was ready to take charge, tugging up my pencil skirt as I spoke.

'Right, you lot, in a line: I want to see those bums.'

Kay and Sophie immediately scrambled into place, tucking their skirts up and pushing down their panties at the back. But Angel stayed as she was, her hands on her hips as she looked down at me.

'Who put *you* in charge?' she demanded. '*I* want a go.'

'Shut up and lick,' I told her, admiring the sweet pink bottoms being presented to me as I pulled the crotch of my panties aside.

'No, *you* lick *me* – you've had your fun,' Angel answered. Then she launched herself on top of me.

I grappled her, both of us laughing as we struggled to get on top. She was strong but light, and I knew I could beat her. The only hard part was getting her to submit so that I could put my bum in her face and get her to lick without making a fuss about it. Or so I thought. I'd just got on top, straddling her, when Sophie yelled out from behind me.

'Let's get Amber, Kay – come on!'

Kay didn't respond, but Sophie had already grabbed my ankle. I tried to shake her off, but she'd got a rope out of the toy chest, wrapping it around my ankle as Angel clung onto me. Only then did Kay join in, but I'd still have dealt with all three of them if I'd been able to stop laughing. Instead I got my ankles lashed to the bed. After that I had no hope at all. Angel held my wrists behind my back as Sophie tied them together, both of them laughing at my struggles. Sophie's panties came off and Angel held my nose as she forced them into my mouth, then tied them off with Kay's tie. Sophie pushed my skirt up around my waist and took down my knickers. Then they stood back.

I was helpless, bound and gagged, reduced from cool dominant Mistress to shivering bare-bottomed plaything in seconds. All I could do was wait, full of apprehension and also consternation, as much for my immediate arousal at being used as for what they had done to me and were no doubt going to do.

'She deserves this,' Angel stated. 'What shall we do, girls?'

'Spank her,' Sophie said with relish.

'Spank her?' Angel queried. 'After what she did to us? You should *cane* her.'

'Both, then,' Sophie agreed, laughing as I immediately began to wriggle.

My cane was on the floor, within all too easy reach. Angel picked it up, running her fingers down the bumpy surface of the malacca with her face set in a grin of pure evil.

'This is some cane. Yeah, six of the best after a spanking – and then what else? The bitch stuck my knickers up my bum! If I hadn't chucked them back at the club, Amber, they'd be in your mouth right now!'

169

'She likes sticking things up our bums, doesn't she?' Sophie remarked.

'Yes, she does,' Angel agreed with feeling. 'I think we should stick something up *hers*.'

'Do you know what she did to me earlier this week?' Kay asked. 'She rubbed boot polish in all over my bum, stuck the brush up me, then made me suck it!'

'Stuck it where?' Sophie queried. 'Pussy or bum?'

'Up my bum!'

'Where's that hairbrush she likes to use?' Sophie enquired. 'We can spank her with it, then in her arse it goes for her caning.'

'Nice one,' Angel agreed.

I twisted around at their words, trying to plead with my eyes as I squirmed in my bonds, but it did me no good at all. Kay fetched my long-handled hairbrush and gave it to Sophie, who climbed onto the bed, straddling my back to pin me down, making me more helpless still as she set to work on my bottom. It stung like anything, and I could do nothing at all to escape the smacks except wriggle my bottom about, which only made them laugh. That didn't stop me wriggling ever more frantically as Sophie belaboured my bottom with the hairbrush, calling out every spank, harder and harder, until I was frantic with pain and jerking in my bonds.

My whole bottom seemed to be on fire. I could feel myself coming on heat through the pain, making my humiliation all the worse as I was punished: fifty smacks, then a hundred, with Angel and even Kay laughing at me and giggling together over the display I was making of myself. They were touching, too, as they watched me being beaten: Angel was holding Kay from behind, one hand down the front of my girlfriend's knickers, the other in her half-open blouse, getting off together on my pain and humiliation.

'One hundred and eighty!' Sophie crowed. 'Tha

should do her. Right, up the bum it goes. See how *you* like it, Amber!'

I went limp as the spanking stopped. They had me, my bottom ablaze with spanking, my fanny eager and moist, ready for use. As Sophie pulled my bottom cheeks apart I even stuck my bum up, showing off my anus for penetration. She spat between my cheeks, then suddenly shifted, a little purring noise coming from her throat as she went down, burying her face in my hot bottom as she began to lick my bumhole.

'Slut!' Angel laughed. 'You're supposed to be dominating her, Sophie.'

Sophie didn't reply. She obviously didn't care, alternately probing my bumhole with her tongue and spitting into it as I slowly came wide. She carried on long after I was ready, and eventually it was Angel who stuck the brush up my bottom, calling Sophie a slut again as she pulled her back by the hair. Then she pushed the end of the handle against my anus, and in.

I felt my ring spread and the shaft slide up, all the way, until I could feel the bristles of the brush head tickling between my bum cheeks. Even Kay laughed as Angel began to bugger me, easing the brush handle in and out until I'd begun to moan through my panty gag despite myself. At last she stopped, only to address Kay.

'Has she got a big dildo or something, for her cunt?'

'Yes,' Kay answered. 'The one she fucks me with.'

All I could do was lie there helpless as they burrowed into my toy chest to find the big strap-on that I liked to use on Kay. They made me lift my hips and pushed three pillows under my tummy to get at my fanny more easily. Then up the dildo went, pushed into my already slippery hole with embarrassing ease, all the way, until the rubbery scrotum was pressed to the lips of my sex.

'Spank her just right,' Kay said, 'and the balls will rub on her pussy. You can probably make her come.'

Angel chuckled and spoke.

'Count on it, girl. But first I get to cane that big white botty. You ready, Amber?'

I shook my head, but she took no notice, whipping the malacca down across my bottom cheeks to send me into a squirming, writhing frenzy as the agonising sting hit me. Again she did it, leaving me no time to recover, and then I completely lost control, thrashing stupidly on the bed as they laughed at me, with the brush up my bum waggling between my cheeks like an obscene tail and the big dildo working in my cunt. I was close to orgasm before she stopped, after far more than six strokes, beaten and molested into submissive ecstasy. As she began to spank me I knew I was going to suffer that final disgrace in seconds.

Angel was spanking me right on my tuck, her hand slapping in under the hairbrush to jam the dildo deep into my cunt with every blow and push the big rubber balls against my clitty. I couldn't help myself, pushing up for more almost immediately, with Kay and Sophie's sweet laughter ringing in my ears as I started to come. When it hit me I nearly passed out, it was so strong. I was still squeezing my bottom and my straining cunt on their loads long after Angel had stopped spanking me, my dignity lost in the ecstasy of my punishment.

172

Seven

The girls didn't stop just because I'd come. After they'd ungagged me they kept my hands tied and made me kiss their bottoms before sitting me in the corner to watch as the three of them played together. Only when Kay was kneeling between Angel's open thighs as Sophie in turn licked her from behind did I finally use my stop word so that I could join them. The sky had already begun to grow light before we finally ceased our games.

I woke at noon, sore but happy, my bottom a mess of welts and bruises, my anus loose and smarting, my fanny aching. The others were in no better a state, all four of us waddling and being distinctly careful as we sat down. None of us minded: both Sophie and Angel were full of life, teasing me mercilessly for letting them have me, and Kay was as cuddly as she'd ever been, clinging on to me even while I was making toast and honey for a late breakfast.

There was only one fly in the ointment, although it was rather a big one: Fat Hannah. She was going to be after me with a vengeance, and if my punishing the four girls in class had been an obvious set-up and so not really to be taken seriously then what we'd done to Jilly was a very different matter. After all, while the gates had been closed by then, they hadn't been locked or guarded. Anybody might have wandered in and found her tied up and gagged, also pretty much naked.

It had been irresponsible of us, and I felt bad about it, almost bad enough to go to Fat Hannah to apologise and ask to take my medicine. Almost. Instead, I decided to send a non-committal letter of apology and accept a spanking from her or Jilly if they demanded it. I wrote the letter before Angel and Sophie left, giving it to them to post before collapsing back into bed with Kay.

Monday felt strange, oddly peaceful after so much misbehaviour over the weekend. As I finished making the bed, with the cool autumn sunlight streaming in through the windows and everything looking so ordinary, it was hard to believe that the same room had been the scene of so much filthy sadistic sex.

Tuesday was much the same, but on Wednesday I got my comeuppance. Fat Hannah Riley rang in the morning, demanding that I come out to where they were setting up the circus in Wanstead and take my punishment. I agreed that she could spank me, telling myself that it was only fair and trying to ignore the immediate tingle of anticipation in my fanny but making her promise it wouldn't be in front of the carnies. Once was more than enough, especially as it had only made their behaviour towards me worse. I told her Jilly could do me too, if she wanted, which really was fair. But I refused to let her have Kay.

I was the usual bundle of nerves as I drove over. The circus was still being set up, with the Big Top in place but most of the stalls disassembled or missing. I saw Hannah immediately, her imposing bulk shrouded in a pink floral dress that made her seem bigger still. The thought that I would shortly be over her knee made my stomach tight and set my bottom cheeks twitching, the more so because I was still a little tender from my session with the hairbrush and the cane.

Hannah saw me as I approached, her expression stern but not actually nasty when she spoke. Jilly was there too, talking to Sean and Mick, who were in their clown costumes but not yet made up. She started towards me as her mother spoke up.

'So you turned up. I thought I'd have to come and get you.'

'No,' I told her. 'I was in the wrong, so it's fair enough.'

'You're dead right it is. And how about that little bitch Angel, and that Sophie Cherwell, and your Kay – where are they?'

'I said you could give me extra in place of Kay,' I reminded her. 'But Sophie and Angel are none of my business.'

'Oh no?' she demanded. 'I don't know how to get hold of Sophie, do I, and Angel told me to fuck off, so you get a straight choice. You tell me where they live –'

'Sorry, I can't do that.'

'– or you get it for all of them.'

I swallowed and shrugged. Hannah wasn't exactly keeping her voice down, and a lot of other people had begun to gather round: both clowns, Maggie, some of the girls and altogether too many leering, sneering male carnies for my liking.

'Can we have this conversation in private, please?' I asked.

'Don't like to be seen, do you?' she answered. 'Offends your precious modesty, don't it? Even after we put you in the stocks.'

'Pillory,' I said automatically.

'Still a stuck-up bitch, ain't you?' she demanded. 'So you don't like it in public? Good, I'm glad you don't like it, 'cause that's where you're going to get it.'

'No, look, Hannah,' I began, backing hastily away – straight into the arms of Gerry.

'Get me a chair!' Hannah shouted. 'There's going to be a spanking!'

'No . . . no, not here. In private!' I squealed as Gerry forced me towards her and others took hold of my arms. 'In private! You said in private, Hannah!'

My voice broke off in a wail of self-pity and despair as I was pushed down over Fat Hannah's lap even as a big wooden crate was pushed up for her to sit on. I lost my balance, sprawling over her knee, and my bottom had been turned up before I could even think of resisting. All I could do was babble for mercy.

It did me no good whatsoever, even as I began to struggle, fighting to stop it happening as Hannah burrowed one big hand under my tummy, groping for the button of my jeans. A scream of mindless distress broke from my lips as the button popped open and I gave another as her hand pushed in down the back. I snatched behind me, clutching at my jeans, kicking, screaming, trying to bite Hannah's legs, anything and everything to stop my bottom being stripped.

I got my fingers in my waistband, holding on just as hard as I possibly could, only for Maggie to snatch my wrist, twisting it until I was forced to let go because of the pain. Down it all came, my desperate sobbing pleas ignored as my jeans and panties were hauled clear of my wriggling bottom. Then I was bare – almost. My bum was still half covered by my knickers as my jeans were hauled clear and I grabbed for them with my free hand.

'Leave it!' Hannah snapped as I snatched my panties back up, too hard, pulling them up into my crease with both cheeks spilled out at the sides.

'Spank her like that, if she wants to hold her knicks up her slit,' Maggie suggested.

'No, she gets it bare,' Hannah answered. 'Let go, you little bitch!'

'No!' I wailed, clinging on to my panties she tried to prise my fingers loose. 'Please, Hannah, no! Do me in the caravan, please, please, please! I beg you! No, not my panties, no!'

My last word was a pitiful drawn-out wail as Gerry leant down and coolly tore the straining cotton where I was holding my knickers up my bum, just above the top of my crease. I felt them split and then Maggie had caught my other wrist, twisting it up with the first as Hannah tugged the remains of my panties out from between my bottom cheeks.

Now I really was bare, the whole fat globe of my bottom on show, cane stripes and all. Then more was revealed as Hannah thrust her knee between my thighs, spreading me out, my fanny naked to the stares of the laughing carnies. I was sobbing as I braced myself for punishment and my whole body was shaking too, utterly defeated as I was held down bare for a public spanking, expecting the first hard smack at any moment. Instead, Fat Hannah's hand settled slowly on my bottom cheeks.

'What did you do with my girls? You pulled their bum cheeks apart, didn't you?' she grated. Then it had been done to me.

I let out another wail of shame and despair as my cheeks were levered apart and my bumhole put on show. The carnies immediately began to clap and cheer, pushing closer to get a better view of my naked sex and my spread anus. I began to squirm again, thinking of hard cocks inserted into tight crevices, but Maggie kept her grip, holding me helpless. Hannah kept hers too, holding me open for that most awful, most intimate of inspections.

'What do you reckon, boys?' she chuckled. 'Ever seen a posh girl's arsehole before? Hoity-toity piece like her, you'd think she'd learn to wipe properly, wouldn't you?'

'I did!' I wailed, unable to hold back against a grossly unjust accusation. But my denial only met with a gale of laughter from the carnies.

I burst into tears, unable to take it any more, and at that Hannah let go, patting my cheeks as she humped my bottom up into a better spanking position.

'Big cry baby,' she chided. 'Can't even take a joke, eh? Ah well, better get your bum spanked then.'

She was laughing as she started to spank me, which made my tears more bitter still as the stinging slaps were applied to my bouncing bum, with the whole ring of carnies laughing at me and making crude jokes, remarking on the size of my bottom and the perfectly natural brown ring around my anus. I was on blatant show, my hips kicked right up and my legs spread by Hannah's knees, my fanny and bumhole well open. The onlookers could see everything, and for once the exposure of my bottom-hole wasn't the worst thing about it. Hannah was spanking hard and well, bringing the heat to my cheeks and, inevitably, to my sex, which had begun to juice. Mick was the first to notice.

'Hey, look, boys! She's getting turned on – what a tart!'

They burst out laughing, Hannah included, and she began to spank lower, right over my sex as fresh tears squirted from my eyes. I lost the last vestige of my control, howling my head off and beating my fists on Hannah's legs and on the ground, waggling my bum in every direction in a vain attempt to hide what I was showing and to escape the pain, waving my free leg in every direction and just showing myself off even more, blubbering out broken apologies and begging for mercy and for the spanking to stop.

It didn't. Smack after smack after smack was applied to my bare cheeks until I really thought I was going to faint, and all the while the carnies were calling out suggestions for what ought to be done to me.

'Come on, mum, give us a go. I want to spank her,' yelled Jilly, a note of petulance in her voice.'

'Yeah, all right,' Hannah answered. And it stopped, just like that, with one word from her, where all my pleas had been utterly ignored.

I tumbled off Hannah's lap as I was released, to sprawl on the ground with my legs apart, providing a fine show of my fanny to the laughing audience. Several of the men had obvious bulges down their trousers and

I found myself scrabbling away on my hot bottom, sure that they'd grab me and fuck me at any moment. Sean was the closest, grinning evilly as he squeezed at his erection through his clown trousers. I was about to offer myself to him in the hope of being spared a gang-banging when Jilly spoke up.

'Come here, you little bitch. Leave the men alone and get over my knee. You're mine.'

She reached out for me as she spoke, grabbing my sleeve. I felt confused, dizzy and scared as she hauled me across her legs. Nobody needed to hold me this time: I was already broken, and all I could manage was a sob as her hands went to the hem of my top.

'Tits out, fatso,' Jilly laughed. 'Jesus, you're big – talk about fucking melons! Hey, boys, how'd you like to fuck between these?'

As she spoke she jerked my top up to leave my breasts hanging heavy in my bra. She began to grope them as the men chorused their agreement that they'd like to fuck my chest. She squeezed one dangling boob and then the other before abruptly flopping them out. Another quick adjustment and both my breasts were completely free of restraint, fat and pendulous beneath my chest, leaving me nude from my neck to my knees save for my ruined panties.

'Now your arsehole, same as you did me,' Jilly said, and for a second time my bottom cheeks had been hauled apart to show off my anus. 'How do *you* like it with a load of blokes staring up your brown-eye?'

I didn't answer, too confused by my feelings even to think straight, never mind explain the agonising mixture of shame and pleasure and self-pity and arousal in my head. She laughed and let go of my cheeks. Then the spanking began, clumsy slaps to my upturned buttocks with the occasional pause to spread my behind and expose my anal star to the audience. I was past reacting, but that only made Jilly angry. She spanked harder still, calling me a bitch and a tart as my cheeks bounced and wobbled under her hand. The men had gone quiet too, a menacing silence, and I found myself looking back at them even through the haze of my pain. I was going to get fucked, made to suck cock, used between my boobs, maybe even buggered. Gerry spoke, echoing my thoughts.

'Do we get to fuck her, Hannah?'

The spanking stopped. I looked back, shaking so badly that I couldn't close my mouth. Jilly chuckled and hauled my legs apart, splaying out my wet fanny.

'Looks like you've got her ready,' Mick said. 'What a slut, eh?'

'I'm going to make her suck me again,' Sean put in. 'She sucks good.'

'I'm going to fuck her arse,' Gerry added. 'Right up it till my dick comes out her mouth.'

Another man growled agreement, and another, making my bumhole twitch in terrified anticipation. I'd been shaking my head frantically as they spoke but I knew it wasn't going to stop them. Then Hannah spoke.

'Don't be such a shit, Gerry. Of course you don't get to fuck her, not if she don't want it. Amber, do you want a fucking?'

'No!' I wailed. 'No, I don't!'

'That ain't what your body's saying!' Sean jeered. 'Come on, Hannah, we all know she wants it really.'

'No!' I repeated. But it was a lie, at least partly.

I was ready, my fanny warm and open and puffy, and I did want to be filled, in there and in my mouth, even up my bum. But not by thirty or forty dirty foul-mouthed carnies, not when they were such pigs to me, and they always were. Yet if they humbled me just a little more, humiliated me just a little more, spanked my hot rosy bottom just a little more . . .

'She's good to spank, isn't she? Nice big bum, plenty of target.'

It was a voice I knew all too well: female, the accent an odd mixture of London's East End and New York – Melody Rathwell.

I jerked my head around to find her standing almost directly behind me, her expression amused as she looked down at my spread bum cheeks and dangling tits. Morris was beyond her, smoking a cigar as he too admired my near-naked body. Immediately I tried to get up, but Jilly tightened her grip.

'Where the fuck do you think you're going?' she demanded. 'We're not finished with you.'

'Yes, but . . .' I began, only to stop. 'Please, Jilly?'

'Let her up,' Hannah ordered. 'We'll finish her off another time. That's one for you and one for your tart, Amber. Don't think you'll be getting away with it, unless you want to tell me where that slut Angel lives? So to what do we owe the pleasure, Mr and Mrs Rathwell?'

Her voice was dripping sarcasm. It drew a scowl from Melody but Morris responded with a happy smile. It was hard not to smile myself as I climbed unsteadily to my feet. My bottom was ablaze, my head still full of shame, but I had escaped what I'd really feared: being gang-banged by carnies. Maybe they'd seen me spanked, maybe they'd seen every rude detail of my body, but they weren't going to have my fanny.

I quickly pulled up my jeans, adjusted my bra and top to cover my breasts, and then joined Melody, who was at least a genuine friend, whatever her attitude to me. Her response was to squeeze my bottom and tell me that she could feel the heat through my jeans. But after what had just been done to me it seemed only playful, and I was very glad of her company. The men standing around looked pretty aggressive but Morris didn't seem to care, taking a long draw on his cigar and blowing smoke into the air before speaking.

'Interesting place you have here, Mrs Riley.'

'What is it you want?' she demanded.

'We have a little problem,' he went on. 'I believe our Christmas parties are on the same date.'

'And?' Hannah responded as she seated herself on the crate, folding her arms across her massive chest.

'And I thought we might come to some arrangement,' Morris said reasonably. 'Perhaps if you were to change dates?'

'*You* change dates,' she told him. 'We've already got our flyers printed. The venue's booked and all.'

'We're in a similar position,' Morris admitted. 'But I'm prepared to make you a good offer if you change.'

'Reckon you can buy me, do you?' Hannah sneered.

'Not at all,' Morris answered. 'But I'm sure you would rather avoid the loss and inconvenience of having your club shut down by the council?'

'You can't threaten me, Morris Rathwell,' Hannah retorted. 'We're above board, we are: legal premises, late licence, the works.'

'You are also planning to sell videos on the night,' he said. 'Unclassified videos showing unfortunate young ladies having their bottoms smacked, and you know what Little Hitlers trading standards officers tend to be – no sense of humour at all.'

Hannah's face had gone red and her mouth was working. But instead of answering Morris she suddenly turned on me.

'You fucking little bitch! I'll –'

'No, no,' Morris broke in, now with a touch of laughter in his voice. 'You mustn't blame poor Amber. She knows nothing about this, and the only thing you could possibly blame her for is introducing you to Angel.'

'Angel!?' Hannah spat. 'That treacherous little –'

'Do calm down, Hannah,' Morris interrupted. 'What's done is done. So how about it?'

'You've got a fucking nerve coming here . . .' Hannah began. I steeled myself to run as the carnies began to close in, but then she stopped, her thoughts visibly flickering across her fat face before she began again. 'So what if I don't sell the videos? Who says I've even got any? It's your word against mine, ain't it?'

Morris shrugged and reached into the deep pocket of his greatcoat, drawing out two videos complete with garish plastic wrappers. The one on top showed Sophie bent over the school desk in her uniform, knickers down and ready for the cane. All I could see of the lower one was the title on the spine, but that was enough. It read, in tall orange and green letters, *The Disgrace of Madame Boobfontaine*.

'Nice vid, Amber,' Melody remarked with a wink, in final confirmation of the awful truth.

'You made a video of me!' I croaked. 'You made a video of me in the pillory! How could you! How dare you! How –'

'Oh shut up, you stuck-up tart,' Hannah interrupted. 'Look, Morris, I don't know how you got hold of those, but . . .'

'How many have you made?' I demanded. 'Have you sold any yet?'

'Will you shut up?' she snapped at me.

'No, I will *not*,' I retorted angrily, my fear set aside as my rage rose higher. 'That was . . . that was totally unacceptable! I'll go to the trading standards people if Morris doesn't, you . . . you horrible old woman!'

'Shut up!' she yelled. 'Who gives a fuck if a load of dirty old wankers get to see your arse? And think about it: if you go to trading standards the vids are going to get passed around in court. They won't get them all, either, I'll make sure of that. But if you're so fucking precious you can buy them back, the lot of them, twenty-five quid a shot.'

'Buy them back?' I echoed. 'Twenty-five pounds each? I will not! You have no right to be selling them in the first place, and what did they cost to make anyway? A pound, two pounds?'

'You want 'em, they're twenty-five quid apiece,' she said.

'You can have this one for nothing,' Melody offered, holding it out to me. 'We've got spares.'

I took it with trembling fingers, my mouth coming open slowly as I took in the picture of me in my riding gear, my head and hands trapped in the pillory, my bare breasts dangling under my chest, my jodhpurs down at the back, but not my knickers. They were still up, with the sponges bulging in my panty pouch as if I'd had the most appalling accident in them. Baffo was lecturing me as Buffo held out my knickers, ready to be pulled down for spanking, so that it looked as if I was about to be punished for going to the toilet in my panties. Despite my dripping hair and the coloured water running down my face I was fully recognisable.

'You bastards!' I managed after a long moment of just staring at the awful picture. 'You utter bastards!'

'Tell you what,' Sean joked. 'Twenty-five quid's about what she's worth for a blow job, so let's say she can pay one blow, one vid. There's only a hundred!'

There was a chorus of laughter at his suggestion, and further embarrassment was added to my boiling emotions.

'Shut up, Sean,' Hannah warned before I could find my voice again. 'I'll make you a deal, Morris. Leave it for this Christmas, and I swear that in future I'll keep off your dates. How's that?'

'And she gives you back the videos,' I added quickly.

'Shut up, Amber!' Hannah hissed. Morris waved me to silence with his hand before he replied.

'I can work with that, maybe. Only from now on I want you to stay out of London. Let's say outside the M25.'

Hannah made a face. But then she nodded, spat on her hand and stuck it out. Morris gave a fastidious grimace but shook hands, then extracted the handkerchief from his top pocket to wipe his palm. I was beginning to panic, picturing videos of me in the pillory, being stripped off, getting spanked, made to suck cock, being fucked from behind and, worst of all, begging for it. Anybody might see it. Kay was bound to. If it got into the shops even my father might.

'Morris, please?' I begged as he turned to leave. 'Help me!'

'Why would he bother?' Mel answered. 'You never come and play with us any more. You'd rather have this lot abuse you.'

'No!' I bleated. 'It's not like that, it's . . . please, Mel. I'll come to a spanking party, OK? How's that?'

'Tempting,' she answered. I felt hope start to flood through me.

'Very tempting,' Morris agreed. 'In fact, I'll do you a deal, seeing as it's you. Mel's right, it's been a while since we had any fun together, and we miss you, you know. I'll buy the videos, all of them, full price. I'll make sure it really *is* all of them, too – that's if you can beat Melody in a little game of one-on-one baseball.'

'And if I lose?' I asked doubtfully.

'Then you'd better be ready to get sucking!' he laughed. But he put his arm around my shoulder as I began to snivel. 'Seriously, I'll see you all right. Come on, you look like you could do with a cuddle and a drink.'

I nodded and allowed Morris to lead me away, my pride far too broken to resist. We went to a restaurant on the far side of the Flats, where Morris ordered up a bottle of wine and some lunch, which slowly revived my spirits as he began to explain what he wanted of me.

'You remember Hudson Staebler, from Fort Lauderdale? Big guy, a bit brash?'

I nodded. 'A bit brash' was an understatement, and Staebler was also extremely dominant, his favourite thing being to treat girls as pet dogs. Morris had tricked me into sucking him off, one of the last such occasions before I'd sworn off it.

'He's a great guy,' Morris went on. 'But he has got a typical Yank ego – reckons they're the best at everything. I was teasing him the other night, saying baseball's really just the same as rounders, and he got a bit hot under the collar. Mel used to play when we lived in New York, and she took his side, so I ended up betting that I could find an English girl who could beat her one on one.'

'OK,' I answered cautiously. 'And you're willing to risk two thousand, five hundred pounds that I can do it?'

'Oh no,' he laughed. 'That's the beauty of it. Hudson's a great guy, like I said, only he's a bit too straight up for his own good. He's bet me five grand that you'll lose.'

'I throw the game,' Mel put in, 'you get your videos and we're all quids in.'

'Won't he notice?' I asked.

'Believe me,' Mel answered, 'I'm good enough to make it look convincing. If it was for real you wouldn't stand a chance.'

'I was team captain at school, as it happens,' I answered her. But she just laughed as Morris went on.

'It can't fail, believe me, but we do have to make it look tight. Your paddock is the best place for it: plenty of space and nice big hedges to keep it private.'

'We're only playing rounders,' I pointed out.

'Sure,' he answered. 'But it has to be nice and fruity no? We're going to run up some cute kit and have a bi of dirt between innings – you know, the winning gir getting a lick from the loser, all that stuff, maybe a bi of spanking.'

'OK,' I sighed. 'But what if I do lose?'

'You'd better not,' Mel warned. 'Or you're going t be sucking pikey cock for the next month if you do.'

I made a face, thinking of the taste of man mixed in with greasepaint as Morris went on.

'You're not going to lose. Listen, this is how the game works. You play five innings, three strikes to an out, three outs and you change. Instead of running, you have to knock the ball beyond a perimeter to get a point . . . maybe we'll have a bigger circle worth two points, I'm not sure. The one with the most innings is the winner, simple, and you play for a draw up until the last innings, with three forfeits each . . .'

'Who chooses the forfeits?' I asked wearily.

'We've thought up a nice one there,' he told me. 'The subbie girls choose before each innings, so if it's your Kay, for instance, she doesn't know if you're going to get what she chooses or if you'll be dishing it out to Mel. Good, huh?'

'I suppose so,' I admitted. 'So we'll have Kay, Annabelle, Harmony – who else? Sophie?'

'Sophie, sure, and maybe Angel.'

'Angel? She's hardly submissive, is she? She'll think up something really horrible.'

'Do you think so?' Morris answered pensively. 'I think you've got more to worry about with Sophie.'

I bit my lip. He was probably right.

'So as I was saying,' he went on, 'you play for a draw up until the last innings. Then you win, Mel takes the last forfeit, and that's the lot.'

'Shouldn't the winner get to choose the last forfeit?' I asked.

'You get to give it,' Mel told me, 'be happy with that.'

It was impossible not to smile at the look on her face. I would have to submit to her, three times but I got to have her four times in return, which had to be worth it.

'I can cope with that,' I told them.

'You'd better be good,' Mel said.

'Come up and practise,' I offered. 'Then we can work out how to do it.'

187

She agreed, and there was a pause as the waiter brought our lunch over. I'd begun to calm down, despite my still-hot bottom, and even if I was letting myself fall into Morris's clutches once again at least I would have my fair share of domination. More importantly, I'd get the videos back, and for once I was extremely grateful for the Rathwell's scheming nature.

'How did you get hold of the videos?' I asked. 'Did Angel steal them?'

'No, no, nothing like that,' Morris said. 'They're blanks. We just picked up some spare cases from the printer.'

'But how did you know who the printer would be?'

'Easy. Angel recommended him to Hannah.'

'So you got me to introduce Angel to Hannah in order to set all this up?'

Morris Rathwell nodded casually.

I expected Morris and Mel to try and take advantage of me, perhaps by driving me up to Epping Forest for her to finish off my spanking while I sucked his penis. For once, though, they left me alone, with nothing worse than a pat on my bum from Mel after she'd given me a last and still badly needed hug.

My equally badly needed climax I got from Kay who cuddled me and stroked my bottom as I cried my out feelings on her shoulder. Then she slipped a hand down between my thighs to bring me off under her fingers. Inevitably that led to full sex, head to tail on the kitchen floor with our faces buried in each other's fannies, equal for once as we licked each other to mutual orgasms.

I was still pulling my jeans up when the shop bell went, setting us both giggling as we hastily wiped our mouths and tidied ourselves up. Our relationship was back as it should have been, made fresh and exciting again by events, so now all I needed were the videos and I would be fully content.

Looking at the case that Mel had given me and thinking back, it became obvious to me how they'd done it. The bright lights and the fixed position of the pillory had made my ordeal easy to film, probably from the window of the big caravan that I'd noticed and possibly with hand-held cameras too, from behind and to the sides. I'd never have noticed with my head jammed in the pillory.

It was a pretty horrible thing to have done, and I felt like an idiot for falling for it. I could understand why Hannah had suddenly relented about paying me, too. Possibly she'd only withheld the money in the first place in order to trap me into doing the video? No, not *possibly*: probably, almost certainly in fact. She'd used me with a vengeance, and if that very thought was enough to make me want to push a hand down the front of my panties, then it also made my blood boil.

I wanted revenge, wanted it badly, but in some way that ensured there would be no consequences for me. That wasn't easy, but that evening it hit me – a foolproof plan. It was a little frightening and involved the added humiliation of having Hannah and others attend the game of rounders and see Mel deal with me, but that was a small price to pay. My revenge wouldn't be sexual. Instead I would deprive her of what she cared about most – money.

Hannah knew that I was supposed to beat Mel before Morris would buy the videos, but that was all. And she loved to gamble. If she thought I was going to throw the game and lose, then she could easily be induced into putting a large sum on the outcome. Not by me, though, as she would immediately be suspicious. She would have to be tipped off as if by accident, or have somebody go to her suggesting the ruse as a moneymaking scheme. The obvious choice was Gavin Bulmer – so long as he was still seeing Jilly.

He was. I made an appointment to visit him the next day, an easy trip as my line goes straight down to Moorgate and his offices were just a short walk from the station. The City had changed even since my last visit, with more great slabs of steel and concrete and glass rising above the streets than ever. Gavin's office was on the fifteenth floor of one of the larger blocks, and while I knew he earned a lot of money and was fairly senior I wasn't entirely prepared for the size of his office, nor for how he looked. In place of the combat gear he was in a perfectly tailored suit set off by a broad salmon-pink tie, making him look wealthy and respectable if still flash. Only his personality was the same.

'Why can't I get a secretary with tits like that?' he greeted me. 'Sit down, Amber, good to see you. So what's up? You say you've got a new game or something?'

'Not exactly,' I told him. 'More of a gambling thing, um . . .'

'Scam? Who's the mark?'

'That's the word, I suppose. Hannah Riley.'

'Fat bitch. I'm in – so what's the deal?'

'I'm playing rounders against Melody Rathwell, on a bet between Morris and this guy Hudson Staebler. It's fixed for me to win, but Hannah doesn't know that –'

'Say no more,' Gavin broke in, grinning. 'Say no more. I tip Jilly the wink that it's fixed the other way, accidentally of course. Hannah goes large on Mel to win and she gets stuffed big time. Who's holding the book?'

'Nobody, as such. Morris's bet is just with Hudson, but I'm sure he could be persuaded.'

'That's a pain. He knows the real deal, so I can't get a side bet in. What's in it for me, then?'

'To see Hannah Riley lose a lot of money?'

'That's good, sure, but she's not stupid. She'll figure it out after the event.'

'Does that matter?'

'Yes. I don't want to get beaten up by a load of pikeys. It's all right for you – you just get your arse smacked and maybe have to suck a cock or two.'

'That's *not* all right, Gavin.'

He just shrugged and put his hands behind his head, leaning back in his big black leather chair as he thought through my proposal. I could well appreciate his argument, and was also trying to find a solution, but he spoke first.

'This is better. I tell Morris what's going on, the truth, and get him to run the book. Then I let slip to Jilly that I've got a lot of money on Mel to win, and hint that I know the game is fixed. Maybe I even pretend to increase my bet when Jilly's with me. Yes, that works. That way, when Mel loses, Fat Hannah thinks I've been done too, and nobody's suggested that she should put any money on it, so she's only got herself to blame.'

'I'm not sure Hannah would see it that way, but yes . . .'

I trailed off. Hannah would be furious, but that was the whole idea, and since Morris had the videos, or she thought he did, she wouldn't dare do anything. Besides, Morris had manipulated *me* often enough, and generally with unfortunate consequences. I thought of what had happened to me at the club in Belfast: Mr Protheroe, Hudson Staebler, Morris himself, the security guard who'd had the Rottweiler . . .

'. . . yes, it works,' I finished.

'It does,' he agreed. 'Now, how about my blow job?'

'What do you mean, your blow job!?'

'I'm doing you a favour here, Amber. Or look on it as a consultancy fee, if you prefer.'

'You're a pig, do you know that, Gavin Bulmer?'

'So they say.'

'Anyway, what if somebody comes in?'

'So you are up for it?'

'No, I am *not*!'

'Spoilsport. At least let me toss off over those gorgeous tits, or show me your arse. You've got to give me something.'

'No, I have not. Anyway, we're in a crowded office building, Gavin!'

'That's no problem. Lock the door and I'll say I'm in conference.'

'No, look . . .'

Gavin had already picked up his phone and quickly told his secretary that he was not to be disturbed. I gave a heavy sigh, telling myself that it would at least ensure he played fairly by me.

'Oh, all right, if you insist. I'll . . . I'll hold my panties down for you, but be quick!'

'You got it, babe,' he answered, pulling down his zip even as I slid the bolt home to fasten the door.

I was feeling nervous, and used, as I turned my back to him and began to tug up my skirt. Gavin watched, grinning as he began to stroke his cock. But his expression slowly changed to one of more intense pleasure as it grew hard. I waited until he was nearly erect, then pushed my thumbs into the waistband of my tights and panties, starting to push them both down.

'Nice,' he groaned. 'You have such a gorgeous arse, Amber. Stick it out a bit more, yeah?'

'Hurry up,' I told him as the full spread of my bottom came on show and I pushed it out to give him a better view.

Gavin began to wank harder, his stare fixed on my bare bottom. I was wondering if he could see my fanny and bumhole and was trying not to let my exposure get to me when he spoke again, his voice rough with excitement.

'Go down, Amber, on all fours . . . show it all . . . show it all, babe . . . please?'

'Oh, for goodness sake!' I snapped. But I quickly got down, a safe distance away from him, in a crawling position, which meant that I was showing everything, my cheeks fully spread to him.

'Such a lovely arse,' he sighed. 'Now I've got to spunk.'

He'd begun to jerk furiously at his cock, pointing it forward so that his mess would go on the floor. But he suddenly pulled his chair forward on its rollers. I realised what was going to happen, too late, managing only a squeal of protest as his come erupted all over my bare bottom, on my cheeks and in between them. A thick strand of it was soon hanging down over my anus, pooling in the little hole as my face screwed up in disgust.

'You bastard!' I managed to gasp.

'Any time,' he told me. 'Do you want to rub off in it? If not, you'd better wipe your bum or you'll make a right mess in your knickers.'

'I'm aware of that, thank you,' I told him, rising carefully.

Gavin watched as I wiped my bottom, his eyes full of that deeply intrusive interest that some men have: not simple lust, but a somehow proprietorial pleasure in seeing a woman bare, as if it gives them some sort of power over us. I ignored him, but I managed a smile as I pulled up my knickers and tights, then smoothed my skirt down.

'Will you call Morris?' I asked.

'Leave it all to me,' he promised.

I left Gavin's office with mixed feelings, and not just because I'd had to hold my panties down for him to wank off over my bum. Hannah was going to be furious, and while she wouldn't have any reason to think that I'd set her up, her behaviour wasn't always entirely rational. Maybe she'd spank me anyway, or worse, just for winning?

It was a worrying thought, and I nearly went back to tell Gavin it was all off. Only the sudden closing of the train doors stopped me, and even then I was left fiddling with my phone as we moved off. What if she realised that I was involved? In theory it didn't matter as I hadn't made her put any money on the outcome but, as I'd said to Gavin, she might well not see it that way. Maybe I should lose anyway? No, then I'd end up having to buy back the videos by sucking the carnies' cocks, about four times each – not to mention what Morris would expect in order to recoup his five thousand pounds.

The thought sent a shiver through me. I'd have to go to his spanking parties, one a month for nearly two years. Horrible old men like Mr Protheroe would put me over their knees, stroke my bottom cheeks, tickle my bumhole, fiddle with my fanny, and spank me, spank me again and again and again. Holding down my panties for Gavin was nothing compared with what they'd do, repeatedly. I'd have to parade myself in the nude, dress up in ridiculous costumes, play the maid, maybe serve wine with the bottle up my straining fanny-hole the way Annabelle had been made to do.

It was unthinkable – or it should have been. I couldn't get it out of my mind. By the time we reached Alexandra Palace I wanted to play with myself and I was very glad that there were other people in my carriage. Unfortunately, as we moved through the suburbs of north London one or two passengers were getting out at every station and hardly anyone was getting in. The last three got out at Enfield Town, but another one did get in.

I relaxed a little, telling myself that he'd probably be going all the way to Hertford. The frustration would be truly awful, driving me to that state of helpless wanton ecstasy I so hated and so loved. I remembered Protheroe telling me that I was a naughty girl and overdue for a spanking: how angry it had made me and how wet I'd been, but maybe no wetter than now. After all, I'd just had to hold my panties down in a City office for a man to masturbate over me, to spunk all over my bottom, to watch me wipe myself . . .

We were in Cuffley, and the last passenger in my carriage had just got out. I told myself that I wouldn't do it, that I'd wait until I'd got home and then I'd play with Kay. I reminded myself that there might be security cameras watching me, but there weren't. I gave in. My tights and panties came down under my skirt as I gave them an angry little jerk. I sat back and closed my eyes, rubbing urgently at my fanny and teasing my bottom-hole, the little pit at the centre still slippery with Gavin's slime.

Why hadn't I gone further? Why hadn't I sucked his cock for him, down on my knees in his office, with my boobs out and my bum bare behind? Why hadn't I shown off for him properly, pulling my cheeks apart and revelling in my humiliation as I showed off my bum-hole? Why hadn't I touched myself, rubbing my fanny and opening my hole, even slipping a finger up my bum? Why hadn't he touched me, easing fingers in up my sticky fanny and my bottom-hole? Why hadn't he just fucked me while he was at it? Or worse, buggered me, jamming his cock up my bottom to the hilt, pumping up my rectum until I was gasping with passion and rubbing at my dirty little cunt to make myself come, just as I was now, my whole body tense as a long, shame-filled orgasm swept over me.

Eight

The game was on Sunday and I was impossibly nervous for the rest of the week. I'd rung Gavin and asked him to call our agreement off but he'd merely laughed and told me to get a grip. He'd seen Jilly too, and Morris had agreed to run the book. I kept telling myself that it would be OK, that I would win and that would be that, but at heart I didn't believe it. I kept telling myself that I should back out, but that hurt my pride and I couldn't bear the thought of Melody's contempt.

Melody came up by train on the Saturday, full of confidence and utterly indifferent to Hannah Riley's anger. When we practised I found myself envying her strength and telling myself that I would at least try to match it. Which might have been easier if she hadn't proved to be far better than me at the game, especially when throwing the ball, although I'd never done so badly in my life. Fortunately Hudson Staebler didn't have the faintest idea whether she was really any good or not, basing his confidence entirely on her boasts and his automatic assumption that anything American had to be better.

We agreed not to try too hard, even in the first few innings, and I was left feeling extremely small. Kay was full of sympathy and quickly had a bottle of wine open and a glass poured for me, but I'd scarcely swallowed my first sip when the bell went again. It was Hannah on her own for once, and as Kay showed her into the kitchen my stomach was tying itself into knots. She seemed friendly enough, accepting a glass of wine and telling us about her plans for the Christmas party, but it wasn't long before she got to the point.

'So what's this I hear about the game with you and Melody Rathwell being a fix?'

'Who told you that?' I asked, attempting to feign surprise as my heart began to hammer.

'Let's just say it was a little bird,' Hannah went on. 'What happens then? You lose and Morris buys your vids back anyway, but a load of punters have gone a bundle on you to win, like muggins here – maybe?'

I merely made a face, not daring to say anything.

'That's it, ain't it?' she said, looking smug. 'Morris says you have to beat Melody to get your vids back, so that I'll hear him, and all the time you're fixed to lose. Sneaky bastard, that Morris.'

There was admiration in Hannah's voice, but also satisfaction. She thought she'd got the better of Morris, but I was trapped. If I claimed that she was right I'd no longer have my excuse and she was sure to spank me, but if I admitted the truth she would do me anyway, for trying to cheat her. She went on before I could decide what to say.

'You're a nice girl, deep down, Amber, for all your stuck-up airs, so I'm not going to get nasty. But let's just say the game went a bit wrong and you accidentally didn't lose. What then?'

My mouth came open to speak, but she carried straight on.

'I'd lose a bit of money, wouldn't I? And if I'd lost money, I'd have to get it back, wouldn't I? Have to push some more videos, probably . . .'

'But you promised!'

'Keep your knickers on, darling. Or maybe, maybe you could make a new one, in a wig and make-up and that, so nobody recognises you. How's that for a proposition?'

'If I win you want me to make a video? What sort?'

'The usual, bit of spankies, bit of dirty stuff. Maybe you're up for it anyway? I pay.'

'No, thank you, but if I win . . . yes, I'll do it, so long as you promise I won't be recognisable. You can spank me, and so can Maggie, but no men, all right?'

'How about just Sean and Mick, and maybe Gerry?'

'No.'

'But you'll do anything Maggie and I say?'

'Yes.'

Hannah spat on her hand and held it out. I was going to be spanked and humiliated, but only by women, and I wasn't getting paid, so I wasn't even prostituting myself. Nobody would recognise me in the video, either.

I had vaguely hoped that Sunday would bring weather so foul that the whole thing would have to be called off. But Kay and I awoke to a perfect November day, cool and crisp, without a breath of wind and the scent of autumn in the air. There was a lot of work to do, so I swallowed a coffee and a bacon sandwich, then got into my overalls. First I mowed the paddock, then got out a line marker that I'd borrowed from the local cricket club. Mel and I had already decided on a single circle, which would make it easiest to keep our scores on course, so I painted a batting plate and made a perfect circle around it, using a peg and a piece of string. I'd let Mel talk me into having a pitcher's mound, and made one using a mixture of rubble and earth from the extension. By the time I'd finished it was late morning. I was just taking the wheelbarrow back when Kay appeared with Morris, Mel, Harmony and Annabelle in tow. Mel immediately went to inspect my pitcher's mound, while Morris handed me a bag.

'Your cossie, Amber, in team colours. Better get changed.'

I peered in, but could only see folds of red and black cloth. After over two hours' hard work I needed a shower and I started for the house. Morris called after me.

'No knickers, Amber, and no bra.'

It wasn't worth answering, and I contented myself with raising my eyebrows heavenwards as I walked away. Nobody else was really due until noon, so I took my time, having a long shower with a scented body-scrub to keep me feeling fresh and comfortable. I took my time drying too, powdering every crease and crevice, also stroking myself a little because if I was going to have to pay forfeits it was best to be turned on.

All the while I could hear Kay's voice and others from downstairs, cars pulling up, doors slamming and all sorts of other noise, making me wonder just how many people there would be. I'd caught more than one voice speaking in pattering Irish, also Home Counties voices, one female and so plummy that for a horrible moment I thought Mrs Mattlin-Jones had turned up.

My outfit was everything I might have expected of Morris. The top was black with a large red number back and front – a five, for no very obvious reason. It was also tight, so that with no bra underneath my breasts were straining against the fabric. My nipples showed through: they were already erect after I'd teased myself, but that would have been inevitable anyway. My skirt was the same bright red as the number, with a black band near the hem, and short, so short that I only had to bend a fraction for my bare bottom to show in the mirror. When I bent to hit a ball, anyone behind me would be able to see everything, but that was no worse than I'd expected. I also had striped red and black socks, and a pair of expensive-looking trainers. Morris might be a pervert, but he was seldom mean. Lastly there was a peaked cap, also in red and black.

Dressed up, I felt vulnerable and exposed, just as I was supposed to. I did my best to ignore the sensation, but it was not easy, especially with my bottom naked to the cool November air, keeping me constantly in mind of the fact that my cheeks showed beneath my skirt. I had been determined to keep my humiliation to a minimum, or at least to have my humiliation witnessed by the minimum number of people. But that had gone by the board and I realised just how much so as I stepped out into the paddock.

Most obvious was Melody, already standing on the plate with her baseball bat over her shoulder. Despite being dressed in the same smutty uniform as I was, only in turquoise blue and gold, she was looking both strong and confident. I could see why Hudson Staebler thought she was likely to win, and I was equally sure that most of those betting would agree with him. Morris would be making a killing.

Morris really did look like a bookie, too, with a hat on and a cigar in the side of his mouth as he took bets at a little table, which looked suspiciously like the one in my living room. He had a considerable queue that included his friends and clients, whom I knew he had no compunction whatsoever about cheating, along with several carnies and various others. Fat Jeff was there, in combats as usual, talking with Jeff Jones. Also present was Mr Protheroe, who waved as he saw me and made a little motion to indicate that I should lift my skirt for him.

I ignored him and continued to look around the paddock. The carnies had occupied one end of the field, using my jumps and other things as seats, with Fat Hannah in the middle on a folding chair. A roughly equal number of Morris's associates stood to one side, while a more mixed group occupied the other, including several trusted members of Razorback Paintball, various club staff, and Hudson Staebler, who had a whistle and so was presumably the umpire. He started towards me, a bat in his hand, his booming voice reaching me long before he did.

'Amber, hi! It's been a long time, huh? You look great, cute as a button and as American as apple pie!'

'Hello, Hudson,' I answered him. 'And thank you, I suppose, although apple pie was being made right here in Hertfordshire long before the USA even existed.'

'Right back at me, huh?' he laughed. 'What, you angling to have that fine ass spanked before you've even started the game? May as well, I figure, 'cause Melody is going to whup it good!'

'We'll see,' I replied, ignoring the spanking hint, only for an all too familiar voice to sound from behind me.

'If anyone's going to spank her before the game, it's me. She's still got two coming to her.'

'What for?' I asked, turning a little so that I could see both Hannah and Hudson. Morris was approaching us, having left Harmony to take the bets.

'You know what for,' Hannah was saying. 'One for your tramp friend Sophie and one for that back-stabbing bitch Angel.'

'Sophie's here,' I pointed out. 'Angel is supposed to be as well.'

'She's coming,' Morris assured me. 'But I don't see there's any need for unpleasantness, Hannah. We've come to an agreement, so why don't we let bygones be bygones?'

'Maybe so,' Hannah answered him. 'But when I say a girl's going to get her arse smacked, I mean she's going to get her arse smacked. Never take back a punishment, that's what I say.'

'Good advice that,' Hudson Staebler agreed. 'The best.'

'So how about it?' Hannah demanded.

'I have no idea why you are asking me,' Morris replied. 'If you think Amber needs to be spanked, then spank her. In fact, yes, good idea. I'm sure it will get her in good fettle for the game.'

Hannah gave a grunt, perhaps not sure whether to take offence at Morris's manner or not. Then he spoke to me.

'All right, one before, one after, or who's to know it's two? Come here.'

'No, look . . .' I began, only to break off as I was sent staggering forward by a firm push.

Stupidly I turned to see who'd done it, and Hannah immediately had me by my wrist. It was Melody, grinning. I was led away, bleating in protest, to where Maggie was already bringing a squat stool forward so that I could be punished where everyone could see. My sense of consternation was already burning in my head as the onlookers turned to see what was going on. Each and every one of them was immediately rewarded with the view of me being hauled unceremoniously across Fat Hannah's lap and my already inadequate skirt being flipped up to expose my bottom, fat and pink and bare in the cool November sunlight.

Somebody laughed, then another, and more guffaws erupted as her hand came down on my bum, hard enough to make me squeak and ensure that absolutely everybody was now watching. I was already near to tears as my bottom cheeks began to bounce and my legs started to kick behind me, in frustration as much as in pain. Not that it didn't hurt – each hard smack flooded my flesh with hot pain – but being done in public immediately before my game with Mel was just so completely unfair.

Yet Hannah had a firm grip around my waist and there was absolutely nothing I could do but lie there, wriggling pathetically as I was spanked, outdoors and bare-bottom in front of maybe seventy people. Soon I'd started to snivel, then to cry openly, only for Hannah to stop just as I'd begun to get snotty.

'That will do,' she said, and leant down so that only I could hear. 'Not just to punish you, but to keep it in your head what happens to girls who break their promises. Remember, you get another one later.'

I was grimacing as I stood up, thinking of the trouble I was in. My immediate future was going to be one long string of spankings and humiliations, probably far more than I'd ever given Kay – and she actively wanted it. Yet there was nothing to be done and I could only start back towards the plate, knowing just how pathetic I looked as I wiped my tears, rubbed at each smarting buttock in turn and tried to sniff up the piece of snot hanging from my nose. Hudson Staebler was smiling and had clearly enjoyed the view, but at least he had the decency to lend me a handkerchief. I accepted it gratefully and cleaned myself up as he took a coin from his pocket.

'Heads,' Mel called as he flipped it. Then she craned forward to look as he turned it up on the back of his hand.

'Tails it is,' he told us. 'Amber, you're up – unless you want to put Melody in?'

'I'll bat,' I said after a moment of hesitation.

'You also get to choose who picks the first forfeit,' he told me, indicating where the five girls were now standing together beside Morris.

I glanced at the girls. Mel and I had agreed to play the first two games more or less fairly, so I had no idea if I'd be giving or receiving. Sophie was out of the question, sure to choose something as filthy and painful as she could get away with just to be certain that whoever got it took it out on her later on. Angel would do the same, more or less, but out of pure sadism. Kay liked to see me punished but wouldn't choose anything too horrible, while Harmony took the same attitude as her sister. Annabelle would be the mildest of all, unless she was sure that Mel would be dishing it out to me.

'Annabelle,' I called.

'You got it,' Hudson replied as she started forward. 'Annabelle, what's it to be?'

Annabelle shot a worried look at Mel and I was sure I caught the faintest of nods in response. Evidently Mel intended to play her best at first, no doubt because she wanted to humiliate me before getting the tables turned on her.

'Well . . . she's just been spanked,' Annabelle began, but I interrupted her.

'What makes you so sure I'm going to lose?'

Annabelle bit her lip but Melody just laughed.

'Make it a good one, Annabelle, something she'll hate.'

I folded my arms across my chest, trying to look stern – not easy with my bottom showing red beneath the hem of my uniform skirt. Annabelle hesitated a moment, then spoke up.

'She can . . . she can play the rest of the game topless, and . . . and in nipple clamps.'

'I don't have any nipple clamps,' I pointed out.

'I do,' Annabelle answered, and pulled her jumper and top up, exposing her bare breasts.

Her nipples were clamped, each fleshy bud caught in the jaws of tiny jewelled crocodile clips, joined to each other by a slim silver chain. I winced, imagining the teeth biting into the sensitive flesh of my nipples and decided to play as well as I could.

'Sounds good to me,' Melody said. 'OK, Amber, prepare to be taken down!'

She walked to the pitcher's mound, tossing the ball in her hand and brimful of confidence. I took the bat from Hudson and went to the plate, trying not to think of the way my bare red bottom stuck out under my skirt as I took position. Mel was the better thrower, but I was sure I could bat just as well, so I'd laid out the field to leave the pitcher throwing into the low winter sun. Mel realised this immediately, tugging her visor down to shade her eyes. I braced myself as she pulled her arm back and swung. I felt my bat catch the ball with a satisfying smack, sending it not merely beyond the ring but in among the carnies, who had to jump quickly back.

'One,' Hudson confirmed and made a mark on his card.

Mel threw again, and again I managed to knock the ball well clear of the ring. She was starting to look annoyed, the more so after I'd driven her third throw right back at her so that she was forced to duck. The fourth I missed, the fifth went in among the carnies again, causing Fat Hannah to yell out that if I did it again I was going back over her knee. The threat completely ruined my concentration and I missed the next, and two more.

'Strike one!' Staebler called.

I forced myself to concentrate and caught the next ball perfectly, to send it clean over the hedge. That made five points, and six with the next. Mel had begun to take me seriously, and had me out again on nine, then for the third time on twelve. I stepped off the plate, moderately pleased with my score but still thinking of the bite of steel teeth on nipple flesh.

'You're up!' Staebler called as we swapped places, and the uncertainty in Mel's eyes had me smiling as she threw the ball to me.

Despite my spanking, or perhaps because of it I was playing far better than the day before. Melody was still warming up but I'd had that across Fat Hannah's knee, and I hurled my first ball down so fast that she barely realised it had gone past her. The second went the same way, but the third clipped her bat, rising in a lazy arc that ended in my hands.

'Strike one,' Staebler said, and for all his reputation for fairness there was a hint of disappointment in his voice.

Mel managed to pick up her game for her second turn, scoring five before she was out, and six for the third. It was not enough, and as Hudson called her third strike her mouth had begun to work in consternation. I was grinning, and clicked my fingers for Annabelle, pointing at the ground beside me. She came, still glancing at Mel for permission, but getting ignored as she knelt down.

'Hands on your head, Annabelle,' I told her as she began to lift her clothes. 'I'm giving the orders just now.'

'Yes, Miss Amber,' she answered, a response that I was sure would cost her a hot bottom, if not more, later.

I pulled up her top and carefully detached each clip from her nipples. Annabelle winced as they came off, and each little bud stayed looking painfully engorged, which was just how I wanted Mel's to be. Taking the clamps, I walked to where she still stood disconsolately on the plate, the bat dangling from her hand.

'Topless, I think your slave said,' I reminded her. 'Then put your hands on your head.'

Mel gave a mild grimace but quickly pulled her top up, spilling out her impressive chest, with each heavy brown breast topped by a big nipple of yet darker flesh. The cool air – or something – had got to her, because both her nipples had begun to rise, poking up into inviting little humps. She had put her hands on her head, reluctantly, and to see her bare and submissive was making my heart hammer as I came close. I took one plump brown globe in my hand and squeezed gently, bringing her nipple into prominence, then to full erection as I pinched it.

'Good girl,' I told her, pulling her nipple out between my forefinger and thumb. 'There, now you're nice and stiff. Hold still.'

I opened the jaws of the clamp, holding it wide to make sure she could take in what was about to be done to her.

'I thought we'd agreed . . . ouch! Amber!' Mel said, just as I released the clamp. I grinned as I watched the tiny jaws dig into her flesh. 'I thought we'd agreed to take the game easy?'

'I hate having my nipples clamped,' I told her. 'Hold still, will you?'

'You wait,' she told me as I lifted her other breast.

'I'm sure you get bigger every time I play with you,' I told her, squeezing her boob to pop the nipple out and applying a pinch.

'You're one to talk!' she answered me, biting her lip as I allowed the clamp to close on her second nipple.

Mel was done, her full brown breasts linked by the silver chain, looking very pretty and very submissive. Her boobs were sure to bounce and swing as she played, which was going to make it difficult for her. Hudson Staebler had watched Mel clamped with unconcealed delight and now he spoke up.

'Who's your forfeit girl, Melody?'

'Kay,' Mel answered without hesitation. 'Kay, come here!'

Kay ran out to us, her smile shy and a little mischievous as she spoke out.

'I think the loser should lick the winner's bottom.'

I felt my stomach tighten. We'd agreed the forfeit in advance, but I'd been thinking of having Melody lick my bottom, which would have been ecstasy in front of so many people. Now it looked like it might be me licking hers, and I could already hear the carnies laughing as my face was smothered between those meaty brown bum cheeks. Yet if I won, I'd have to take whatever Harmony and Angel chose. Both knew how things were fixed, and both would make me suffer. Maybe it was best to lick.

'Ass-licking it is,' Hudson called out, loud enough to make sure that the entire audience could hear. 'You're up, Mel.'

She took her place on the plate and I went back to the pitcher's mound. Mel looked comic with her top off and her breasts lolling forward as she got ready, which might have put me off. She caught my first ball squarely, sending it well outside the circle, and the next. On the third she made a mistake and it went almost vertically upwards, allowing me a simple catch. Her second innings took her to six and her third to ten, leaving me with a reasonable target that I still wasn't sure if I should try to beat.

I needn't have bothered. Now Mel was throwing for all she was worth, fast and on ever-changing lines. I was out once before I'd even managed to score, and caught for the second on just three. By then I'd decided I might as well lose anyway, only to send my first attempt at a deliberate miss backwards off the bat and over the circle. That was still only four, and I was resigned to licking Melody's bottom, and soon, as I managed to drive the next ball right at her and got caught out.

Mel raised her hands in triumph and came forward, grinning and swinging her hips. I dropped my bat and got down on my knees, not waiting for her order. But she had already stopped midway down the pitch, where she turned her back to me and stuck out her bottom, full and brown and meaty beneath the hem of her skirt.

'Crawl to me, Amber,' she told me. 'Come and lick me clean.'

I had no choice but to go down on all fours and do as I was told, crawling up behind her. As I drew close Mel pushed her bottom out further, making her cheeks part to show off her anus, darker even than the surrounding flesh, a glistening black pouch of meat – and clogged with little bits of pink lavatory paper that I was about to have to lick up. She was looking back at me and she laughed as she saw the expression on my face.

'You might have wiped!' I hissed as I drew close.

'I did,' she pointed out. 'Now come on, lick me.'

Every single person there was watching as I steeled myself to put my face between Mel's bottom cheeks. Some were laughing at me, especially the carnies, who obviously thought that one woman being made to lick another's bottom clean was hilarious. I didn't. I thought it was disgusting and one of the deepest, most intimate acts possible, an act of utter submission, which I was now performing, my face pushed forward against the firm meaty cheeks, and between them to the puckered musky black star of her anus into which I poked my tongue.

Mel sighed in pleasure as my tongue began to flick in her tight hole. Her hand came back, locking in my hair to pull me tighter in, smothering me in plump bottom flesh and her thick feminine scent. I began to give up, assuaging my feelings by telling myself that I was being forced to do it as I burrowed my tongue in, licking up the little bits of loo paper. As my mouth began to fill with an acrid taste I knew I'd surrendered completely.

My hands went to Mel's bum cheeks, spreading them in my face as I began to lap inside her crease. Again she sighed and began to rub my face against her bottom, but I didn't need any more encouragement. I was enjoying cleaning her, licking around her ring and in deep, eager to be made to do a thorough job of it. She laughed at me for the state I was in, sending a powerful shock of deep and erotic humiliation through me.

'Lick it all up, Amber,' she taunted. 'Come on, get your tongue in my hole. Taste my shit and swallow it down. Why don't you frig off while you do it?'

I could have done it easily if it hadn't been for the leering, laughing carnies. But I wasn't that far down, not yet. Instead, Mel's voice brought me down to earth a little but not enough to stop me doing as I was told and swallowing before giving her bottom-hole a last kiss and rocking back on my haunches. My mouth was full of specks of rolled-up loo paper and thick with the taste of her anus, keeping me firmly in a state of submission as I stood up, so that I had to force myself to concentrate on continuing with the game. Fortunately Hudson had a flask of spirits, some of which he poured into the flask's cap and passed to me.

'Who's it to be?' he asked as I swallowed the smooth rich bourbon down, an exquisite taste after Mel's bumhole.

'Harmony,' I told him, having already decided that I was going to lose.

'You're up, then,' he said and turned to the crowd. 'Harmony!'

Harmony stepped out from the crowd, smiling and smacking her palm against her sister's in congratulation. I took my place on the plate and picked up my bat again, swinging it as Harmony and Mel whispered together.

'What's it to be?' Hudson demanded.

'Six of the cane,' Harmony answered.

I winced, but from Angel it would have been twelve. It was definitely time to lose.

Unfortunately Mel had evidently decided the same, pretending that her shoulder hurt and throwing balls so easy I could hardly fail to hit them. I was wishing I'd thought of the trick first as my score quickly began to rise. It was obviously better for her to do it, as she had to lose, but that did nothing for my feelings.

I tried to miss. I tried to give her easy catches. Still my score increased, past ten, past twenty, and it was obviously pointless not to play well, or Hudson Staeble would be sure to realise that something was amiss. I began to bat seriously – and promptly struck out. Then I put up a catch that even Melody couldn't avoid. With one out already that left me on twenty-four.

To watch Mel bat was painful. She grimaced. She winced. She rubbed her shoulder. As I was so far ahead of her it was hardly worth trying to let her score and so I threw as well as I could. She'd scored precisely three before she struck out for the third and last time. I'd won the innings, the right to cane her, and whatever horrible punishment Angel was likely to choose.

Or had I? What mattered was that I won, not that I won by three innings to two. Having faked her hurt shoulder Mel could hardly start playing her best again, and if I won the next innings the game was over, three to one. I could even choose Sophie to give the forfeit.

'How's the shoulder, Melody?' Hudson was asking as the three of us came together.

'Not too bad,' Melody answered, rubbing it and putting on a face.

'If you want to call it a draw?' he suggested.

'No,' she answered. 'I can still win.'

'You're a brave girl,' he told her. 'Better touch your toes, then.'

Mel pulled a face but bent down, her skirt turned up behind, as Kay ran out to us with one of my canes. I took it and got behind Mel, making sure that everyone had a good view of her full dark bottom as I laid the cane across it, tapped twice and gave her a carefully aimed hard stroke. She barely cried out, and I gave her the second one harder still, and lower, catching her across the swell of her cheeks. This time she yelped, and the next, filling me with cruel excitement for her pain and exposure.

She was nicely decorated, with three purple-black welts showing on her dark skin, evenly spaced. I gave her the fourth a little higher, the fifth higher still, each time making her cry and gasp. The sixth I laid diagonally across the others, marking her with a neat five-bar gate across her bottom, marking her plainly as a girl who'd been caned by an expert.

I was clapped for my efforts, mainly by Morris's people, who appreciated not only skill but seeing

Melody get punished for a change. Hudson Staebler bent close to inspect the welts before addressing me again.

'So, Amber, who's next to choose?'

'Sophie,' I answered him.

Mel gave me a puzzled look and I smiled back. Hudson called for Sophie to come out. She was rubbing her hands with glee as she approached.

'You two have been so mean to me,' she said happily as she reached us. 'So mean, and I know you'll be mean to me again, so . . . so, the loser has to pee in front of everyone, into a potty, and the winner gets to give her an enema with the pee, and then she's made to –'

'One forfeit, Sophie,' Hudson pointed out, laughing.

Sophie looked crestfallen for a moment. Then she spoke again.

'The loser gets an enema with her own pee, OK? I've got the potty and a turkey baster.'

Mel and I shared a look. It was about what I'd expected, but to actually think of peeing in a potty in front of a crowd and having the contents squirted up my bottom really brought it home. Not that it was going to happen to me. It was going to happen to Melody, which was an entirely different matter. I turned back to Sophie.

'OK, you little pervert,' I sighed.

'Yes!' she crowed. 'I'll get the gear.'

I shrugged and smiled for Mel as Sophie ran off.

'You're up, Amber,' Hudson said.

I went to the plate, feeling well pleased with myself. Mel climbed up onto the mound opposite me, spent a moment limbering up her supposedly hurt shoulder and threw. I swung, meaning to hit the ball clean over the hedge, but missed completely and so unexpectedly that I lost my balance and sat down hard on the ground. There was a ripple of laughter from the carnies as the ball was thrown back, and Mel was grinning at me.

'Curve ball,' she said. 'Try another?'

Hudson gave a wry chuckle. I had no idea what they meant, only that I had no intention of taking a pee enema in public. This time I put everything into concentrating on the ball, and missed. I missed the next one too and so had gone one strike down with no score. Mel was grinning like the Cheshire cat and I was beginning to panic, with my bottom-hole twitching and my bladder suddenly uncomfortable. Again Mel threw, and at last I managed to hit it – straight up in the air to fall so easily into her hands that she barely had to move to catch it.

I was two down with no score and I could already hear the carnies laughing as my pee squirted from my fanny or the nozzle of the turkey baster was eased up my bum. Near to panic, I swung at the ball the moment Mel threw, far too early. Hudson's call of 'strike one' seemed to come from a thousand miles away and I was praying as I readied myself again. At last I got a proper connection, sending the ball soaring high over the heads of the crowd and onto the Razorback land, which left me wishing I'd painted more circles for higher scores.

Mel waited calmly until Gavin brought the ball back, her arms folded under her bare breasts. I braced myself, knowing that I had a mountain to climb, and managed to knock the next ball well outside the circle again. The next I missed. The next I hit but not hard enough to score. The next I caught well, sending it high into the air over Mel's head, forcing her to run well out beyond the ring – where she caught the ball neatly.

'Out!' Hudson called.

I had two points. My body felt numb as I climbed up onto the pitcher's mound, except for my bottom-hole, which was twitching uncontrollably. Mel stood poised, her shoulder apparently no longer a problem, her stare locked on mine as I threw. My ball was sent soaring into the trees. I missed catching the next by an inch as it was

213

driven back at me. The next she missed. The next rose high, a perfect shot, to land among the carnies – and I'd lost.

The smile on Mel's face was pure evil as she pointed to the ground a little way to the side.

'Kneel down,' she ordered. 'Bum to the crowd.'

I went, defeated, onto my knees in a rude squat as Sophie ran out, laughing. She had the potty and the baster – a huge thing that looked like it was designed more for ostrich than for turkey – and a pot of anal lubricant. Mel took all three, but Sophie stayed, smiling down at me as the potty was eased under my bum. I closed my eyes, trying not to think of the ogling men as my skirt was turned up to expose my bottom fully. They could see everything: my fanny, my bumhole, and the pee squirting out to splash in the potty as I let go.

A lot of the spectators laughed, some gave gasps of shock or disgust, others clapped, all of them watching as I urinated in full view, my piddle gurgling and splashing into the pot beneath me. My bumhole wanted to open too, forcing me to squeeze it shut and leave my pee erupting in little jets, some of the stream going to the side to wet my fanny lips and run down one thigh.

Mel watched calmly until I'd finished before reaching down to slap my cheeks and make the last few drops fall into the potty. I looked back, pouting despite myself as she inserted the turkey baster into my puddle, the cool metal touching between my bottom cheeks as she sucked the pee up, as much as would go.

'Stick it out,' she ordered. 'Right out.'

I obeyed, lifting my bottom and pulling my back in to make my bum cheeks open fully. Mel took the pot of lubricant that Sophie had given her, twisted the lid free and pushed in a finger to bring up a fat blob of glistening white ointment. I gasped as she pushed it between my cheeks, cold and slippery against my bumhole, and again as she eased a finger in, working it deep up inside my rectum where she began to wiggle it about.

All I could do was sob out my feelings as I was lubricated. Mel made a thorough job of it, slipping a second finger in and pushing both digits in and out for a while to make sure that I was fully open and relaxed. Only then did she pull out, leaving me gaping behind, my anus an easy receptacle for the nozzle of the baster.

Up it went, cold and hard as Mel pushed it in deep, suddenly warm as she pressed home the plunger and my bottom was filled with my own pee. I cried out as I felt it, not in pain, but in raw emotion. It felt lovely, hot and heavy, making me want to squeeze my cheeks and wriggle my toes as my rectum began to swell inside me. But the humiliation of having it done at all was agony, never mind having it done in public.

'Why not frig off now?' Sophie suggested gleefully.

I burst into tears, choking with sobs for what had been done to me. Yet I urgently wanted to masturbate, knowing that I'd had perhaps a pint of my own piddle forced up my bumhole with maybe a hundred people watching. Not that I could have held it during orgasm, but to squirt it all out as I came would have been the final agony, more than I could have borne.

'Better expel into your potty,' Mel whispered as she eased the nozzle from my bumhole.

'Yes, so everyone can see!' Sophie chortled. 'Go on, Amber, let it all out – do it!'

She finished with a giggle of delight and disgust. I couldn't do it. Clutching my cheeks and squeezing my slippery bumhole as tight as I could I jumped up and ran for the house, biting my lip in consternation and because of the pressure in my swollen belly and against my anus. Gales of loud Irish laughter followed me, growing louder still as I tripped and went down on all fours, losing control of my ring at the shock. My bum stuck up high as my enema exploded from my gaping anus in a high dirty arc of discoloured liquid.

I heard it splash on the ground behind me as I cried out in unbearable shame. The onlookers just laughed all the louder, and were still laughing as I continued to expel, too broken to care any more as my piddle squirted and oozed from my open bottom-hole to trickle down my fanny and down my thighs, dripping from my pubic hair and soiling my skirt. Numb with reaction, I stayed down until it had all come out and until at last I heard Melody's voice.

'Quit playing the fool, Amber. We have to finish the match.'

'Sorry,' I managed to mutter, such a stupid thing to say when she'd just given me a public enema.

She helped me up at least, and took me into the yard to wash down. She also took my skirt off so that as I came back into the paddock I was stark naked between my top and my stripy socks, bum and fanny on full show. But really I was too far gone to care. Mel was talking gently as she led me towards the plate, where Hudson Staebler was standing with Angel.

'Remember to win, yes?'

I nodded, struggling to pull myself together. It wasn't easy. The only way to cope with my feelings was to be appreciated sexually, to be watched as I came off under my own fingers, maybe to be made to lick Mel's bottom again as I came, maybe to be put out for fucking by anyone who came by – anything, so long as they found my degradation exciting. The alternative I couldn't bear.

'. . . going to take a bit of beating,' Angel was saying. 'Um . . . how about the loser gets a fucking from that guy Gerry's . . .'

'No,' Mel said firmly before she could finish.

'What, then?' she demanded. 'OK, OK, I know: the loser gets her cunt lips sewn up.'

'Angel!'

'There's no pleasing some people . . . all right, seeing as we're here, the loser gets hunted down, and the winner and the first five to touch her can do as they like with her.'

Mel bit her lip, but nodded. I followed suit as Hudson glanced at me and I took the bat from him. I was shaking so badly that I could barely hold it, and nothing seemed quite real any more. People were clustering around Morris's table, and I knew they weren't betting on me. But they seemed to be miles away and quite irrelevant to my situation. All I could think of was that I'd just been given an enema with my own pee, in front of so many people, and all my blood seemed to have gone to my sex in response, leaving me weak and dizzy as I stepped up to the plate.

'Let's play ball!' Hudson called out. But as Mel began to flex her arm I could only think of how it would feel to suck his cock again.

The ball came at me, straight and fast. I missed completely, swinging the bat long after it had gone by.

'Strike one!' Hudson called as I tried to force myself to think straight.

Again Mel wound up. Again the ball came, and by some miracle I hit it, not well, but she failed to react in time for a catch and it landed beyond the circle. One point. That was the best I had to give. I hit the next too, but so badly that Mel couldn't possibly drop it.

As she readied herself again I was trying to force myself to remember what I was supposed to be doing. With the first ball it worked and I had one more point, but three later and I'd struck out for the second time. Again I tried to will myself to do it properly, but it was as if my body had turned to jelly. I hit the first, just, and it fell too short for a point. I missed the second, put the third up for an easy catch that Mel somehow managed to fumble, missed, missed again and before I knew it I was out, with a miserable two points.

Fat Hannah Riley was looking at me as I walked forward to swap over with Mel, her expression openly smug. She was going to get her winnings, while I was going to be in trouble with Morris and left to suck cock if I wanted my videos back: a hundred videos, with one of Hannah's men coming in my mouth or over my face to pay for each and every one.

At that thought my adrenalin finally began to pump. I steeled myself. Mel only had to miss, that was all. I hurled the first ball down so fast that she didn't even react. The second she missed completely, and the third. One out.

Again I hurled the ball down with every ounce of my strength. Again Mel missed. The next caught her bat to fly high up behind her and land well over the line. The next she hit too, and again it went high, this time to land safely in my hands. Two out.

Three more balls and I'd be there, the winner. I'd also be over Fat Hannah's knee, but what difference did it make? She spanked me when she pleased anyway. I threw the ball with more determination than ever and grinned as Mel missed it. Two more balls. I threw. She missed. One more ball. I threw, she waved her bat and hit, but not hard, sending the ball up in a lazy arc.

I had to catch the thing and I hurled myself after it, only to realise that it wasn't going to land beyond the circle anyway but just inside. Only it didn't. It hit my arm, bounced and fell just inches beyond the line leaving me staring at it as what I'd done sank in.

We were drawn. Mel could no longer lose. I walked back feeling numb, unable to think at all, and hurled the next ball down with all my strength. She missed, but as the ball was tossed back to me I realised that I now had to let her win or I would be in trouble with both Morris and Hannah. But Mel didn't know that.

I threw feebly. She missed. I tried to make faces at her, not daring to be too obvious in front of Hudson

She took no notice. I threw again, a truly pathetic lob, which she missed.

'Drawn game,' Hudson laughed. 'Well, who'd have thought it?'

I barely heard, dropping to my knees on the pitcher's mound. Everybody was making for Morris's table where he was quickly surrounded by a dense crowd, all talking at once at the tops of their voices. I couldn't face them: I was supposed to run for them so I did, indoors and upstairs where I sat on the bed, fiddling with the baseball bat I'd picked up with some ridiculous notion of defending myself, trying to ignore my desperate need to masturbate over what they were going to do to me. When the doorbell went downstairs I was nearly sick, only to relax as I heard Kay's voice and then stiffen abruptly as Morris Rathwell answered her. A moment later there were footsteps on the stairs, heavy male footsteps. Kay spoke again.

'Please, Morris, she didn't mean to mess it up!'

He ignored her and a moment later the door was thrown open. I'd never seen Morris genuinely angry before, not with me, but now his eyes were blazing and his fingers were working as he looked down on me. I lowered my gaze and spread my hands in a gesture of helpless pathetic resignation.

'I'm sorry, Morris . . .'

My words broke off in a cry of shock and surprise as he grabbed at me, twisting me across his knees with a single motion, my naked bum stuck high. Before I could so much as bleat out a protest he'd begun to spank me, furiously hard, raining slaps down on my bare cheeks as I kicked in his grip and howled for mercy. All I got was my hairbrush, snatched up from my bedside table and applied to my bottom with all his strength.

It hurt more than his hand, far more, setting me blubbering and beating my fists on the bed in furious, pointless remonstrance. I just got more strokes as he took the full weight of his anger out on my bottom, stopping only when the brush slipped from his hand to crash against the door. Kay had come in and stood looking down on me with her hand to her mouth as I babbled out apologies through my tears.

Morris didn't bother to answer me and kept his grip. I heard Kay squeak and felt something round and hard press between my legs. It was the end of the baseball bat, spreading the mouth of my fanny so wide that my protest came out as a wordless grunt, breaking to a cry of pain as I stretched to take it in.

'No, Morris – you'll split me! Oh God!'

He'd twisted the bat, and it was in me, well up, which was how it stayed as he dropped me on the bed to lie gasping with the thick handle protruding obscenely from my well-stuffed cunt.

'That's just for starters,' he snapped, and strode out of the room.

Nine

I knelt on the sand in the middle of Hannah Riley's Big Top, my hands folded in my lap, my head hung down. I was dressed in Buffo's clown suit, the peppermint-striped material loose around my waist but awkwardly tight over my bottom and across my breasts. One change had been made: a flap had been added at the rear to allow access to my bum cheeks. It was fastened with big green buttons. My face was made up in Buffo's style too, painted white and red and black, with a huge drooping mouth and sorry-looking eyes. His absurd green wig was on my head.

Hannah had kept her promise. I would be unrecognisable in a video that was to be made portraying my shame, to be sold by both Hannah and Morris, as I was made to buy back the previous one at a price of one session of oral sex for each and every copy. That meant sucking cock for twenty-eight male carnies, seven of the men from Razorback Paintball, and some of Morris's regulars to make up the numbers, including Mr Proheroe – thirty-one of this last category in all. Some of them I'd never even met but I was still going to suck their cocks: sixty-six cocks. Hannah counted too, and Maggie, and other women from the circus, my own friends as well, which amounted to another thirty-four, making a total of one hundred people, all entitled to use my mouth for their pleasure.

I'd barely put up a fight, listening to them hammer out the terms of my degradation as I knelt on the floor of my own kitchen, nude but for my shoes and socks, my mouth thick with the taste of come. Once Morris had cooled down a bit he'd come back into my room to apologise for spanking me in anger and sticking my baseball bat up me. I'm been in such a state that I'd ended up apologising in turn. He'd made me suck his cock to say sorry properly.

The fight had come later, after I'd come down from the state I'd been left in after the game. I'd tried every possible argument, begging, cajoling, trying to negotiate different terms, anything short of flatly refusing to accept what every single one of them seemed to see as my just deserts. Only Kay had stuck up for me and even she had been doubtful, pointing out that as she had given herself over to my discipline I should accept what was coming to me in the same way. At that I'd given in.

They'd been laughing and joking by the time they'd agreed what to do with me. Morris had even patted Hannah on the back. A few days later it had all been set up, my hundred molesters chosen, my fate sealed. I was fairly sure that Morris's people had paid too, prostituting me to add yet one more touch to my humiliation, which was about to begin.

Gerry had closed the flap of the tent and sealed it against intrusion, with his great sleek Alsatian beside him to make doubly sure. Maggie arrived carrying a big painted drum, which she set down in front of me. I looked up to find her fat slovenly face split by a wide cruel grin. A cigarette hung from one corner of her mouth, and she flicked a maggot of ash into my ridiculous green wig before she spoke.

'You've still got a spanking coming to you first – one of Hannah's hairbrush specials.'

I nodded, not even bothering to protest. If I was going to have to suck cock it would be far, far easier to

accept it once my bottom had been warmed up for me.
Hannah would be first, putting me straight to my knees
once I'd been spanked. Morris would come next, Kay
last by my own request. The others would be done by
lottery, with Sean as Baffo the clown drawing the
tickets, and it was he who came next as Maggie waddled
away. He capered back and forth with a ridiculous top
hat in one hand, three feet tall at least and decorated
with red and green stripes. Next came Mick, stark naked
but for a pair of outsize underpants and huge red shoes,
looking affronted as well as absurd, but no more absurd
than I did in his costume and make-up.

Hannah followed, massive in a bright red dress, the
great swells of her belly and breasts and hips moving
beneath the cotton, her fat face set in smug satisfaction,
one hand lifted in response to the claps and cheers of
the carnies. In her hand she held her hairbrush, the same
one she had spanked me with the first time we'd met. I
swallowed and my bottom cheeks tightened in the frilly
panties I'd been put in under my clown's costume. I
looked up as Hannah approached me, showing off to
the camera by smacking the hairbrush against the palm
of her hand. She sat down, making a lap for me, which
she patted as she spoke.

'Over you go – let's get that big fat bottom of yours
warm, shall we?'

'Yes, please, and I'm sorry,' I answered her.

'Sorry for what?' she demanded.

'Sorry for being a bad girl,' I told her. 'Sorry for
resenting my spankings. Sorry for being so stuck-up.
Sorry for thinking . . . for thinking I'm too good to go
down for you, and . . . to suck cock for your men.'

The last part was hard to get out at all, and my voice
had sunk to a whisper as I said it.

'I beg your pardon?' Hannah demanded. 'What was
that you said?'

'I . . . I said I'm sorry for . . . for thinking I'm too

223

good for you ... to good to go down for you and to suck cock for your men ... but, but it's not fair! I've never been like that, and it's just not true, and it's not fair! It's not fair!'

I was shouting, the script they'd made me learn completely forgotten in the agony of my emotion. But Hannah just laughed and reached forward to take a firm hold on the scruff of my neck, once more hauling me over her knee.

'I can see you need this,' she laughed. 'And you are going to get it, again and again, until you learn to do as you are told, and until you learn to like it!'

As Hannah spoke she had begun to fumble with the buttons holding the rear flap of my clown suit shut. One came undone, then the other, and then the flap had dropped loose, exposing the seat of my big pink frillies, bulging from the open back as she brought her knee up to bring my bottom into full prominence.

'Well, boys and girls,' she called out. 'Do you want to see this? Shall I show her bum, all big and bare for her spanking?'

Immediately they were calling for me to be stripped behind and cameras were zooming in on my bottom. Hannah's hand closed on the waistband of my frillies and the tears began to trickle down my face as the undergarment was slowly pulled down. Every instant and every detail was recorded as she unveiled me, my crease and cheeks exposed inch by inch until the full chubby swell of my bottom was out of my pants. More, my frillies were pushed down into the baggy legs of my clown suit to make sure my fanny lips showed behind.

'Not so proud now, are you?' Hannah chuckled. 'Not with your cunt on show. Let's do that again, boys, and get some close-ups.'

She pulled my frillies back up and buttoned my clown suit. I was forced to go through the whole agonising process again, and again, and yet again, my frillies going up and down like a yo-yo as they shot my exposure from different angles and distances. Soon enough I was beating my fists on the sand in a rage of frustration as they filmed my fanny from just inches away, recording every tiny secret wrinkle of flesh. But at least I managed to keep quiet until Hannah spoke again.

'Hang on, boys, I forgot to show off her arsehole. We'll have to start again.'

I screamed, even as my bottom cheeks were hauled apart and my anus was put on show, but that wasn't enough for them. My frillies came up again, my buttons were fastened. Then my buttons were unfastened and my frillies pulled down, and again, and again, only this time at the end of each exposure Hannah would haul my cheeks wide, displaying the rude pink and brown hole between them to the cameras, so that when they zoomed in it was not just my fanny that they recorded in detail, but everything, every wrinkle and crevice, so close that my anal star must have filled the entire screen. All the while my frustration was growing stronger, my sobs more bitter. But at last it was done and Hannah was laying the hairbrush across my cheeks to spank me – only for Sean to speak up.

'Don't forget her titties, Mother Riley. After all, this is Madame Boobfontaine, so her titties must be out, no?'

'You're right,' Hannah answered. 'Sorry, boys, we'll get it right in the end.'

Again I screamed in frustration, but there was no apology for me. I was told to shut up and then I was put through the whole agonising process again, only this time with the front of my clown suit unbuttoned and my breasts flopped out for Hannah to grope and slap. Then they were left swinging fat and heavy under my chest with one camera still on them as the exposure of my bottom was filmed again, and yet again, until at last I could stand it no more.

'Just spank me!' I screamed. 'Spank me, you horrible old woman!'

'Temper, temper,' Hannah joked as she brought the hairbrush down across my bottom with a meaty smack, sending a jolt of pain through me and instantly making me wish that I'd kept my mouth shut.

Hannah chuckled as she adjusted me over her lap, bringing my bottom up a little more so that my bumhole would show without her having to pull my cheeks open. The cameramen moved back a little, one to my side to record the full view of my punishment and the expressions on my face, another behind me to make sure that no rude detail was missed. Again the brush landed on my bottom and it had begun, just pats really so that I could speak clearly.

'You really do need this, don't you?' she asked. 'You need this regularly, don't you?'

I was supposed to admit it but I couldn't, not with the cameras there to record my every word. Instead I gave a defiant shake of my head. But Hannah merely laughed and began to spank a little harder, setting me whimpering and gasping as she went on.

'No? What a shame, 'cause you're going to get it anyway. What shall we say, once a fortnight over Hannah's lap? How about that?'

'No,' I managed to gasp and the smacks immediately got harder.

'You need it,' she said. 'You may not want it, but you do need it. Now, come on, admit it. You need Ma Riley to pull your pants down now and again, don't you? And you need your big arse spanked now and again, don't you?'

Again I shook my head, my lips pursed against the pain as the smacks grew harder still. My bottom had begun to bounce and I was fighting not to start making a display of myself. Not that I had any modesty left, and not much pride, not with what I was showing to the cameras. But it still mattered.

'Going to be a brat, are you?' Hannah demanded, her grip on my waist tightening. 'No more play, then. Let's see how you get on with a proper old-fashioned hairbrush spanking.'

She had laid into me even as she spoke, whacking the brush down on my poor burning bottom with all her strength. Any pathetic ideas that I might have had about resistance vanished with the first smack. I began to kick and howl and squirm, my fists beating a furious tattoo on the sand and my boobs bouncing wildly and slapping together. The more fuss I made the harder she spanked, belabouring my bottom with the brush until I was crazy with pain and outrage, screaming and blubbering, thrashing my limbs and shaking my hair.

It stopped suddenly and I was left gasping out my feelings, my entire body shaking violently. Once more Hannah adjusted me, hooking one leg around my ankle to spread me out behind, with my frillies taut between my thighs and my fanny open to the audience, my bumhole too, winking between my cheeks as my pain slowly faded to be replaced by heat. Again the hairbrush began its work on my bottom but no longer were the strokes hard. Hannah now applied firm pats to the chubby tuck of my cheeks and across it, right on my sweet spot. I'd been beaten – now she was getting me ready.

I could hear the crowd, full of happy laughter as they watched me being warmed up for sex, each and every one of them waiting their turn to use me once I was done. To my utter consternation I found myself wanting it, wanting to be made to suck cock and lick fanny, just the way a spanked girl should. The word 'no' burst from my lips in a last feeble effort at resistance, and then I'd broken, sticking my bottom up to receive the smacks, eager and wanton.

Hannah chuckled as she saw, but continued to work on me as before, applying the hairbrush firmly but gently to my sweet spot to bring me up to helpless arousal. I was going to get it anyway and made no effort to fight until she spoke again.

'Pop it in, Sean.'

I looked up in shock as Sean's huge clown boots appeared in front of me. I found myself staring right at his straining cock, which had been pushed at my face before I could do more than squeal in hopeless protest. An extra-hard smack made me gasp and then my mouth was filled, my eyes popping and my cheeks bulging as he thrust the full length of his prick right down my throat. Still Hannah spanked me, now laying into my bottom with a will as the crowd cheered and stamped and clapped their approval to see me have my throat fucked by Baffo the clown.

Sean came in moments, right down my throat, forcing me to swallow. But I wasn't fast enough. I began to choke, my throat spasming around his cockhead, something I was sure he'd done on purpose, a truly horrid trick to play on any girl. A mixture of spunk and snot exploded from my nose as I went into a coughing fit, unable to breathe and still being spanked, so that I'd begun to thrash around in panic before he pulled out.

Sean danced away, laughing and waving his spit-wet cock at the crowd in triumph and glee, and at last Hannah stopped spanking. I was gasping for breath, unable to speak, clinging on to her leg until she gently detached me to ease me up a little, turning my face to hers.

'Do you need it?' she asked.

My resistance had been spanked out of me and I nodded. I was shaking all over and snivelling badly, snot and spunk bubbles frothing from my nose and dribbling from my mouth. My vision was hazy with tears and every last scrap of my dignity was gone. I was a little spanked brat, punished and ready to be put to good use by the woman who'd had the courage and power to beat me. Yes, I needed it.

'Do you need it?' she asked again. 'Do you need Hannah to spank your naughty bottom? Tell me.'

'I need it,' I sobbed. And I meant it.

Maybe I hadn't found the woman I really wanted for my discipline. But Hannah had found me, and I was going to get my discipline whether I liked it or not.

'What do you need, and how often? Say it.'

'I . . . I need to be spanked, regularly.'

'Good girl,' she said and ruffled my hair. 'That's better, isn't it, now it's out? Come to Mother.'

Hannah took me in her arms, cradling me against her gigantic breasts. My mouth came open to suckle by instinct, but I was already being guided lower, onto my knees as she began to pull up her dress. Her hand gripped my hair tight, making very sure that I didn't try to get away. I was pulled in underneath her dress as her thighs opened wide and I was faced with the fat bulge of her fanny, hidden beneath stained white panties.

'Pull my knicks aside,' she ordered.

I could only obey. Her hand stayed twisted in my hair as I fumbled her panty crotch open to expose the broad musky gash of her sex. She pulled me in, so suddenly that it made me squeak in surprise, and began to rub my face in the wet mushy flesh between her lips. I could barely breathe, and my feet had started to kick in the sand, drawing an amused chuckle from the cameraman behind me. I thought of how I must look, my head and shoulders hidden under Hannah's dress while my bottom stuck out of the open flap in my clown suit, bare and red, panties down and showing everything as I licked Hannah's fanny.

Not licked, really, although I was trying, with my tongue poking between the fleshy folds of her sex. Mainly she was using my face to masturbate with, her fingers gripping painfully hard in my hair to control me as she rubbed my nose against her big ugly clitoris. She was already groaning and a moment later my head had been pulled up, my mouth pressed to her hard bud. I took the horrid little thing between my lips, sucking, and was immediately rewarded with a long sigh of pleasure. Hannah's thighs squeezed tight around my head as she came, squashing me, and my nose was now pressed so hard to the great hairy bulge of her pubic mound that I was being smothered, completely unable to breathe. My feet had begun to drum on the ground in panic before I was released.

I rocked back, gasping as Hannah spoke.

'Good girl. Now you're going to suck my boys, aren't you?'

I managed a nod, knowing that I had to although I was already in a state. My face was smeared with Hannah's juice as well as with my own snot and Sean's spunk, my jaw was already sore, and I'd pleasured just two of them out of a hundred. Yet there was no towel for me, not even any water, just Morris stepping forward to shake hands with Hannah as they changed places. I found myself pulling a face. They'd sorted themselves out, reaching agreement on everything, but I still ended up having to buy back videos of myself by sucking cock.

Morris sat down, his thighs wide open, his zip already down to reveal purple underpants.

'Spanking club next Friday?' he asked politely as he extracted his cock from his trousers.

'OK,' I answered. Then I took him in my mouth.

I was sucking Morris Rathwell's cock. I was being put on video sucking Morris Rathwell's cock. He'd probably play it at the club, before I was put over some dirty old man's knee for spanking. They always fondled me too, groping and tickling and even sticking fingers in places they had no right to. I knew perfectly well that I'd lose control as well, and end up down on my knees to suck their cocks and let them wank in my mouth, just as Morris had begun to do.

'Mustn't hold up the queue, must we?' he chuckled.

He pulled my head back, his cock jerking in his hand right in front of my face. I closed my eyes just in time as I realised where he was aiming. Hot wet spunk splashed in my face, across my nose and on both eyelids, over my forehead too. Morris was chuckling happily as he wiped his cock on my cheek, then he was gone.

I managed to open one eye a crack, peering out through a veil of Morris's spunk as Baffo drew a ticket from a hat. He called out the number and somebody responded from the audience, a big elderly man who drove one of the lorries. I didn't even know his name and I was going to suck him off and swallow his spunk or take it in my face. It had begun in earnest.

The lorry driver came down to the sand, his cock already in his hand as he reached me. It was big and ugly, with a thick brown foreskin and a bend in the middle. That didn't matter. It went in my mouth and I sucked him off, even stroking on his shaft and squeezing his balls to make sure he was quick. He was, erupting a great gout of semen down my throat so soon and with so little fuss that he took me completely by surprise, making me gag. I was left coughing up spunk down across my boobs and into the sand as he raised his arms in triumph, with Baffo already calling out the next number.

It was another of Hannah's men, another one whom I didn't know, another one whose cock I sucked to erection and then to orgasm, swallowing his spunk like the obedient little tart they'd made me. One of Morris's clients came next, the enormously fat Mr Enos, who took for ever to come and did it in my face. Next was another of the carnies, an old woman who called me a slut when I made her come, and meant it. Another man followed, and another, until my world had become a blur of cocks and balls and spunk, broken only by the occasional fanny as I was made to lick one of the girls.

Only the people I'd already met stood out. Maggie came behind me and gave my bottom a few slaps before putting my face to her fanny. Gavin Bulmer made me deep-throat him and slapped me on the back when he was done to make the spunk come out of my nose. Mick had painted his cock and balls with greasepaint, white and green, smearing it into the mess already on my face and leaving me feeling sick. Little Hannah was cruel, pulling my hair and slapping my face before she made me lick her. Melody made me do her bumhole again and asked the cameraman to come in close to get a shot of my tongue-tip working in her tiny dirty hole.

By then I was masturbating and he filmed that too, coming behind me to zoom in on my bare bum, with my fanny sticking out and my fingers busy between its lips. I was lost and I began to show off, wiggling my bottom and reaching back to tickle my anus and then slip a finger into the tightness of my ring. My tongue was still up Mel's bum, and I came like that to be filmed in orgasm, masturbating my anus as I licked hers.

Mel came first, under her own fingers, then me, wriggling myself onto my hand and pushing my tongue as deep up her bottom as it would go as wave after wave of ecstasy swept through me. Before I'd even come down from that another cock had been stuck in my mouth – a carnie again, as crude and dirty as the others, calling me his bitch and telling me to suck his helmet as he began to wank.

He came in my mouth and made me show his spunk to him on my tongue, which inevitably got filmed. Another man replaced him, and another, but by now no longer knew how many I'd had. Baffo was still calling out the numbers but I had no idea, beyond the obvious ones, who had had me and who was waiting. My face was a mess, plastered with spunk, and m' make-up was smeared into a dirty pink paste. My hair was thick with mess, full of blobs and strings of stick white come. My stomach felt bloated and my mouth was overflowing, goo dribbling down my chin to fall on my tits, which were already filthy where I'd been rubbing it in as I grew excited.

The molesters didn't seem to care, happily fucking my mouth, and when one of them tried to put his cock between my slimy tits I didn't resist at all but held them up for him. He fucked them and came in my cleavage. After that my tits were fair game. I didn't care, holding them up to have cocks rubbed on my nipples and stuck in between, rubbing in the spunk as I licked fanny, and wondering how long it would be before one of those pricks went up my own cunt.

It was Fat Jeff who did me, not even bothering to ask but making me suck him hard and then going behind me to lift my hips into the doggy position and slide himself in up my hole. I took it, his fat belly squashing against my spanked bottom as he fucked me, and when the others saw that I could be used anyway they pleased the whole thing broke down. Fat Jeff had barely spunked over my bottom before another man had replaced him in my mouth. I was sucking too, spit-roasted just as Baffo and Buffo had done with me before.

Now it wasn't just two of them. Half the crowd seemed to be trying to get to me, jostling each other for the right to use my body, most of their cocks already erect. Hands groped at my body, tearing my clown suit wide to get my tits right out and my bum showing properly. Soon it was just a rag around my knees, along with my spunk-sodden frillies. With me bare they really crowded in, hard cocks rubbing against my skin, some even spunking on my back if they couldn't wait their turn.

I struggled bravely to take it, but it really made no difference if I wanted it or not. Cock after cock after cock was thrust into my body – mouth and fanny – load after load after load of spunk was ejaculated into my mouth or over my face, up my vagina or over my bum and between my cheeks, to leave my anus slimy and fuckable.

Any one of them could have done it, but it was Mr Protheroe who chose to bugger me. Most of the carnies were done by the time he got behind me, shuffling up on his knees and rubbing himself in my slimy crease to get his cock hard. I was sucking another man's prick and never even realised that it was him until he spoke, at the same moment as he pushed the head of his cock into my bottom-hole.

'One up the bum from an old friend, my dear?'

'Pig!' I managed to splutter as the man in my mouth pulled out.

I didn't try to stop Mr Protheroe, far from it. My mouth went wide in ecstasy and was promptly filled with spunk. My nose was held and I was forced to swallow as my bum ring spread to accommodate Mr Protheroe's cock. My mouth was filled yet again and my cheeks were bulging as I struggled to suck at the same time that my bottom was forced. Protheroe's cock eased in up my rectum bit by bit until at last his balls met my empty fanny.

Buggered, and sucking too, I was only dimly aware that they were the only two still with me. I'd done it save for my own darling Kay, who came to hold me a Protheroe and the man in my mouth rocked me back and forth between them. She was naked and didn't seem to care about the mess, cuddling up and sliding a hand under my belly to rub my fanny and stroke my tits.

I just came, almost instantly, in helpless ecstasy as Kay fiddled with my clitty. My buggered bottom-hole wen tight on Mr Protheroe's cock, whoever was in my mouth jammed himself deep, and even as I came I was being given a double load of spunk, in my mouth and up my bum. I'd done it, I knew, every one of them, and as the last two men vacated my body I was filled with triumph

Kay kept hold of me, easing my head between her thighs as she sat down on the drum, more open, more in control than I'd ever known her. I began to lick and took hold of her, cuddling her to my face with my hands on her sweet little bottom. She was giggling, then sighing, and a moment later she'd come, wriggling herself against me in dirty delight, obviously drunk but aroused and loving, just as I wanted her.

We cuddled up as she finished, kissing, nude and happy together, our bodies utterly filthy but simply not caring. I didn't, anyway. I didn't care that I'd had my bottom spanked in public, nor that I'd sucked all the carnies' cocks and more, nor that Fat Jeff had fucked me on camera, nor even that I had Mr Protheroe's spunk dribbling out of my bottom-hole. That was all fine, just as long as I had Kay.

'Ladies and Gentlemen!' Sean's voice sounded from somewhere behind me. 'We have one hundred! Didn't she do well, and what a slut she is! So let's have a big hand for the one and only Madame Boobfontaine!'

Cheers and clapping filled the Big Top, but as it died Mick's voice called out.

'How about the master copy, Baffo?'

'Good point, Buffo!' Sean responded. 'How about the master copy indeed, but let us not make life difficult for the poor dear. Madame, can you take one more cock?'

I managed a weak nod, smiling through my mask of spunk. One more was nothing.

'Who, then?' Sean called out. 'What sturdy fellow will fill her up for a second time. Gerry? Yes, why not, an excellent finale!'

'Do it, Amber,' Kay said softly. 'Do it again like you did in Belfast.'

'For you,' I answered her.

Suddenly every person there was clapping and cheering as I got back on all fours. It was going to happen: couldn't stop it, I was just too high to hold back. He came to me and I stuck up my bum, not even really caring which hole he went up. What I didn't expect was to have it put in my mouth, Kay stroking my back and whispering to me, Gerry holding me firmly by my hair as I was fed the thick meaty cock.

I sucked, not just holding it in my mouth but getting busy with my lips, drawing wild applause and raucous laughter from the carnies. Just that was enough to make me want to come again, but I knew he was going up me and I held back, letting my head fill with his taste and the feel of his great bulging cock. Kay was giggling as she watched, nervous and urgent in her excitement, and then she was holding him and feeding him into my mouth. I pulled her down, knowing that she wanted it, and we were doing it together, licking at the thick red shaft of his penis, taking turns to put it in each other's mouth, utterly wanton together.

'Now up you,' Gerry demanded.

I pulled back, nodding. Kay gave an excited little whimper and I lifted my bottom, making my cheeks spread in willing acceptance of what was to be done to me. He came behind and I felt him touch me, rubbing against my bottom, between my cheeks, exploring my anus and my fanny. Kay took my head, cradling me to her chest to let me take a nipple in my mouth, suckling her, so soothing, as he moved behind me to touch between my cheeks again and to clamber up, mounting me, his weight on my back and his cock . . . his cock probing between my thighs, finding my hole, and sliding in, deep up inside my slippery aching cunt, to fuck me.

'Let him come in you,' Kay sighed. 'Let him come up your pussy, and do yourself . . . do yourself while he fucks you, Amber, you lovely dirty bitch, you bitch . . .'

My hand went back immediately, clutching at myself, touching the big cock in my hole as he pumped into me, making my bottom wobble and my tits swing and slap together, all fat and sticky and lovely. Kay held or tighter, whispering my name, and suddenly she'd pushed me lower, making me lick her as he pumped into me, calling me a bitch again and again as I was fucked, faster and faster, his huge cock pumping inside me at a furious pace as I clawed at my spunk-sodden cunt and came even as Kay did too, both of us together in perfect ecstasy as spunk exploded into my well-fucked hole.

nexus

The leading publisher of fetish and adult fiction

TELL US WHAT YOU THINK!

Readers' ideas and opinions matter to us. Take a few minutes to fill in the questionnaire below and you'll be entered into a prize draw to win a year's worth of Nexus books (36 titles)

Terms and conditions apply – see end of questionnaire.

1. Sex: Are you male ☐   female ☐   a couple ☐?

2. Age: Under 21 ☐   21–30 ☐   31–40 ☐   41–50 ☐   51–60 ☐   over 60 ☐

3. Where do you buy your Nexus books from?
☐ A chain book shop. If so, which one(s)?
_____

☐ An independent book shop. If so, which one(s)?
_____

☐ A used book shop/charity shop
☐ Online book store. If so, which one(s)?
_____

4. How did you find out about Nexus books?
☐ Browsing in a book shop
☐ A review in a magazine
☐ Online
☐ Recommendation
☐ Other _____

5. In terms of settings, which do you prefer? (Tick as many as you like)
☐ Down to earth and as realistic as possible
☐ Historical settings. If so, which period do you prefer?
_____

☐ Fantasy settings – barbarian worlds
☐ Completely escapist/surreal fantasy

☐ Institutional or secret academy
☐ Futuristic/sci fi
☐ Escapist but still believable
☐ Any settings you dislike?

_____

☐ Where would you like to see an adult novel set?

_____

6. In terms of storylines, would you prefer:

☐ Simple stories that concentrate on adult interests?
☐ More plot and character-driven stories with less explicit adult activity?
☐ We value your ideas, so give us your opinion of this book:

_____

_____

_____

7. In terms of your adult interests, what do you like to read about? (Tick as many as you like)

☐ Traditional corporal punishment (CP)
☐ Modern corporal punishment
☐ Spanking
☐ Restraint/bondage
☐ Rope bondage
☐ Latex/rubber
☐ Leather
☐ Female domination and male submission
☐ Female domination and female submission
☐ Male domination and female submission
☐ Willing captivity
☐ Uniforms
☐ Lingerie/underwear/hosiery/footwear (boots and high heels)
☐ Sex rituals
☐ Vanilla sex
☐ Swinging
☐ Cross-dressing/TV

☐ Enforced feminisation

☐ Others – tell us what you don't see enough of in adult fiction:

_____

_____

_____

8. Would you prefer books with a more specialised approach to your interests, i.e. a novel specifically about uniforms? If so, which subject(s) would you like to read a Nexus novel about?

_____

_____

_____

9. Would you like to read true stories in Nexus books? For instance, the true story of a submissive woman, or a male slave? Tell us which true revelations you would most like to read about:

_____

_____

_____

10. What do you like best about Nexus books?

_____

_____

11. What do you like least about Nexus books?

_____

_____

12. Which are your favourite titles?

_____

_____

13. Who are your favourite authors?

_____

_____

14. Which covers do you prefer? Those featuring:
   (tick as many as you like)

☐ Fetish outfits
☐ More nudity
☐ Two models
☐ Unusual models or settings
☐ Classic erotic photography
☐ More contemporary images and poses
☐ A blank/non-erotic cover
☐ What would your ideal cover look like?

_____

15. Describe your ideal Nexus novel in the space provided:

_____

_____

_____

_____

16. Which celebrity would feature in one of your Nexus-style fantasies?
   We'll post the best suggestions on our website – anonymously!

_____

THANKS FOR YOUR TIME

Now simply write the title of this book in the space below and cut out the
questionnaire pages. Post to: Nexus, Marketing Dept., Thames Wharf Studios,
Rainville Rd, London W6 9HA

Book title: _____

TERMS AND CONDITIONS

NEXUS NEW BOOKS

To be published in November 2006

STRIP GIRL
Aishling Morgan

Shy, self-conscious Sarah is all too used to attracting male attention to her ample bust and well-formed bottom, despite never really knowing what to do about it. Offered her dream job as a cartoonist, she is willing to sacrifice a little of her own dignity by drawing cartoons for men's magazines. Unfortunately, the job also means sacrificing every last scrape of propriety for Sarah's heroine, the exquisite Celeste du Musigny, which has unforeseen repercussions, ensuring that Sarah comes to live out every last detail of her darkest and most secret fantasies.

£6.99   ISBN 0 352 34077 0

SLAVE OF THE SPARTANS
Yolanda Celbridge

Ben Fraunce goes up to Oxford to read classics, and is sucked into the Society of Spartans: a cult of female domination specialising in the cruel punishment of innocent males, by bare-bottom flogging, and humiliating cross-dressing. When he is allowed by the Spartan dommes to spend his summer vacation on their Greek island, toiling as a naked slave, under their whips or with his young skirted body used to satisfy their most lustful and decadent desires, he at last understands that no male is ever innocent.

£6.99   ISBN 0 352 34078

OVER THE KNEE
Fiona Locke

This is the life story of a girl addicted to the sensual pleasures of spanking. A girl who feels compelled to manipulate and engineer situations in which older authority figures punish her, over their knees.

And as *Nexus Enthusiast* publishes convincing and exciting literature, written by the devotee of a single fetish for the large number of enthusiasts of that same kink, the author is fully qualified, as an adult corporal punishment film star, and active participant of the S&M scene.

£6.99   ISBN 0 352 34079 7

If you would like more information about Nexus titles, please visit our website at www.nexus-books.co.uk, or send a large stamped addressed envelope to:

Nexus, Thames Wharf Studios,
Rainville Road, London W6 9HA

This information is correct at time of printing. For up-to-date information, please visit our website at www.nexus-books.co.uk

All books are priced at £6.99 unless another price is given.

Please send me the books I have ticked above.

Name ....

Address ....

....

....

.... Post code ....

Send to: **Virgin Books Cash Sales, Thames Wharf Studios, Rainville Road, London W6 9HA**

US customers: for prices and details of how to order books for delivery by mail, call 888-330-8477.

Please enclose a cheque or postal order, made payable to **Nexus Books Ltd**, to the value of the books you have ordered plus postage and packing costs as follows:

UK and BFPO – £1.00 for the first book, 50p for each subsequent book.

Overseas (including Republic of Ireland) – £2.00 for the first book, £1.00 for each subsequent book.

If you would prefer to pay by VISA, ACCESS/MASTERCARD, AMEX, DINERS CLUB or SWITCH, please write your card number and expiry date here:

....

Please allow up to 28 days for delivery.

Signature ....

Our privacy policy

We will not disclose information you supply us to any other parties. We will not disclose any information which identifies you personally to any person without your express consent.

From time to time we may send out information about Nexus books and special offers. Please tick here if you do *not* wish to receive Nexus information. ☐